BUBBLE OFF PLUMB

EDITED BY:
KG FINFROCK, SARAH KALIN,
AND DAN M. KALIN

FERAL CAT PUBLISHERS
Melbourne, FL USA

2018

Feral Cat
PUBLISHERS

Published by Feral Cat Publishers, Melbourne, FL 32940

www.feralcatpublishers.com

Version 1.0, December 2018

Cover Art by Priscilla Thomas

KDP Print ISBN: 978-1970-087000

IngramSpark Print ISBN: 978-1970-087024

ebook ISBN: 978-1970-087017

Contents

FOREWORD

When Feral Cat Publishers was first formed, I had a conversation with a friend about the kind of things we should do here. Among other suggestions, she recommended publishing an anthology as a fast way to kick things off, but initially the idea didn't take hold. Only later, after reading several genre-specific anthologies, did the idea for Bubble Off Plumb emerge.

Excited, I went back to her and pitched the idea for a genre-neutral anthology of offbeat stories, titled 'Bubble Off Plumb'. She initially wasn't keen on the theme because it ran counter to current publishing dogma which serves strictly-defined customer marketing segments and, more importantly, she had no idea what the phrase meant. I later found she wasn't alone there, but I stuck with it regardless. Given the trouble finding bridging metaphors to explain BoP, it was probably a good thing I didn't start with my first notion which was 'Red-Shift Stories', a similar concept but even less accessible.

Armed with a concept, I posted a call for cover art and found quickly others had the same problem, especially the English-as-a-second-language artists overseas. Extremely literal cover art featuring carpenter levels, bubbles, and blocky letters was produced. I thought we might have to settle for a less creative solution, until Priscilla Thomas came in at the last moment with a perfect understanding of what we were looking for.

With all the difficulties, we weren't sure how many submissions we'd receive. Maybe the concept was too hard to wrap your head around. But we needn't have worried - more than 850 authors presented their off-plumb stories for consideration, and they were predominately excellent stories. Authors understood the concept very well, as it turns out, which was a very gratifying result for me personally.

Now, it is up to you, the reader, to determine whether bucking conventional publishing wisdom was a good idea. The jury is out!

Dan M. Kalin
Publisher

SERPENT, WOLF, AND HALF-DEAD THING

By: Marie Brennan

With his fangs still buried in the thick meat of his own tail, the great serpent says, "I wondered when you would come."

She scowls at him with the dead half of her face. Her tangled, knotted hair floats weed-like around her, but the harsh croak of her voice is as clear as if she stood in the open air. "What do you know, old snake?"

It's cold down here, in the depths of the sea that encircles the world. He is sluggish with the chill, but his mind is more awake than she's ever seen it, since the day they flung him out here. Something has wakened him. "Know?" the serpent asks, thoughtfully. "Many things. There is wisdom here the Allfather has not: the secret movements of the hafgufa and lyngbakr, the shape of stone that has never seen light, the pattern of the currents of the deep. This wisdom is mine alone."

Her lip curls in disgust. He's grown strange, this past age—from the chill, the darkness, the loneliness of his exile? She hardly cares. Her visits are rare, and growing rarer; she stirs less and less often from her own lonely realm. What do the three of them have to say to each other, or to anyone?

Until now. "I saw the light dim," he admits after a thoughtful pause. "And I heard the beasts of the sea weep—a thing never heard before."

One enormous golden eye regards her. How much *does* he know? She says, "They wept for the death of light."

The tip of his tail shifts, rippling the water. Ships will shudder in the waves high above. "Father's work," the serpent says.

Of course. Who else would devise such a malicious trick? "And he is punished for it," she tells her monstrous brother. "Bound beneath the earth, with venom dripping upon his face." One trick too many. They've forgiven his evils before, but not now. Not with the Allfather's own son struck down, pierced with mistletoe, his shining beauty dimmed by death.

Another ripple, that in a human creature might have been a shrug. But they are not human, none of them—not even she, for all that she has the look. Their shapeshifter father takes any form he chooses, but their mother is a giant, and gave birth to monsters.

Monsters who could not be trusted in the world of men, nor gods neither. And so the gods flung this one out into the sea, where he grew beyond even the ken of his mother's race. The serpent says, "It matters not to me. Norns wove our fates before they began, and the fates of the nine worlds."

This is what her brother has fallen to, here in the depths of the sea. Apathy. He may have wisdom, but to no purpose. He does not care what their father has done.

Even the brief wakefulness it brought is fading. "What will you do, old snake?"

Drowsy amusement fills the eye she can see. "Poison the sky. Slay a god. Then die. But the time has not yet come."

The time when he will take his fangs from out his great tail and uncoil his length from around the world of men. The final battle, the twilight of the gods. Many know the fates they will find there. She imagines it to be a cruel thing, knowing one's own end so clearly - but not half so cruel as ignorance. The Allfather claims her people will be there when the battle comes, fighting at her father's side; but of her he has said nothing.

The eye is drooping shut. Her brother is subsiding once more, back into the half-dreaming sleep that consumes the span of his life. She watches with contempt. This is his kingdom, beyond even the reach of the sea-god, but he cannot be troubled to rule it.

When at last she turns to go, she thinks she hears a whisper from behind her. "Farewell, sister."

But when she glances back, her brother is fast asleep.

***

The black surface of the lake barely ripples as she passes over it to the heather-strewn island beyond. No one comes here, even less than to the depths of the sea; this was a sacred place once, but now is haunted by the howls of the wolf.

He thrashes when he sees her. No apathy, not here; his hatred only burns hotter with every passing age. It's a hatred he shares with all, but not equally. She has a relatively small portion of it as such things go.

In part because she is the only one who will take the sword from within his jaws. The hilt rests on his lower gums, and the point gouges a bloody hole in the upper. Though smaller than their serpentine brother, he is still the mightiest wolf the nine worlds have ever seen. Little wonder the gods grew to fear him.

She reaches in, grasps the leather-bound hilt with her living hand, pries the sword free. The wolf spits blood into the river of saliva that flows from his mouth. They call that river Hope; it's fitting that its waters should sometimes run red.

"I bring news," she says.

Golden eyes glare at her. It's the one thing all three of them share, the only mark of kinship among them. Their mother does not have such eyes. Perhaps their father does — but who can tell, behind the lies?

"Unbind me," the wolf snarls, as he always does.

She does not even bother to look. She knows well the silken ribbon that binds him, woven of six impossible things, beyond even his strength to break; she knows the fetter that leads from it, the slab to which the fetter is bound, the stone that anchors it all to the earth. Unlike their mother, she is no giant. She can move none of it.

Instead she surprises herself by echoing the serpent's words. "The time has not yet come."

The wolf snaps at her arm, so that she has to lift the sword to warn him back. He would have claimed more than a single hand, had they not wedged his jaws open. "The time will come when I escape my bonds. Let it be *now*. I will feast upon them all, and howl my victory to the desolation."

He hears only as much of his doom as he wishes to. That is not how it will go. He will die, just as the serpent will; his mouth will be torn apart, so he can howl no more. It is a bloody fate that has been woven for them, when they were but new-born.

For two of them, at least.

She says, "I came to tell you that Father is bound."

The wolf bares his teeth, slaver dripping from his jaws. "What do I care? *I* have been bound for ages. If he shares my fate, it's only fitting. Why should any of us walk free?"

The binding upon him will not break before the end of the world; that knowledge is the only thing that keeps her from stepping back. This is the hate he reserves for her, that she, alone of the three, can go where she wills. It's a freedom she rarely enjoys, and he hates her all the more for that. But there is no welcome for her anywhere outside her realm, not even in the company of her kin, and certainly not among the gods.

Her lupine brother, though, is not the only one who bears hatred in his heart. "Why should any of us have enjoyed the warmth of the gods' own halls?" she spits. "I am not the one who played the faithful hound, accepting scraps from my master's hand, all for the hope that they would accept me among them. That they would *love* me."

She can scarcely hear her own words in the end, drowned out by the wolf's fury. This is what he despises above all: not her, nor the gods, nor even the one who betrayed his trust, but himself, for having given that trust to begin with. He played their games, let them place fetters on his limbs, because he hoped it would earn him a place among them. And the one he called friend, the only one brave enough to come near him, promised it would be so.

Perhaps the gods also deceived their fellow. His honesty is renowned as much as his courage, even now, when the stump of his wrist proclaims his lie. It hardly matters. That lost hand rots in the wolf's belly, and her brother will never trust again.

A necessary thread, dyed black with blood. The wolf could never be their faithful hound; they knew that when he was still a pup, and that is why they bound him. Their binding created his hatred—and thus is the tapestry woven.

She chooses her moment with care. When the wolf lunges against his silken chain, hoping to claim a taste of her flesh, she thrusts the sword once more into place. Fresh blood springs free as it digs once more into his gums. It is necessary; the guardian of the gods sees all, and he must see the wolf as he was before she came. But she feels a touch of pleasure, too, as she forces the blade into her brother's mouth. He knows what she never will: what it is like to dwell among the gods. To pretend, however briefly, that she belongs with them.

With the wolf's howls once more wordless in her ears, she turns her back on the river Hope and leaves her brother to his fate.

***

The earth bucks like a horse fighting to throw its rider, like the sea heaving in a storm. She waits until it calms before she approaches the mouth of the cave.

Darkness envelops her as if welcoming her home. But this is not her realm, and she is not welcome here.

Her father's wife makes that very plain. The goddess sits patiently by her bound husband's side, hands clasping a wide, shallow bowl. Above waits a snake; his venom hisses as it strikes the basin, and foul smoke wisps into the air. Beneath lies the maker of mischief, the thief from giants, the great liar himself—her father.

His breath comes quick, and his hands still clench and flex as if to purge the pain. Red weals mark his face where the venom struck, in the moment when his wife turned aside to empty the bowl. It was his convulsions she felt a moment before, shaking all the earth, so that men everywhere might remember his torment, and his crime.

It will end only when the world does. When he rises from his chains to fight against the gods, and those who were once his companions.

Perhaps it is better to have always been alone. She cannot betray, when she has no friends. And she cannot be betrayed.

She looks to the goddess and says, "I will hold it for a time."

Her father's wife hesitates. This is not her mother; what sons the goddess bore have fallen to their own fates. The guts of one now bind his father to the stone, bloody ropes transformed to iron bands that will endure until the end of time. And she hates the children the giantess bore.

But her vigil is long, and the goddess loses nothing by letting another bear her burden for a while.

The stone bowl weighs heavy in mismatched hands— one living flesh, one dead claw. She waits until the goddess is gone, and then she speaks.

"Why?"

Her father lets out a ragged breath, something like a laugh. "You look well. On the right side, at least. Let your hair fall across the left; otherwise you will never get a husband."

The bowl trembles. She wants to fling its contents into his face, hear him scream in pain. But then the goddess would return, and there is more she must say first.

"I tried to save you," she tells her father. The words have to be forced out, a harsher rasp than usual. "When their messenger came … I was willing to give him up." The light of the gods, the Allfather's brightest child. He lit her gloomy hall like the sun, turning its chill, sleeting rains to showers of gold. But there need be no vengeance for one who is not dead, and so she promised that if all the world wept for him, she would let him go.

And all the world wept—except one.

This time her father's laugh is stronger. "They speak wrongly who say that because the heart lies on the left, yours must be a black and rotted thing."

Always mocking. She wonders if he knows how to do anything else. Gritting her teeth, she asks again. "Why? Why did you kill him, why did you disguise yourself and refuse to mourn?"

"Perhaps I did it for you."

She spits a curse at him.

"No," he agrees, in the same friendly tone. "I didn't think you would believe it. Though that would be a wondrous gift, would it not? A companion in your dark and freezing realm. The sort of thing a loving father might do for his lonely daughter."

"You have never been a loving father." But she does not bother to dispute the other.

He sighs, and his eyes move restlessly, as if already bored with the view: the bowl, her hands, and the stone roof above. "The tapestry is woven, its threads long since spun. This was always the place I would come to."

"And so you ran to meet it? The one crime he could never forgive—and when it seemed you might be spared his wrath, you made sure to seal your doom. But if this was always where you would come, why did it have to be by that road? Why help fate in its work?"

The light in this cave is dim; his eyes hold no color, only darkness. But she sees something in them that might be amusement, or pity, or both. "You don't care what I've done, or why. Your real question is more interesting: you want to know how to face your *own* fate."

She shakes her head, and the tangles fall forward, masking the living side of her face, leaving him only the sight of death. "My fate is secret, known only to the norns."

He shrugs as much as he can, with stones beneath his shoulders and hips and knees, and the guts of his own slaughtered son binding him in place. "Whether you know it or not, your fate is fixed. And so you wonder whether our choices even matter. Whether *your* choices matter."

"Do they?"

Her father smiles. Despite the red weals, despite his prison, despite that he is the greatest traitor the gods have ever known, she still sees it there in his smile: the sly charm, beguiling her against her will, whispering that even if she can't trust him, she still wants to listen. No wonder they tolerated him for so long.

"Of course," he says. "Our choices are the only thing that matters. Whether you cringe from your fate or embrace it, you end up in the same place. You might as well keep your pride."

She stares at him, and he grins back, until the goddess returns. Then she leaves him to his torment, knowing she will not see him again before the end of the world.

***

Her hall is dark and cold again. Her bright companion she has banished from her sight, for she cannot bear his company. Not for more than a few moments at a time. This has been her realm for too long, since the Allfather cast her down here to rule over the inglorious dead. She is used to the shadows and chill.

To her belong the forgotten ones, those not fortunate enough to perish in battle and thereby join the Allfather's host. His dead pass their time in feasting and fighting; hers enjoy no such comforts, and all for the sin of unremarkable death. She does not wonder why they will fight against him in the end.

She wonders instead about herself. What deeds she will do, when that end comes.

The gods fear all three of them: serpent, wolf, and half-dead thing. She understands the first two, but not the third. What doom awaits her, what evil will she commit? For now she is a queen, ruling over her great hall of frozen mist, and that is more than her brothers have; but in the end she will have less. The dead will go to fight for her father, and what happens then, only the Allfather knows.

So she cannot take refuge in her serpentine brother's uncaring patience. Nor can she, like the wolf, reach with hungry jaws for the blood of her foes. She cannot even follow her father's advice, to keep her pride and embrace her fate.

Our choices are the only thing that matters.

To choose blindly …

Her mismatched hands tighten on the arms of her throne.

To *choose.*

Half living, half dead. Half of this realm, and half not. If she had dwelt all this time among the gods …

Their actions create their fates, a net that none can escape. Yet if her fate is to choose, then why would the Allfather send her among the dead, to live lonely and cold, with no cause to love anyone at all? Not the gods, nor the monsters that are her kin. But it could have been different, had they not cast her out.

Perhaps he fears what he does not know. And just as she cannot understand what it is to know one's own fate, the Allfather cannot understand what it is to choose.

Perhaps all of this is mere delusion: a story she has spun for herself, like the neglected child who pretends her real parents will come for her someday. A scrap of warmth against the cold. Her fate might be as fixed as anyone else's.

But she might as well keep her pride.

Hel straightens on her throne, and considers her choice.

BARN RAISING

By: Buzz Dixon

"We're here for the barn raising."

Bob blinked. "Barn raising?"

"Barn raising."

"We don't need a barn."

The big raw-boned farmer, dressed incongruously like an Amish field hand only with bright pink headphones, waved his hand dismissively. "*Every*body needs a barn."

"But we already *have* a barn," Bob said, pointing to the old grey structure a hundred yards away.

Another dismissive wave. "Feh. You call *that* a barn?"

"Well, as a matter of fact, I do."

Carol stepped up to join Bob at the door. "What's going on?"

"Barn raising," said the technologically inconsistent Amish farmer.

"Barn raising," said Bob.

"'Barn raising'?" Carol's inflection almost perfectly matched Bob's earlier utterance.

"Barn raising," said the Amish farmer.

"Barn raising," said Bob.

"But we don't *need* a barn," said Carol.

Bob started to speak but the farmer cut him off. "Enough! Got a barn to raise."

Now for the first time Bob and Carol noticed the mass of farmers and workers, male and female, young and old, on their front lawn. They had come in flat bed trucks, in hay wagons, in pick-ups, in rusty old hippie vans. Several helped unload a large pile of gleaming white pine lumber.

The Amish farmer stepped off the porch to organize his co-raisers of barns.

Carol turned to Bob. "What are we going to do?"

"I don't know, honey. Call the sheriff, I suppose."

The sheriff arrived about the time the farmer and his co-raisers finished the frame of the first wall. "Howdy! How can I help you folks?"

"They're building a barn."

"'Raising a barn' is how we say it 'round here. Yessir, I can see that. Mighty fine barn it's gonna be, too, once they get it finished."

"But we didn't *ask* them to build a barn."

"Well, that's the nice thing 'bout folks in these here parts. You don't hafta ask 'em nothing, they'll just see a need and go out and do it. Right nice of them. Real friendly folk."

"But we don't *need* a barn," Carol said. "We've already got one."

The sheriff peered at the dilapidated old structure, then turned back to Bob and Carol, a little less friendly this time. "Yes, ma'am, I see it. Not much of a barn, is it? I reckon if I were to call my cousin the county agricultural agent, she'd condemn it on sight."

"We were told this property met all structural requirements when we bought it."

"Yes, ma'am, I'm sure it did. The house, that is. But the barn, that's something else."

Carol started to speak again but the sheriff cut her off, his former friendliness returning. "Thing is, these folks just want to help, show you some kindness. It would be a mite rude to refuse 'em."

Carol and Bob hesitated, looking at each other.

"You folks come from the city," the sheriff said. "Bought this place as a country home, you'll commute to work, right?"

Bob and Carol nodded.

"I thought so. Well, these folks, they're trying as best they can to make you feel welcome, part of the community. You can understand that, right?"

"Well…yeah," said Bob.

"There ya go, we're half way to understanding one another already. Barn raising is what these folks do to welcome people into their community."

"But that knife cuts both ways. They do something for you, you gotta do something for them."

Carol and Bob looked puzzled.

"They'll be expecting you to lay out a bit of a spread for them. Food. Lunch, at the very least maybe some snacks on the side."

The sheriff peered at the busily laboring barn raisers. "I don't see any water for 'em, much less any ice cold lemonade." Less friendly now. "You wouldn't want these folks working so hard on a hot day like this without offering them any lemonade, would you?"

Bob and Carol looked at each other again. "Well, I've got some instant lemonade mix," said Carol. "I suppose I could make some for them."

"Ain't you got any fresh lemons?" the sheriff asked, belatedly adding: "Ma'am."

Bob shifted uncomfortably; he did not like the way this was going but saw no way of avoiding it without causing more problems.

"I suppose I could run down to the store, get a couple of bags of fresh lemons —"

"You'll need at least four," said the sheriff. "Five, just to make sure."

"Five bags of lemons," said Bob.

Carol said, "And some fruit and pastries — donuts should do — and if they have any roasted chicken buy seven or eight —"

"Ten, ma'am."

"Ten, as well as some vegetables — here, I'll make you a list."

Carol went back into the house leaving Bob alone with the sheriff. Bob smiled weakly, spreading his hands as if in submission. The sheriff smiled broadly. "I can see you folks are gonna fit right in."

Bob went and bought the food. Carol made instant lemonade as a stop gap until he returned. The barn raisers looked at her instant lemonade disdainfully, but drank it without comment.

Bob returned and they laid out a spread using sawhorses and wooden planks as tables.

The barn stood half-finished, and as soon as the raisers polished off their lunch, they resumed work. By late afternoon they finished raising the barn, and Bob and Carol had to admit it was much better than the old barn that came with the property.

The barn raisers packed their tools, those who wore hats tipped them, and departed; Carol and Bob thanked them profusely as they left.

Before climbing into his battered old flat bed truck, the atypical Amish farmer said to them, "The donuts was nice but next time see if you can get the kind with pink icing." Then he climbed in his truck and drove off.

Carol and Bob looked at each other in befuddlement. "'Next time'?"

Then they laughed, shaking their heads at the quaint country ways of their new neighbors.

The knock at the front door came just after dawn. Pulling a robe around him, Bob answered it.

The Amish farmer stood on his porch. "Barn raising."

Bob blinked in surprise. "You just built a barn for us yesterday. Raised a barn," he said, correcting himself.

"Raising another," said the farmer. He turned and whistled and a crew of barn raisers, much larger than the previous day's crew, swarmed onto the property.

Another phone call to the sheriff. This time he appeared a mite peeved. "What is it? I've got better things to do than babysit a couple of new comers."

"They're building a barn," Carol said.

"'Raising' a barn. Ma'am."

"They're raising *another* barn!"

"So? Ain't no law stopping them."

"But this is *our* property," said Bob.

"Then what're you beefing for? These folks are just trying to be helpful —"

"We didn't need a new barn in the first place," said Bob, "much less two."

The sheriff's eyes narrowed. "Sounds to me like we got a pair of ungrateful city folks here."

"No, no, no! Nothing like that! We just — well, we *have* a barn, we don't really need two...do we?"

"Why don't you learn to be a little more trusting of your neighbors, let them decide what you need or don't need. They know these parts better than you."

Bob could sense the hostility lurking shark-like just below the surface of the sheriff's words.

So…more food, more lemons. Donuts with pink icing this time.

As the barn raisers drove off, Carol said, "What do we need two barns for?"

And the next day: "What do we need three barns for?"

And the day after that: "What do we need four barns for?"

And it wasn't just the food for an ever increasing number of barn raisers (gluten free / peanut free / organic / vegan / kosher sub-menus provided). The sheriff made some pointed comments on the day of the fourth barn raising about folks having to stand up and eat, not have a proper sit down meal at proper tables. So Bob rented chairs and tables.

And rented them again on the next day.

And again on the sixth day.

And bought them outright on the seventh day.

By then Carol and Bob were feeding barn raisers in two shifts, their number increasing with each new barn.

And the barns themselves started to become more ornate, more elaborate.

Cupolas began appearing on the eighth barn, and the barns' meandering side sheds spread out vastly over the farm, crowding out the landscape. By the eleventh day, the cupolas evolved into ornate and intricate spires rising over the barns, requiring whole new teams of specialists to execute them.

They tore down the old original barn, replacing it with a phalanx of porta-potties; Carol found herself cleaning them whenever not making lemonade or setting out the lunches.

Bob kept busy acquiring new supplies and arranging for larger and larger deliveries.

On the night of the fifteenth barn, he said, "We just can't keep this up. Our bank account is nearly exhausted, our credit cards are maxed out."

"They just won't listen and that sheriff won't help," said Carol.

"They must want us out and this is their passive aggressive way of doing it."

They knew they were beaten. They called their real estate agent that night and the next day, between cleaning porta-potties and laying out food for six shifts of workers, they sealed a deal to let the agent sell the property at a loss.

After the barn raisers left that evening, a moving van came, loaded up Bob and Carol's personal possessions, and took them to a storage facility.

Luckily one of Carol's friends in the city was vacationing with her family for the summer and let Bob and Carol stay at her apartment while they looked for a new place of their own.

"I guess we weren't cut out for country life," Bob said as they turned in for the night.

"I guess not," said Carol, thinking about all the money they'd spent and lost, money that meant to have gone towards a nice home for their future.

Early the next morning there was a knock at the door of their borrowed apartment. Bob answered it, assuming it was a neighbor who didn't know their hosts were away.

The Amish farmer with the pink headphones stood in the high rise's hallway.

"Barn raising," he said.

GOOD THOUGHTS

By: KG Finfrock

"Inmate Roy James Burney, is this you?"

Roy slouched in a plastic chair across from the suit. "Yeah. Who else would it be?"

The suit flipped through the file in front of him as if he hadn't seen it before. "It says here you like setting fires."

Roy counted the dots in the ceiling panels.

The suit cleared his throat. "Well?"

Roy stopped counting. "Thought you were making a statement."

"You know why you're here?"

Roy exhaled a heavy breath. "Something about an experimental program. Advancing technology bullshit."

"What makes you think you're a good candidate?"

Roy bent and gave his ankle a scratch. "Look Boss. Let's cut the crap." He held his palms out. "I'm not going anywhere. You need a chimp. I can be a chimp." The left corner of his mouth lifted. The inside joke being he could participate in a hundred experiments and still be serving his sentence on his old age deathbed. "Let's get the ball moving."

"Tell me about the fire."

Roy scooted the chair back. He glanced at the camera in the corner. "Is this some kind of trick?"

The suit removed a photo from the file and centered it on the table. "No trick. Just a request."

"I'm not supposed to talk about it. There are consequences for talking about it. Painful consequences." His whisper was conspiratorial.

The suit looked over his shoulder at the camera. "Good thoughts, Roy. Nothing you say in this room will be used against you or to …. punish you further."

"Says you. You won't be here later. You won't be here when they …"

"You won't be returned to your cell if you answer my questions truthfully and to my satisfaction. Instead, you'll be transferred immediately to a sanctioned wing where you won't be locked up. You might be able to earn access to the outside without fences."

Roy thought of the possibilities. This place was pretty tight. Maybe the science wing would offer a chance of escape. Sounded too good to be true. "The warden would never allow me out of here."

The suit shook his head. "Warden Redstone recommended you. All you have to do is answer my questions."

The hair rose on the back of Roy's neck. "He blames me for his granddaughter's death. He won't let me out of here." He chewed on his bottom lip. "Bastard's got it in for me. He ain't never letting me go after what I did."

The suit flicked the corner of the manila folder under his nail. "Rumor has it the strain of you being here is having a bad effect on his health. Another rumor is the governor requested your participation. It's only a rumor, of course."

Roy mulled this over. The governor was Warden Redstone's boss. The governor received a lot of publicity in the hunt for Roy. A lot of voter support. It would make sense the governor would feel beholden after what Roy had done for him. His chest began to puff out. Roy's sentence probably wouldn't have been as heavy if the governor hadn't made such a brouhaha out of the case. The fact is Roy had helped him get elected the second term. The governor owed him. His shoulders relaxed.

He leaned over to the table and peeked at the photo. It looked like black and white film. It wasn't. Not much color to ashes mixed with charred bones.

"How does this photo make you feel?" the suit asked.

Roy shrugged. "How do you feel when you look at a used ashtray?"

The suit pulled out six photographs and placed them across the table, three above three. Pictures of smiling children. A large rectangle square with a name tagged to each photo. Robbie Whittle, a boy with red hair and freckles across his nose. Selma Stein, a girl missing her front tooth with a white bow in her hair. Amanda Miles with blonde curls. Jamal Washington stood with a baseball and mitt smiling an ear to ear grin. Jesus Marinex, a small child with limp hair and large glasses. Nicole Redstone posed for her school photo with a shy smile and large dimples.

"And these…? You know who they are?"

"Sure. They were plastered all over the courtroom."

"And…"

Roy looked at the suit with a blank stare.

"Any regret?"

"Not really. I don't like kids. They're like vermin. You ever wonder why everyone gets sick at certain times of the year? It's those damn kids spreading germs around. Sticky hands touching everything. Fingers in their noses spreading snot everywhere. They're worse than rats."

"Is this the reason why you burned the schoolroom?"

"Fire cleans and purges. I tried to get my punk lawyer to point out there was no flu epidemic in my town the year of the fire. He said we needed proof. I said proof was right there in front of everyone."

"It wasn't just schools you burned, was it?

Roy flicked his finger as if shooing away a fly on his leg. "Little vermin grow into large vermin. Big fat dirty rats thinking they're king shit." He snickered. "King of ashes is what they are now."

"No empathy for the victims?"

Roy shrugged his shoulders. "I already told you."

Roy heard a low subtle buzz from across the table. The suit pressed his hand against his ear. He gathered the photos into the file folder. "Thank you for your honesty. Officer Billings will escort you to the orientation room. An attorney will be present. Once you agree to the terms and sign the contract, you'll be transferred to your new cell block."

The door opened and Officer Billings stood there with his thumbs hooked into his belt loops.

"This is too easy. There's got to be a catch. What if I don't want to go through with it?"

"Good thoughts, Roy. You have the right to refuse. Each person who participates is a volunteer. No gun to their head. Should you not accept the terms, your attorney will have you sign a paper stating such and you will be returned to your cell to serve your remaining time. No harm. No foul. No penalties."

Roy smirked. "There are always penalties."

GOOD THOUGHTS

***

Prone in the bed with his hands behind his head, Roy contemplated the light emitting from the rectangle window shaped like a door within a door. He thought of a small window to the boiler, a patch where you could watch everything burn. He was still searching for the catch. The deal he had made didn't sit well with him. He wondered if his downfall was in one minor sentence buried in the ream of paper that consisted of the contract. His appointed attorney, a greasy long haired pansy, had sworn he had read every page as it was the same contract he represented to the other inmates chosen for the D.U.O. project. He encouraged him to sign it. Roy knew he was getting screwed. He drank three cups of coffee while he tried to make sense of the small print. Since he didn't have anything to lose, he signed it, but not before asking if the signature needed to be in blood. The pansy blanched before saying normal ink was preferred. Roy signed.

Four uniforms he had never seen before escorted him to the new wing. They stood before a thick steel door. Each uniform took turns punching a series of numbers into the key panel. The door opened outward with a large exhale. Roy stepped inside expecting the uniforms to follow. They did not. The door closed behind him. He was in a small room facing a plexiglass door. A series of colored lights beamed across him from head to toe. A door on the opposite side slid open to a sterile hallway with steel blue colored floor tile. The door closed behind him.

A small disc flashing red rolled across the floor. "Announcement. Follow the circles. Follow the path now. They will show you the way. Good thoughts, Roy James Burney.

The disc stopped flashing. An opening in the baseboard appeared. The disc rolled through the opening and disappeared.

Red and orange circles appeared on the floor beckoning him to follow. He passed blue trimmed identical doors. Each with a single rectangle window. It wasn't until later Roy realized there were no door handles or locks on the doors.

***

Sleep wasn't coming. The light from the cutout in the door was bright as a lighthouse beacon peering into his room. Roy punched his pillow and tossed it across the room. His feet hung over the side of the bed. It was a real room. Nothing like his old cellroom. Everything was voice activated. All he had to say was the name Allan and tell Allan what he wanted. Lock or unlock the door, change the temperature, or play music. The room was furnished like a studio apartment he once lived in except the furniture was a higher quality. The bed was firm, but not too firm. A steel wardrobe large enough for him to fit inside stood in the far corner. Shelf space at the top for undergarments, two pairs of jeans, and four shirts. A single gray jumpsuit hung inside. No prison uniforms.

A private bath was provided with a large shower. The downside was no windows other than the one in the door.

Roy hadn't decided if the room being soundproof was a positive or negative aspect. He knew the room was soundproof because no one screamed for him to shut up when he sang at the top of his lungs in the shower.

He had met a few of the volunteers at dinner call. The climate appeared jovial with an underlying sense of unease.

He walked to the door shuffling his feet and found the pillow. He returned to his bed. He fluffed the pillow and settled his head into the soft down. He flinched each time the light flickered as a shadow walked by the door.

The light from the door imprinted his vision. He watched a yellow blotch dance and fade on the ceiling with each blink in the darkness.

***

Roy had followed the flashing lights as the disc had instructed. The path stopped at an open doorway. Roy leaned forward and peeked inside. A red slim recliner with thin armrests sat in the center of a narrow room. An empty bag with long tubes attached hung from a pole. A tall man with premature balding and long gangly arms waved him in.

"Come on in, Roy. I've been expecting you. I'm Charles. Have a seat. Take a load off." The corner of his eye twitched. "Can I offer you something to drink?"

"A shot of tequila would be nice."

Charles laughed. "Do you mind if there's a worm in the bottle?"

"Not at all."

To Roy's surprise, Charles pulled a bottle and two shot glasses from the drawer behind him. He poured the drink and handed it to Roy who promptly slammed it down without hesitation.

Charles grimaced. "Perhaps I should have given that to you afterward."

"After what?" Roy held out the glass shaking it.

Charles laughed. "More? Absolutely, but first I need a little of your blood for testing."

A short stout woman entered the room. She looked at the two men, her eyebrows arched. The corner of her lip lifted in a sneer.

"Don't be mad, Audrey." Charles pleaded. "It was just one drink."

"You didn't prep him."

Charles' eye twitched. "He is a little."

"All right you two lovebirds. Let's get on with it. Don't forget you promised me another drink."

Audrey snapped the tourniquet around his arm and inserted the needle into his vein. Roy tried to relax his arm. This bitch was going to jam the needle in hard enough to make his toes curl. She surprised him. He watched as her eyes widen. She took a deep inhale. She glanced at Charles. Roy was positive an unsaid message exchanged between them.

"Good thoughts, Audrey," Charles said in a quiet voice.

Audrey exhaled. Her smile was weak. "Good thoughts, Charles."

She inserted the needle in Roy's vein with a touch so gentle, he didn't feel the prick. He didn't realize she had inserted the needle until he saw his blood flowing into the vacutainer tube.

She removed the blood filled tube and without so much a thank you, she left the room.

Roy smirked. "Think I ought to ask her to kiss my boo-boo?"

"Sure, as long as you like snake venom. She'll be back in a few minutes."

"How about that drink?"

Charles shook his head. "Not yet."

Roy considered getting up and helping himself, but the truth was he felt just fine with the one drink. Unnaturally calm to be honest. He began to question if there was something in the drink besides tequila. He smiled. Maybe the worm.

Audrey returned to the room carrying a plastic bag filled with a teal blue liquid. Was it the way the fluorescent light reflected off the bag or was the fluid glowing? Roy couldn't tell.

Audrey hung the bag from the pole. "Pour me three fingers while I hook him up."

"Hold on there. How is it you can drink on the job?"

"A perk of being in the science wing. Consider it medicinal." She took his arm and stretched it out. "Prison food isn't sufficient for your needs. This bag is filled with liquid nutrients and will balance your body's requirements."

Roy pulled his arm back. "What if I refuse?

Audrey's brows raised high like rainbows. "Do you?"

He shrugged. "I'm just asking."

"You'll be released from your contract and returned to your previous wing with a new cell and new roommate. And of course, you won't have access to our fine brew." She took the paper cup from Charles and took a sip. "What's it going to be? Intravenous nutrition or back to shitty food and company you don't want?"

Roy watched the colors in the fluid dance. "What else besides nutrients?"

"Are you in or out?" Audrey slammed the remainder tequila. She wiped her mouth with the back of her gloved hand.

"Do it."

***

And she did, not once, but an additional three times. One for each day he had been their guinea pig. She was arrogant as the first time. He smiled as he thought of her office burning. His grin grew wider as he pictured her burning inside it.

Roy coughed and wiped tears from his eyes. They were burning as if he had a speck of dirt in them. He turned in his bed to look at the yellow light. The sharp edges blurred. The light diluted.

Smoke. The room was filling with smoke. He tasted it. He yanked his shirt up to cover his nose and mouth while he dropped to the floor. On his hands and knees, he crawled to the door. It was cool to the touch. He peeked out the window. No smoke in the hallway. "Allan, unlock the door." The door remained closed. "Allan, respond. Open the damn door." The automatic system did not respond or open the door. Roy coughed, almost choking on his inhale. Dizziness brought him to his knees. He crawled to the wardrobe and climbed inside. He pulled the jumpsuit off the hanger and stuffed it along the bottom of the doors. He pulled back to the corner with his knees pulled up to his chest.

Tears burned down his cheeks. He wiped his face feeling the heat. His cough racked behind his ribs. He tried to shout out. His voice reduced to a hoarse whisper. His fingernails peeled back as he scratched inside the walls reaching for air that wasn't there.

***

He rolled to his side and fell out his bed. The room's morning lights blazed. The baseboard door slid open. The small disc rolled to the front of Roy's head. "Announcement. Breakfast in thirty minutes."

"Where's the snooze alarm on you?" Roy knew not to touch the little disc. Steve had tried to kick one across the cafeteria room. Steve went to the infirmary after the disc shredded his foot.

Roy sat up and laughed at the bad dream. He stopped laughing when his airway cut off and he pissed his pants a wee bit. He fell back. He took shallow breaths, increasing the expansion of intake with each subsequent breath. He stood on shaky legs and made his way to the bathroom.

He stripped and dropped his soiled clothing on the floor. The automatic wall vacuum sucked them away. The shower sensor released a stream of cool water. He stepped under the spray. "Allan, increase temperature ten degrees."

"Water temperature increased by ten degrees." Allan's automated voice responded.

Rising steam unlocked the tightness in his chest.

***

Roy sat at the table which was more of a conveyor belt with place settings. Empty plates rolled down the belt and disappeared into the walls much like his soiled clothing. This morning Felix sat across from him. Felix had a black eye.

Felix picked up a fork and shoveled scrambled eggs into his mouth. "You look hung over this morning. Charles give a bottle of that sweet tequila?"

Roy took a sip from his mug. "Who did you tussle with?" He pointed to the swollen eye.

Felix smirked. "You wouldn't believe me if I told you."

Roy shrugged. "Try me."

Felix leaned forward moving the eggs around his plate with his fork. "Wish I had a cigarette. Always liked a smoke after …" He threw the fork down. "It's not what you think. No one touched me. I did this to myself." He pulled his shirt collar down. Large finger-shaped bruises lined the side of his throat wrapping around his neck. "Check this out. My own hand did this." His fingers fit inside the bruising like a glove.

"Maybe someone the same size as you came in your room."

Felix shook his head. "Nah. It was me. I was dreaming about Mandy except I was Mandy. It was the night I … I could feel everything she felt." His finger rapped the table. "Never had a dream like that before. It was like I could feel her fear which turned into one pissed off broad. Then when she knew she was dying, I could feel her sadness and she was so worried about her family and what her death would do to them. Crazy shit, huh?"

Roy sipped his coffee. "Yeah, crazy." He tried to clear the raspiness from his voice.

"What's with you? Why are your eyes so red? You ain't breathing so good either. You sick?"

"Feel like I smoked four packs of cigarettes, butt to butt. Dreamed the place was on fire. My room was filled with smoke."

"Maybe you should hit the infirmary. Get checked out."

"Yeah, you should have your eye checked before it falls out of your skull. Maybe Audrey will give you a shot of love."

Felix stood up. "Nah. I'm gonna head back to my room. See if I can get some sleep."

Roy watched Felix limp away as if someone had slapped a two by four board between his legs.

The small disc rolled next to Roy. "Announcement," as if it was the host welcoming him to an amusement park ride. "Charles request immediate follow up physical. Follow me." Roy wanted to kick the little booger, but he had learned from Steve the consequences of abusing the equipment.

He finished his coffee, grimacing at the bitterness, and followed the little weed whacker he had nicknamed Puck2 down the hall to the examining room.

Charles sat on the stool and waved Roy to the dentist chair.

"Looking a bit rough this morning."

"Feeling a bit rough. Why am I here?" Roy glanced at the drawer where the tequila resided.

"Allan reported you were having difficulty breathing."

"Did Allan, by chance, report my room being filled with smoke?"

Charles pursed his lips. "You think your room was filled with smoke? Interesting."

"Look jackoff. I didn't imagine it. I been around a few fires. I know the effects of smoke inhalation."

"The rooms are state of the art. Smoke from a single cigarette, hell, even a vape would set off the sensors. The sensors would also alert smoke particles on your clothing or body."

"The sensors are faulty."

"Possible for a few, not likely, but possible. The other sensors would pick up what they missed. There was no smoke."

"You're saying it's in my mind."

"It isn't for me to say. However, I do know what will make you feel better. How about a ..."

"I'd love a drink."

"... a walk outside. Get some fresh air and sun." Charles pressed his hand to his ear. "Hold up here for a few minutes, Roy. I'll be right back."

Roy went straight to the door and pulled out the alcohol. He shook the bottle. Sure enough, a small worm swirled at the bottom. He twisted the cap and drank from the straight from the neck. Shivers ran down the nerves in his legs. He put the bottle back and sat down.

Charles peeked around the corner of the door. He tipped his head toward Roy. "Come on. Let's go."

The two men followed the flashing green lights on the floor.

"Do you think Sergio's out in the yard. We don't get along real well?"

"The yard? You're not going to the yard. You're going outside."

The lights stopped flashing. A door leading to a cylinder similar to the one he first entered the wing slid open. Charles took a step back. "Good thoughts, Roy." He turned and walked away.

Roy could feel the stomach acid rolling, threatening to send his breakfast in reverse. It was too easy. Everything was volunteer in this wing. He didn't have to go through the door if he didn't want to go.

Outside Charles had said. Fresh air. Real sunlight. Roy realized he had no idea what the weather would be like. Hot and humid most likely, but storms were known to blow in with little notice. Any change would be good. Roy realized what he really desired was unfiltered air. He stepped into the cylinder and placed his hands on the sidebars. As before, a series of light beams crisscrossed his body from head to toe. The cylinder twisted and the door slid open.

Roy shielded his eyes against the bright sun and stepped outside. His mouth gaped open. He had expected chain fences and asphalt. He saw neither. He was standing on a dirt path. Waist high dried weeds bordered a narrow trail leading up a hill. Perspiration began beading on Roy's head. It was a hot day. Roy guessed triple digit, dry heat. Zero moisture content could be felt in the air.

He tried to swallow; his throat already parched. He needed a hat and some water. He searched for a panel to open the door and found none. He pounded on the closed door. He, for a brief moment, wondered if he could find a piece of glass. There was more than enough dry kindling. He'd burn the door down just like he did when his mother sent him outside to play and locked him out of the house. "How's that for good thoughts, Charles?" he shouted.

He looked around and spotted a backpack under a tumbleweed. Inside the bag was a bright orange cap with a large brim, a bandana, several bottles of water, and a can of sunscreen with a note attached from Charles. "Good thoughts."

Roy twisted the bottle cap off and tossed it into a shrub. He drank half the bottle in one swig. He drenched the bandana with the other half and placed it on his head under the cap. He slung the backpack over his shoulders and headed up the trail.

He was breathing heavy when he reached the top. He picked a foxtail out his sock. He turned and looked behind. The science wing wall blocked the rest of the prison. He twisted around. No fences anywhere. Nothing but dried out mesquite and creosote bushes as far as he could see. The trail leading along the ridge was almost non-existent.

No fences. No guards. No lookouts. What's the catch? He moved his leg away from the prickly bush stabbing the back of his knee. His shoe caught on a vine. He slipped, down the side, arms flailing to his side, reaching out to grab anything to stop his descent. He stopped midway. The back of his shirt pulled up to his neck. His backside on fire. Profanity spewed from his mouth. He stopped swearing when he saw the spiraling wisp of smoke. It grew darker and wider. The flames climbed up the hill small at first but grew in height with each foot the fire ate.

The sizzling blaze drove directly toward Roy at an unnatural accelerated rate. Roy turned and grabbed the roots for leverage as he climbed. His hand slipped from the stem. He could smell it now. The flammable concoction that painted the hillside.

He tried not to scream when his pants caught on fire. Tried to bury his face to stop the flames from searing his lungs. Tried, but failed.

***

Warden Redstone stood with his hands clasped behind his back looking out his office window down at the yard. "He survived the session?"

Charles waited as the warden sat at his desk before sitting. "Yes. He has burns over ninety percent of his body. His legs are charred to the bone."

The warden smiled. "Just like Captain Rosen in the Arnette fire Roy started."

"Yes, sir."

"The bots did this to his body? There was no real fire involved to cause his injuries?"

"There was no fire. Roy first ingested the nanobots we placed in the coffee he drank while signing the volunteer contract. Programming began when he set foot in the cylinder as he entered the wing. First event was triggered and he suffered severe smoke inhalation symptoms. I'd say the bots got a good feel for the way Roy thinks considering the severity of the next event."

"How long before his body heals?"

"Two, maybe three weeks?"

"Not a lot of time, is it?"

"His body will heal, but the bots will make him think he's spending the next five years in treatment and therapy. The scars will be gone on his physical body, but he will see and feel them."

"And the next time he thinks about starting a fire?"

Charles shrugged. "The bots will drop him to the floor and create a new scenario where he is the victim. He'll feel everything his victims experienced over and over."

"Excellent." The warden pulled out a bottle of whiskey and two crystal cut square glasses. He poured and handed a glass to Charles.

"Imagine a world where people are kind to each other. A world where they do the right thing, knowing that what they do is going to come right back at them." He took a sip.

"We're going to have a penal system where only the guilty are punished. A system where they are punished for the true crime they did, not the one they were convicted of. No punishment for the innocent." He lifted his glass in a toast.

"Good thoughts, Warden. It is a rare person truly innocent of evil thoughts."

The warden sipped from his glass. "Let me know when you're ready to expand the program to the rest of the population."

"Yes, sir." Charles rose to leave.

"One more thing. What's with the worm in the tequila?"

Charles shrugged, "I like the brand."

"Why give it to the test subjects?"

"I don't like to drink alone."

The warden nodded. "Good thoughts, Charles."

"Yes, sir. You as well."

HOW MUSIC MOVES US
By: Veronica Brush

The tears in my eyes made it hard to see the sheet music on my stand. Luckily I had practiced this piece enough that my fingers knew their way along the neck of my violin without my brain telling them the notes. Music often moved me, but this was the first time I had actually cried during a performance. This new piece wasn't the most intricate or emotionally charged that I had ever played. There was something different about this piece; something powerful. The sound reverberated inside me. It almost felt like the music was taking me over. I wanted to let it, but I had to keep playing.

This was the first time I had heard the song played by the full orchestra. Rehearsals had been conducted separately for each section of the orchestra, so I had only ever heard the parts for stringed instruments. Not allowing us all to play together until opening night was the unusual whim of our guest conductor.

This conductor was somewhat of a larger-than-life character, but geniuses are always allowed to be eccentric. He was a prolific composer, often compared to all the old greats: Mozart, Brahms, Beethoven, Hayden. He always demanded to conduct the first performance of each of his songs, but always refused to personally conduct any further performances. He also never worked with the same orchestra more than once. He had already performed his way through the most well-known orchestras. Although ours was fairly popular along the west coast, we were not on the level of what he was used to. We weren't sure why he had chosen us to premier his newest composition, but no one wanted to look a gift horse in the mouth. We hadn't ever played to a sold-out audience before and this conductor came with his own crowd of devoted followers.

Despite the excellent ticket pre-sales, there had been a lot of grumbling among the musicians. None of us had ever performed a song without practicing at as a group before. How would we know how loud to play to not overpower another section but also not be overpowered ourselves? How we sounded together was not something any of us wanted to find out in front of an audience.

But the conductor had insisted. As strange as it was, we were now playing together gorgeously; not at all like this was the first time we had played this particular piece as a group. The sound was beyond enjoyable. It was intoxicating. I rocked and moved with the motion of my bow, fighting to keep from getting distracted by the feeling of it all.

As I looked at the conductor now, he, too, seemed greatly moved by the music, his eyes clenched and arms flowing powerfully; extending and straining as though trying to physically pull ever more passion from our instruments.

The music was carrying us all on the crescendo. I was finding it hard to breathe. The world around us - the audience, the stage lights, the backstage crew standing just off stage, even the music stands - had all faded away. There was just us now: musicians, instruments, and conductor. And the music was there, binding all our souls together.

At the peak, I closed my own eyes, taking in the sensation of floating that I thought was just a feeling. The chair wasn't holding me up anymore. I was flying, carried by the purity of the notes blending together from all the different instruments.

As we neared the end I had to open my eyes again to keep the pace. I saw nothing but the conductor's baton guiding the speed of my bow. The baton must have been dancing in and out of the light because it seemed to flash with bright sparks. It was cruel how fast the baton made us race for the ending. I longed to slow down, to linger over the final notes so as to savor the few moments before the song would end and these feelings would fade.

The final note started quiet as a breath and built until it could be heard crying out in the heavens.

Then the song was over. I closed my eyes again to listen to the quickly fading memory of the final sound ringing in my ears.

There was no applause; just a moment of silence. I remembered the audience and believed that they were experiencing the same overwhelming sensations, In a moment they would recover and burst forth in a deafening applause for the journey we had taken them on.

But no applause came. A quiet murmur started, but it wasn't coming from the audience. It was coming from other orchestra members.

I opened my eyes. We were no longer in the theater; no longer indoors at all. I was seated on the ground, still clutching my violin.

The ground was hard and solid like rock and painted with streaks of pink and blue. A green mist rolled along the flat ground around us. The ground rose into giant cliffs on three sides. Carved into the cliffs were castle-like towers. There was no grass or trees or plants of any kind. Up in the sky, there was something yellow like the sun, but I could look straight at it without pain. It was accompanied by two other suns, one blue and one pink.

We were no longer on Earth.

The murmuring grew louder as the initial silent shock faded. Some people stood up and rushed around in circles, looking for anything familiar. Other people started asking questions, getting louder and louder when no one was able to answer them.

Dumbfounded, I looked to the conductor, as though he would know what to do.

He was staring straight up into the sky. The baton had dropped out of his hand and there were tears in his eyes. He wasn't scared or confused or in shock. He smiled broadly. His face still upturned, his body drifted slowly down to his knees, swirling the green mist.

"I finally found the right song!" he exclaimed. "I'm finally home!"

BUDGET DEMON

By: Dan M. Kalin

"I've got a mojo box,
with your head on top"
Southern Culture on the Skids, 2004

Stuart could not accept Bella's abrupt departure, even after a long month had passed. She played the old "I need to understand who I am becoming, alone. I have to honor my process." card, rather than just stating the relationship had ceased to work for her. Also left unsaid was that she expected Stuart's sole contribution to the process to be his continued absence.

Stuart was the type of person who was seldom noticed in a crowd. Not handsome or ugly, reasonably fit, forgettable haircut, decent but not expensive tastes in clothes. Non-threatening, but with a nimble mind and wit (when he chose to use it). Stuart was a corporate fixer or strategist by profession. His core talent was being able to evaluate the opposition (however defined) and help clients prevail by whatever creative means were most effective. He could find an exploitable weakness in almost anything.

Bella, in marked contrast, was an artist; volatile, wildly creative, and delightful in conversation. Her look was angular and thin, but not too terribly fit. These days she sported short Goth-black hair atop upscale hippy clothing, which actually had to be paid for rather than having its origins in a bargain bin. Completing the picture was an abundance of art jewelry, mostly silver. Everyone noticed Bella, wherever she went.

There wasn't lengthy discussion before she left. No heated arguments or other unpleasantness as her things were loaded and moved to the truck. Just a quick hug, a kiss on his cheek, an admonition to "Take care of yourself" as well as an "I'll always treasure what we had!" and she was gone.

Stuart thought he objected less to what Bella did than the way in which she did it. Abrupt, unilateral, and final. He had expected something of the sort eventually, but simply wasn't ready to take such a drastic decision himself. They had mostly run out of things to say to one another for some time, but had continued to be comfortable and warm in each other's company.

Of course, it hadn't helped his peace of mind to later hear from mutual friends she had moved in with one of her male occult group friends. Why couldn't she have just said she was doing that rather than an artful-dodge which felt like a lie?

In the days which followed, Stuart reclaimed all of the things she had shared, the extra closet space, refrigerator shelves, and the demands on his time. However, the hole in his heart persisted and still rankled.

So one day when she telephoned, unexpected and irrational hope had blossomed.

"How have you been? For some reason, I have been thinking of you. How has your work been going?"

Stuart had been spending more time with clients, preferring to be paid if he was going to be miserable anyway, but didn't really want to talk much about it.

"I've been fine, working mostly. I did write a short poem last week which I thought had some legs. Do you want to hear it? It's short," he said.

Several beats of silence and "Sure, let's hear it."

"Every day, missing
Every day, hating
Every day, loving
Every day, waiting
Every day."

Stuart recited, with pauses in all of the right places, as it is always important.

"What do you think?" he asked.

"I liked the theme repetition and the order of the activities. It begs the question as to whether the waiting is actually for love or hate? The best verse doesn't always lend certainty, in my opinion, so well done!" she said noncommittally.

Yes, Bella, those things are certainly observable, Stuart thought to himself, *but how do you feel about it?*

The question was not going to be answered by Bella, not least because she hadn't heard it. Stuart found he had no further interest in casual conversation. Casual conversation, after such a long mental intimacy, created even more wounds which could not be overtly acknowledged. Stuart saw no benefit or future in being a friendly acquaintance. So he thanked her politely for the call and, transparently inventing a client meeting for which he was late, rang off.

Several days later, he met his friend Brian at a local brewpub for happy hour. Over the loud Two-Drink-for-One ambient bar atmosphere, he shared his inability to move on from Bella.

"Stu, the real problem here is that you were too civilized. The bridge between you two isn't well and truly burned, so you don't know what to do next."

Stuart thought he understood but, being thorough, asked "What exactly do you mean?"

"It all comes down to a difference in the way that men and women view past relationships. Women have an imaginary curio cupboard where all of their past loves are kept as figurines. Women will periodically take one down in remembrance, dust it off, heave a deep meaningful sigh and then put it back in its place on the shelf. They then will continue their day as though nothing had happened. Men, on the other hand, tend to break the figurines as well as the shelf (and perhaps the wall behind it) in order to move on. Remembering all of the good things only exacerbates the loss, for men."

"You, my friend, have not broken the figurine and cannot, therefore, move on."

Brian said this with the certainty which comes from self-knowledge and being halfway through his second round of happy hour beer.

Stuart thought for a few moments and said, "I'm not really interested in hurting her just so I can burn a bridge. I wouldn't mind doing something which would make her appreciate, or provide a taste of, my feelings in all of this. We didn't work out, it happens. But she should feel some of the disconnect and accept some of the negative as well. Not sure how I would go about doing just that."

"The answer is staring you in the face, Stuart. What do you do for a living? You find and exploit the weaknesses in things. Why don't you treat her as an opponent? You already have your rules for the proper types of revenge, and yes what we are talking about here is revenge. How would you create enough cognitive dissonance or angst to make her uncomfortable and recognize what she lost in you? How much effect is needed before you feel some closure?"

Brian drained his glass, "Look, Stu. I'm about done with the New-Age-Sensitive-Guy routine for tonight. In fact, I'm planning to go ugly, early. You might want to consider it as an alternative to my suggestion, nothing like a new romance to cauterize the loss of an old one!" With that said, Brian lurched off towards a loud gaggle of women on his own mission.

You know, Stuart thought as he headed home to his empty house, *Brian might have a point*. Where would I find such a weakness in Bella? What is there about her which could lend itself to the creation of discomfort, rather than tangible injury? She was honest, for the most part, so dishonesty was not an opening. Greed or avarice provides an avenue for many people, but neither really applied to Bella. What about her belief in the occult and supernatural? Bingo! That might be a good choice, but how?

Stuart considered this aspect of Bella's life to be nothing more than superstitious nonsense. While he hadn't made it an issue during their time together, he viewed it as one of her little quirks. During the entire time, he had never seen anything tangible which would support such a belief system. Bella herself wasn't concerned about his views on the topic other than to state there were many more things in the universe than ever met the eyes of someone prone to skepticism. Usually, she would follow it up with a hug or a kiss, as though to prove she wasn't bothered or being critical.

She believed in spells. How about doing something along those lines? Spells probably weren't the best choice, he decided, as spells seemed to be fairly predictable in effect. Stuart was really striving for something to create persistent anxiety or non-specific angst. The best result, from his perspective, would be for Bella to be uncomfortable or anxious, without being able to prepare against or counteract an imaginary threat. No, a spell would just enable her, or her new roommate, to simply cast a "counterspell" and consider the issue dealt with. He chuckled an aside to himself, the counterspell would work just as well as the spell itself, i.e. not at all. No, this had to be something which would linger in her mind, even in the absence of tangible effect.

What about demons? She had mentioned on more than one occasion she and others from her family could "see" demons. She also maintained that all demons were dangerous and should not be engaged for frivolous ends. Since Stuart didn't believe in the supernatural, he heard those cautions as stories, little different from those of the religious. You either had faith, believing the stories in the absence of tangible proof, or you didn't believe them at all.

I think I will summon a demon to bother her, Stuart decided. *That should blow a cold wind up her skirt. Of course, I can't just say I have summoned a demon; she has almost always been able to know when I am lying. Therefore, I must do some preliminary research, follow the guidelines or process of summoning and tasking a demon, tell her what I have done afterwards, and let the fun commence.*

Having a plan felt much better than not having one, Stuart fired up his computer and started researching online. Unfortunately, most of the search engine returns were fan sites for various television shows which featured the supernatural. Clearly, those were not the right sources. He even checked the website of the occult group to which Bella belonged, SealsofFate.com, but there weren't any obvious resources for spells or summoning, just a lot of member conversation threads on where to best find ingredients which would be put to unspecified uses.

Stuart was about to give up when a popup advertisement appeared for "Blazin' Bob's One Stop Occult Shop - Locations near You!" Stuart thought, *why not?* He clicked the banner marked Shop Locations and entered his zip code into the form. A new browser screen opened with details of a local store which, oddly enough, was located within the Streedle Beat Mall, near Stuart's home. Perfect and convenient.

Thinking there was no time like the present, Stuart walked to the mall concourse, looking for a store directory. The Streedle Beat Mall had the usual assortment of retail establishments, a food court, and about a million teenagers no matter the time of day. Looking down the directory, he found the listing. The Blazin' Bob store was located in the space formerly occupied by a Radio Shack, and a motley crew of successor firms which never seemed to last long.

Dodging teenagers the entire way, Stuart walked across the mall towards the store. He noticed the teenager density gradually diminished as he approached the door. That's odd, he thought, I would have expected a place like this to be a magnet for teenagers, Goths, if no one else.

As he entered the shop, an old-fashioned bell hung over the door rang.

"I'll be right out," a voice shouted from the backroom of the store.

Stuart headed over to the occult bookshelves and started browsing. The first few he looked through were written in Middle or Early English, without notes or references of any kind. No table of contents either, clearly these books were meant to be read cover-to-cover. Stuart was an impatient sort of reader when it came to how-to books, he generally referred to the table of contents or index prior to turning directly to the section he needed. Facing the prospect of reading through all the tomes, sifting for the important information, did not appeal to him.

"Can I help you?" a voice from behind him asked.

Stuart started and turned. The small thin man was dressed in clean but shabby clothes, covered by a store smock with the Blazin' Bob logo foremost. On a small pocket, which had several writing utensils parked, almost as an afterthought was a name tag labeled "Bob".

"Yes, I believe I do need some help with my project," Stuart said. The name tag registered at that point and he asked, "Are you THE Bob?"

Bob laughed and replied, "I get the question a lot. No, I am not THE Bob; merely one of the many Bob's which run a Blazin' Bob franchise. Blazin' Bob only sells franchises to persons named Bob, something to do with the franchise branding and name tag economies of scale. Of course people could always change their name to Bob, as some have done, to get round that requirement. But enough of that, how can I help you today, sir?"

"I'll get to that in a sec, because I have another off-topic question. Isn't it odd that there aren't any teenagers hanging around the store, I would have thought they'd be everywhere since this kind of thing would appeal to a large number of them?"

"Not odd at all, sir. What you are seeing is the result of Blazin' Bob's standard Teenager Repelling Ward Kit. We find that most of our target customers are put off by having teenagers around; therefore we make sure teenagers don't interfere with our business. Since we are in a mall, the issue is even more pronounced. Also, we are a responsible corporate entity, and we don't think non-adult persons should be involved in occult matters."

Stuart laughed, "I may want to buy one of those as well. Several of the neighborhood children are getting on into their teenage years and you never know how that will turn out."

"Very good, sir. I'll make a note. Now, how else can I help you?"

"Well, I'm a bit of a novice, but I want to summon a demon. Looking through some of these texts, it is difficult to find the right section based on what I have seen so far. I'd prefer not to have to wade through a lot of extraneous text before I get to demon summoning."

Bob took out a handkerchief which had seen better, and cleaner, days and blew his nose soundly. "That, sir, is fairly advanced magic. Furthermore, there is a wide range of what types of entities can be summoned, as well as what it takes to do so. It might help a bit to know what type of entities for which you are aiming."

"Can you give me some examples?" Stuart said, "I'm not familiar with the specific names or types which would be available."

"Certainly. In general, they can range in power from small imps, say, to a prince of Hell. The difficulty or cost increases more or less proportionately with their power. The risk to the summoner is also more or less proportional. Here, let me show you some examples from the tome you're holding. So, if you are summoning a run-of-the-mill demon, you need something to scribe a ward which restrains the demon from attacking you (very important). For small demons, common household chalk would work. Large demons might require something as rare as charcoal from a saint's bones. Sometimes the ingredients have to be gathered over time, such as nightshade leaves harvested in Cornwall under the light of a gibbous moon using a pure silver knife untouched by human hands. We have a standing policy at Blazin' Bob's that we never inquire as to why a customer wants something, but in this case it might be helpful to understand the scale for which you're striving."

Stuart thought for a second and mused, "I don't really have a need for large scale. In fact, I think it should be something which only requires a reasonable amount of effort. I'm looking to do this as soon as possible, so travel to far-flung places and the need for special timing should be minimized if at all possible."

"Thank you, sir. I think I have just the thing. Have you heard of Mystic Mort's 'Summoning for the Mostly Moronic', part of the Mostly Moronic line of how-to books? It's even indexed so that you can easily find what you want."

"I have the Mostly Moronic books on French Cuisine and HTML Programming, so that should do very well I think, they've always been very helpful in the past," Stuart confirmed.

"You'll likely want the section for summoning an imp. It is the least difficult, both in terms of risk and materials needed. As for materials, you can probably find everything you need at Stallmart, my cousin Robert runs a mystic materials stall there. Tell him I sent you if it is not too much trouble."

"Thanks, I'll take the book! And throw in a couple of Teenager Repelling Ward Kits while we are at it, one extra in the event that the first one doesn't take," Stuart took out his credit card and handed it over. Revenge had never been acquired at such a reasonable price.

Bob placed the items in a shopping bag and handed it over to Stuart. "Don't forget to be very careful on the instructions; even small demons can be a handful if you are not careful."

"Thanks, I will," Stuart replied, then he walked back to his home.

Stallmart was close by, and since Stuart had decided to get everything the same day, he turned to page 187 of the Summoning book and quickly copied the list which was shown in the box labeled, "You'll Need:" onto a convenient sticky note.

Frederick Stall of Gothenburg, Nebraska was the founder of the Stallmart national chain of shopping stores. Stall had always been fascinated by the concept of rural marketplaces and resolved to create little stores within the enclosed spaces of large buildings across the nation. The idea was similar to an indoor shopping mall, with an important difference. Instead of just leasing space to smaller stores which managed their own businesses, Stall's vision was to provide identical services and products in every Stallmart, and selling franchises to operate the "stalls" to operators. Stall's parent company set operations and product standards, marketed, managed inventories and drove high-level economies of national scale. The franchisees ran the stalls.

Every Stallmart had a grocery, home goods, electronics, pharmacy, optometry, and automotive stalls. Each Stallmart also had a wide assortment of lesser-known stalls, such as the Mystic Materials stall managed by Bob's cousin Robert.

Stuart parked his car in the "Stallmart Car Detailing" stall and went inside the grand promenade to reference the store directory. *I get lost every time I come in here*, he thought to himself. Normally, Stuart only did weekly grocery shopping there, as the pricing was excellent, but normally didn't walk the entire store and browse.

Looking through the listing he found the Mystic Materials location, it was a small stall next to a wireless device boutique. Skirting the aggressive tout at the wireless device stall, he scuttled into the Mystic Materials shop.

Looking around, the closely spaced row shelves were jam-packed with small containers and the room itself smelled slightly musty. Seeing a counter bell, Stuart rang it.

"Hello? I'll be right there," a surprisingly resonant voice came from a small slightly-framed man. "Ah, here you are. My name is Robert, what can I help you find?"

Robert pronounced his name 'Row Bear', which amused Stuart. Thinking there might be an additional discount available he asked, "Yes, I have a list of the ingredients needed for a project of mine and I was referred to you by your cousin Bob over at the Blazin' Bob shop."

"Which Blazin' Bob shop are we talking about? The one at the Streedle Beat Mall or the one off of Highway 15?" Robert asked.

"Why, the one at Streedle Beat."

"Thank you; I have two cousins with Blazin' Bob franchises."

"Both named Bob, I suppose?"

"Of course! All the males in our family are named Robert. Some of us change how it is pronounced in order to maintain some semblance of the individual, not to mention it being a convenient conversational shortcut when talking in-family. One cousin even pronounces his name as 'Frank', but that is less common than simple plays on the same name like Rob or Bert."

"Interesting, Row-Bear. Here is the list of items I'll need. Do you have all of them available?" Stuart said while handing over the sticky note.

Robert read down the list, nodding his head with each entry. "Yes, we do have all of these items; however, you will also have a fair amount of each left over. While the sold quantities come in small amounts, your project doesn't require very much. One of the minor issues imposed by working with Stallmart is that we only sell pre-packaged items. However, you'll find the prices are quite comparable to competitors selling by the unit. Is this list from the Mystic Mort's 'Summoning' book? Yes, I thought so. Then you'll have plenty of leftover ingredients for other uses, Mystic Mort specifies a lot of the same ingredients in his formulations." As he spoke, his hands were picking items off of the shelves as he ran down the list.

Stuart shook his head, "I'm only working the one project, but I'm sure your pricing will not be an obstacle. Was there a referral discount connected with Bob's reference?"

"Absolutely, very little I wouldn't do for dear cousin Bob. I'll include your discount when I ring up the charges. Now, will you be paying with cash, debit or credit card?"

Robert deftly worked the register, processing the transaction. Stuart declined being added to the list receiving a newsletter but was nice about it.

Robert handed the bag over to Stuart, "Thank you for your business, please refer your friends to us. Have a great day, and if it isn't great, the spell for fixing that is on page 287," he said with a wink.

What an odd experience, Stuart thought. He quite enjoyed the conversations with Bob and Robert, it reminded him of the slightly off-kilter effect Bella always had on him. Of course, the thought of Bella dampened his mood somewhat as he remembered why he was engaged in the summoning of an imp in the first place.

He picked up his newly-clean car and drove home. He resolved to do the summoning itself the next evening, which should give him more than adequate time to read and fully understand the instructions.

As Stuart read the section, he realized his old photography equipment would be useful, as he already had readily available beakers and various other chemical-handling utensils. He hadn't previously thought about it, but not having to use the dishes he ate off of was probably a better approach.

Stuart started the next day full of expectation. He planned to contact Bella shortly after the summoning, checking in to see how "she was doing". He would casually drop a comment he had summoned something to keep her up at night, with an evil chuckle. He longed for a mustache to twirl. He'd then listen for the first indications of concern and ring off. That would put paid to all remaining angst concerning her abandoning him, and he could move forward with his life. Who knows, maybe Brian would be available for a late dinner?

The first step was mixing a cleansing bathing fluid. Stuart had a magnetic mixer from his photography kit that served the bill nicely for mixing things in a glass beaker. As he dropped each ingredient into the swirling mix, he solemnly spoke the prescribed words. Once it was complete, he set the mixture aside in a fresh flask and started on a priming solution after he had washed the mixing beaker. This one required simmering heat during the preparation, which Stuart supplied using his kitchen gas cooktop. It too was set aside in a separate clean glass flask.

So far, so good, Stuart thought as he reviewed the next step. *I guess I need to decide where the ritual should take place. Someplace convenient to the kitchen, I suppose. The granite countertop is quite expansive, although probably too slick to accept the necessary chalk ward lines. I'll just use a portion of the last large cardboard box I got from Amazon over the countertop.*

He cut the box into a 24-inch by 24-inch square, which he set atop the granite countertop. Getting his masking tape from the workroom, he taped the entire cardboard square down so that it wouldn't slip or move. Stuart then lined up the balance of the ingredients next to the square for easy access.

Drawing the pentagram ward design was a fairly simple exercise for Stuart. He took the special drawing stick, which acted like chalk even though it was not, strictly speaking, chalk, and drew the interconnecting straight lines into the familiar pentagram design. The center of the five-sided design was approximately 4-inch by 4-inch, plenty of room to center the provided special candle. Looking it over, Stuart considered it a credible effort. He went on to complete the full circle around the pentagram and poured salt onto the boundary of the entire circle.

Stuart placed the candle and holder in the middle of the pentagram, dipping his fingers into the cleansing solution which he then flicked over the complete tableau while saying words specified in the instructions. He dried his fingers on a clean hand-towel and picked up the candle lighting taper. He lit the wax taper, moving it slowly to the candle centerpiece, which caught almost immediately.

Blowing out the taper, a small tail of smoke wisped up past his nose. There was an unusual smell in Stuart's kitchen. *Must be a fragrance in the taper or candle*, he thought.

Now for the final step, he dipped his fingers in the priming solution and this time flicked the solution into the flame while saying, "I summon you to bedevil, Bella my lost love, and be a blight on her happiness from this day forth."

Stuart was rather proud of the text he had come up with and couldn't wait to tell Bella about it. As he flicked the solution onto the flame, it flared several feet towards the ceiling and receded back to just the normal candle flame height. *Must have been something in the priming mix to do that, but it's a nice visual effect.* He flicked a few more drops onto the flame but this time didn't see any unusual effect other than making the candle sputter.

Well, it doesn't matter, it's time call Bella!

He dialed Bella's number and she answered after a couple of rings.

"Hi Bella, this is Stuart! I wanted to check in on you to see how you are doing?"

"Hi Stu, things have been just fine here, how are you?" Bella asked.

"I've been busy on some new projects. Throughout, I was thinking of you and all of your occult studies and it occurred to me, you could use a demon over at your house. So I went ahead, summoned one, and ordered it to head your way."

"Demon? I thought you didn't hold much stock in the topic," Bella said.

Before Stuart could answer, a large crash was heard through the phone. Bella yelled something unintelligible before she turned the same vocal volume at Stuart, "Stuart, you complete idiot! What have you done?"

Stuart was about to answer, but the phone connection went dead in his hand. He redialed Bella, but evidently, she was not picking up. This had gone even better than he had imagined!

His mood lifted, he walked over to the refrigerator to pour himself a glass of wine. He lifted the glass and readied a toast to himself.

"Oh, what occasion are we toasting?" asked a cavernous deep voice behind Stuart.

Stuart whirled, spilling just a bit of wine, and saw something coming through the wall of his kitchen. It was approximately human in shape, but very hard to see as the edges seemed to be blurry. The air within the kitchen seemed to also be under greater pressure as the dark figure fully entered the room.

"Who are you?" Stuart cried, "You've given me such a start!"

"My name you couldn't pronounce and I likely wouldn't tell you regardless. You can call me Buz if it matters to you. Are you the one I have to thank for the delightful snack I just had?"

"Snack?"

"Yes, someone sent a smallish imp over to Bella's. They aren't much good for anything except a quick bite, but as hungry as I have been, it was quite welcome."

"What are you?" Stuart inquired as panic started to have its way with him.

"A much better question than who I am. I am a greater demon, currently under geas to serve as Bella's home security system. Evidently, it was easier to summon me than spend $39.99 a month for a human-monitored system. Luckily for me, my self-worth isn't tied to that information," Buz said with good humor. "Did I mention I am still hungry?"

"I also see from the apparatus lying about the imp indeed came from here. I knew it already, having tracked it back, but it pays to follow the forms when engaged in this type of activity," Buz said fastidiously. "Based on the rules under which I am bound, I am now permitted to eat you for breaching Bella's home security. When last I saw her, she was unconscious underneath a fallen bookshelf, so I should probably get on with the eating as she might try to stop me, were she awake. Nothing personal, and I did appreciate the snack." Buz slowly moved towards Stuart, his face a black nothingness. His form seemed to expand with each step.

Stuart backed away from the oncoming presence, running into the countertop. His mind, unable to comprehend matters, searched wildly for any option. Maybe this person, who thinks he's a demon, is also superstitious. Quickly, he grabbed the beaker of cleansing solution and poured it all into the primer flask. A chemical bubbling rose up and Stuart flung the entire fluid contents of the combined flask onto Buz's immense chest.

Buz, looked down the front of his body in stunned disbelief, "You are the luckiest son of a bitch I have ever met! That's Mystic Mort's Geas Remover Potion or I'm a prince of Hell!"

"Now I have even more for which to thank you. However, I am still very hungry. Therefore I will still eat you, but I'll show you a mercy and make sure you don't suffer any more than is absolutely necessary. Win-Win! How does that sound?" Buz asked reasonably, resuming his inexorable advance towards Stuart.

Stuart's mind was in disarray, no solution presented itself. Finally, just as the shadow of Buz's fingers touched Stuart's body, he cried "But I don't believe in demons!"

Buz chuckled, "Skeptics taste the best of all!"

The screaming was abrupt and mercifully short-lived.

The sound of chewing, however, went on for quite some time.

"Now that was a meal!" a deep voice exclaimed accompanied by a lengthy belch. "I do have some room left for dessert, though."

Several minutes later, in a kitchen not too far away, the deep voiced words "Bella, I'm home!" were heard.

THE WAY IT WAS WITH JONAH

By: Arthur Weil

I guess maybe a lot of people never even heard about my friend Jonah Schmeltzle. I maybe never would have heard of him myself except every Friday after I get my pay, I usually stop for a couple of brews at the Gourmet Room. This is a joint run by Tony Santucci, used to be friends with my brother, Bill.

So anyway, it's a Friday evening and I stop into the Gourmet Room with some of the other guys from the can factory. We make tin cans which other places put food into. I load a top stamper. For all I know, it may be a bottom stamper, as who can tell the difference?

I get there earlier than most as I am good getting first into the pay line, so I climb on a bar stool next to a little guy I never seen before. He's maybe forty with a small moustache on a small face and a build to match. Not much. But there isn't anyone else around, so I say, "How's things, buddy?"

"Fine, thank you," says the little guy, very polite, "and how's things with you?"

Well I tell him how things is with me and we finish our beers and still the regular guys don't show up. So, I offer to buy the little guy a beer. Well, sir, his face lights up and I can see right away that here is a poor little guy who appreciates big guys like me being friendly. I never got much use for big guys that pick on little guys.

So the beers come. "By the way", he says, "My name is Jonah. Jonah Schmeltzle."

"Please-ta-meetcha," I says to him, and whip my hand out for a shake. Except the hand never gets there.

It seems the way I'm sitting, the elbow—my elbow—is crocked around the beer glass. And when I whip my hand out, the beer spills with glass and all into my lap.

"Oh," says Jonah, "I'm dreadfully sorry. I really am."

But I can see it ain't his fault so I start mopping up and cussing a bit at myself. Of course, if this Jonah guy had laughed or maybe snickered, I'd of bust him one right on the chops. But he don't snicker, don't even smile, and all the time apologizing as if he'd done it.

Well, I calm him down and order another beer, and he insists on paying for it, which is OK with me. One beer leads to another and pretty soon Augie joins us. Augie is my friend—Augie Donatio—a welder at the can factory. What he welds at the can factory, I don t know, but he says he's a welder and that's OK with me.

Like I says, Augie joins us and sits on a stool next to me and promptly falls off with the head of the stool, or rather the seat, right on top of him. This is funny, so I give him a loud "Ha, Ha," all the while preparing to defend myself.

But it ain't that way. He picks himself up and says to the little guy, Jonah, "Can't you never turn it off?"

Naturally, this is not what I expect and on my last "Ha", my mouth is still open. Augie dusts himself off and says sort of matter of fact, "Whatsa matter? You never hear about Jonah?"

Frankly, I don't know what he's talking about, so I say, "What are ya talking about?"

"Jonah," he says slow, like I was a kid or something,

"Jonah here who things happen to people when he's around. Ain't nothing happened to you yet?"

"No," I says.

"The beer," corrects Jonah, apologetically.

"What about the beer?" says Augie like a private eye.

"I spilled a beer," I says, "Jonah didn't do nothing. I spilled beer before, lots of beer, lots of times."

"Yeh, I know," says Augie, like I 'm still a kid, "That's the way it is with Jonah."

Jonah turns away like he's bashful. He dips a lip into a new brew.

"He's accident prone," says Augie, "for other people."

"Whattaya mean," I says, "for other people? People what are accident prone have accidents for their personal selves. Besides, I spill lots of beers, lots of times."

"You don't understand," says Augie. "Things happen around Jonah. People fall down, spill beer, fall off seats, stuff like that. You ever see a bar stool come off under me before?"

"No, but..."

"I'll show you. Come on. You too Jonah."

Well Jonah polishes off the beer and we go out, me tripping on a soft spot on the floor and Augie banging his elbow on the door.

It ain't long before I begin to get the Idea.

We haven't walked half a block before two cars lock bumpers at the curve. Next block, a little old lady drops a bottle of milk or something right through the bag she's carrying. Jonah stops for a minute to lean against a lamppost. The bulb goes out. Finally, we end up at my place. I can't seem to get the door open. So I hand the key to Jonah and the door opens and we go in.

As you can see, I get convinced.

Augie and me, we always see a lot of each other, you know, shooting pool and watching TV and drinking booze. And Jonah, he sort of joins us once in a while. Nothing serious ever happens and Augie and me sort of feel sorry for the little guy. He's quiet and seems to like having Augie and me around, you know, not whacking him one every time we get a stubbed toe."

One night, Jonah says on the phone, how about the ball game?

I says, "How about?"

So I call Augie and he says maybe a ballgame ain't a good place to take Jonah since the Bees are fighting for first. But we go anyway.

In the first inning, the guy in front of Jonah reaches up for a foul tip and catches it on his head. In the second inning, the lady behind him spills a hotdog, mustard and all, down her—you know, right between—well, it was some show how she tried to get it out. Third inning someone in the balcony hits me with a bag of water. I figure I get off light.

Right then, Augie gets a brainstorm. "Let's go sit behind the Gull bench."

"Yeah, all right," says Jonah, and I tag along. Lots of times the box seats aren't full and after the first few innings the ushers don't pay no mind who comes to sit there. I would have like to see one of them snippy ushers try to pitch Jonah out, though. That would be good.

The Bees score four in the fifth, three in the sixth and eight in the seventh, and we go home.

Augie, he gets real quiet, so I talk to Jonah. He's downed a few at the ballpark and this always makes him sentimental.

He tells me about his Ma and his Pa and about how people always keep clear of him. Even in school and the army. He figures with him in the army during a war, maybe we lose the war. The worst that happens in peace, though, is a Sergeant gets the mumps, two corporals get the crud for a month, the army loses a tank in the mud, and a coast defense gun gets hit with lightning. At, least that's all he takes credit for. Jonah tells me how glad he is that we, me and Augie, like him. I don't tell him we consider it a challenge, and we all get to my joint with me merely losing a heel off my shoe. Jonah offers to pay the repairs and I say OK. This makes him feel good, like a part of the team.

Up at my place, Augie looks real hard at Jonah. "We're going into business," he says. Just like that, he says it, knocking a full ashtray off the arm of his chair.

"What business," I say. "You drunk?"

"Jonah is a natural with a natural talent," Augie says.

"What are ya talking?" I says. "Maybe we start a protection racket and keep Jonah away from people if they kick in?"

Jonah winces, so I add, "Nothing personal, mind you."

"You seen what happened tonight," says Augie. "Jonah sits near the Gulls and the Bees shellac 'em. We rent him to the Bees. We rent him to the can factory to get a job in the Armstrong Can Co. We rent him to the Mayor during election to go to the opponent's rallies. We rent…"

"Now wait a minute…." starts Jonah.

"Shut up," says Augie, warming to his subject.

And so it goes on. That Augie…always full of ideas.

The long and short of it is we rent him to the Bees. It ain't easy and we really only rent him to Sock Guffin, the manager. Next day Augie goes up to Sock before the game and says he can win the pennant for him with Jonah and, naturally, Sock throws him out of the office.

Augie keeps at it though. He changes his tack. "Today," he writes in a letter to Sock Guffin, "you will lose by 20 runs or more."

We buy three boxes right behind the Bees bench and settle down with scorecards and beers, only my scorecard is a blank that got mixed in and Augie's beer spills on his pants. And the Bees start out OK. After all, Moose Dooley is pitching for his third straight shutout against the Miners who are last in the league by a hatful.

The third inning is still nothing to nothing. The fourth sees the Miners score six, the fifth gives them four, and the sixth gets Sock thrown out of the game for raising his voice to an umpire. Coming back to the bench, he looks up and scowls at Augie.

Next day Augie writes a similar note and mentions where we sit and all. Same thing. The Bees lose 18-1. Augie has to go to the john in the seventh, and the Bees score a run. Sock scowls but he don't say anything. I guess he thinks it's too silly to say anything about. Next day, in the seventh with the Bees behind 12-0, he turns to Augie and says, "Sit over there tomorrow. The whole double-header."

I tell Augie things better start showing a profit as I cannot afford to be off work much longer. He says they will.

The next day, which is a Sunday, The Bees take two real easy and Augie calls Sock after the game, says he's coming over.

He comes over and we sit Jonah over in a far corner so the manager will not get knocked around too much.

"This is nuts" says Sock Guffin. "You mean to tell me this guy makes me win or lose?"

"It's this way," says Augie, like he was talking to a kid again. "Jonah is accident-prone to other people. Things go wrong around him. Now what we propose is to put scientific controls on this propensity of his and get the maximum benefit from his unexplored talents."

I don't know about Sock, but these kinds of words coming out of Augie stop me cold. I listen like I know what he's talking about.

"This is nuts," says Sock again, and he stands up to leave.

Fortunately, his belt breaks. Right at the buckle.

So we get our first job. It ain't nothing on paper and Sock says if we ever tell a living soul, he'll break all three of our cotton-picking heads, but he agrees. When the team is in town, we're commissioned to sit behind the opponent's bench every game if the Bees are not at least three games on top of the league. For this we get $50.00 a game out of Sock's pocket which he will make up double from his bonus and share of the playoff money.

That season we work sixteen games and the Bees win by five, some on their own merits.

So you can see we come out with $800.00, split three ways. Of course, four of the games are day games and we lose a day at work each time. But at least it's money earned honest and on our own. I begin to know how an independent businessman feels making his own money by use of his talent and brains—or maybe Jonah's talent and Augie's brain. Anyway, the $800.00 is the only money we make.

With ball season over, we hold a council of war to decide where next to turn a buck from Jonah's talent. Jonah and Augie come up to my place about eight o'clock on a Tuesday after the final game. Augie had his coat tore where he caught it getting out of the car.

"Well," says Augie, "What next?"

"I've always wanted to travel," says Jonah with a sort of faraway look in his eye. "1 always wanted to go to Washington and New York and see the Empire State building and the Washington monument and the Eiffel Tower."

"The Eiffel Tower ain't in Washington or New York," says Augie.

"No," says I, "Everyone knows it's in Europe. London."

And there the conversation rests. So we drink a few and Augie says we got a gold mine by the tail. Augie thinks we ought to rent him to the Mayor. Jonah says baseball is OK, but he wouldn't want anyone to be mayor of his town if the guy got in by causing his opponent any particular harm. Augie says they're both crooks anyway so who cares, but Jonah can't see it that way and neither can I. So we quick get out of politics.

Then I start getting lyrical. I call to mind how lucky we are, bachelors, $800.00 extra clams in the sock, able to go anywhere, do anything, no wife-people around to say things like don't go bowling and mow the lawn. Not like Monahan. Morris Monahan at the plant. Always griping about his wife and his mother-in-law. The mother-in-law had made a two week visit ever year the last seven years. "Seven years bad luck," says Monahan, "And I didn't t even break no mirror." Monahan used to be a regular guy before the battle axe staked a claim. Just shows what the guy says. A guy don't marry just a girl; he gets a raft of people.

"That's it!" says Augie, jumping up, and tripping both him and the coffee table to the floor.

"We are in the mother-in-law removing business."

"Now Augie," I say as he picks himself up. "You been gettin' TV eyes. Besides, Monahan may not want the old bat killed."

"Not killed, ya dope," says Augie. "Monahan introduces Jonah and nature takes its course. She starts having accidents and all of a sudden she don't like it here anymore."

Well, I don't think much of the idea but who am I to stand in the way of Augie's business acumen? Anyway, I get out of the evening unscathed. At least I think so until I find both my alarm clock and my wristwatch don't work anymore. Expensive, this Jonah? I'll say.

So Augie talks to Monahan and Augie says one hundred dollars, special price for our first client. Monahan has met Jonah and sort or half-believes maybe Jonah can do it. Anyway, it's a breath of life in a dull existence. Monahan says fifty bucks. Augie says seventy-five. Around sixty they shake—money after results.

It's a short business venture.

Monahan Takes Jonah and Augie home from work. Jonah don't work with people. He stays home and makes rhymes for birthday cards. He's always available, which is an asset.

Like I say, Monahan takes Augie and Jonah home. He opens the door. The wife is there and so is the old biddy.

"This is my friend, Jonah," says Monahan. "Jonah Schmeltzle, meet the wife and the wife's mother, Mrs. Ryan." The mother-in-law raises the hand to shake, takes one step forward, out goes the throw rug, and down goes the battle axe.

Broken hip.

Six months in bed.

At Monahan's.

Well, Monahan is not known for being a reasonable gentleman when catastrophe strikes, so Augie forgoes asking him for payment. In fact, Augie is all for taking a week off to visit foreign shores.

"Washington," says Jonah. So Washington it is.

I don't know about London, but there sure isn't any Eiffel Tower in Washington. There's lots of other towers, though, and lots of white buildings and statues and all.

We stay at a real nice hotel, too. Clean sheets every day. Stationary in the drawer. And the morning paper stuck in the door.

That's how I find out about the bomb.

You know all about it by now.

It made all the headlines.

What you don't know is about Jonah and how he played the most important part of all.

Well, the bomb was like a satellite. There was this ban on atomic tests and all, but that didn't keep us (and them too) from putting atom bombs in orbit around the Earth ready to be aimed back at a minute's notice. I don't know how many there were. We both claimed the most. But we said ours were further away and safer and they wouldn't fall accidently. They said the same thing.

So the cold war went on.

We're on our way to see the White House when we hear all the fire engines and police sirens and loudspeakers. "Off the Streets," seem to be what they're saying. Later I find out what happened. There wasn't any time. That's why all the bombs have been aimed into outer space and detonated now. Theirs and ours—I think.

But this one bomb WAS set off. No one still says who it belonged to. All they knew for sure was that it was heading down and it seemed like for Washington. It only took a few seconds. We were walking along by the White House, people running here and there and all over.

Then we hear someone say, "Look there!"

We look up and there is a glow like a star in daylight. It gets brighter fast.

Augie runs, and I run, and Jonah runs. But Jonah runs the other way. Right across the White House lawn.

BOOM!

It hits.

Augie and me go flying, but no bones broke. We look around for Jonah on the lawn. There ain't no Jonah.

You remember the headlines. A crater eight feet deep and twenty-six feet across. One casualty. An innocent bystander. Wouldn't you know it? Poor Jonah.

I keep thinking Jonah knew what he was doing. Where he was running.

Anyway, with his luck, the damned thing didn't work.

That's the way it was with Jonah.

THE HOLE

By: Tim Jeffreys

As Josh had said on the day of the viewing, the house was everything they were looking for in a starter home. Though Marion agreed, having herself fallen in love with the place from the moment she stepped through the front door, something about it hadn't felt quite right. It was nothing she could put her finger on. The kitchen was small, but since there was a separate dining room this didn't worry her. The garden too was small, but as Josh said that would make it easier to manage. The other rooms, including the bedrooms, were of a reasonable size. There was even a downstairs toilet.

Perhaps it was the price that bothered her. "The owners want a quick sale," the Estate Agent had told them, which Marion — seasoned house-hunter she'd become — had thought to be an excuse. She imagined all would become clear at the viewing, as was usually the case, but on arriving at number 28 Arcadia Street she could find nothing to explain the low asking price. Perhaps it was true then. The owners only wanted a quick sale.

The owners were a thirty-something couple named Carrie and Wayne who had two children in their early teens, both girls. The girls sat in silence on the sofa for the duration of the viewing. They didn't even look up when Marion said hello to them, though she noticed how their hands wrestled in their laps. It was Carrie who showed Josh and Marion around the house. She seemed weary and put-upon, but determined to show a brave face.

"Marion's obsessed with finding her dream home," Josh told Carrie as they climbed the stairs. "You wouldn't believe how many hours she spends on the internet every evening searching."

"It's true," Marion said, smiling. "Josh has been feeling neglected. He's about ready to divorce me, aren't you, honey?"

They laughed, but Carrie only showed them a thin smile and indicated the master bedroom.

Marion was resolved to uncovering something to explain the asking price. "Such a lovely home," she said to Carrie. "And such a steal. You must be going somewhere amazing after this."

"We want to get away," Carrie said. "Get our lives back."

"Get your lives back?"

"It's for the children mainly. They need a fresh start."

"Oh," Marion said, though she didn't press for further information. She imagined this meant trouble at school, or a bad crowd. Drugs or boyfriends or bullying or peer pressure, or *something*. Nothing to do with the house then, after all; only some hardship this particular family wanted to get away from.

The husband, Wayne, had spent the duration of the viewing looking at his mobile phone; until the visiting party returned from upstairs and his wife snapped at him to put it away. Her reprimand, which seemed overly harsh, and Wayne's expression of shame set Marion's imagination into gear again. She thought maybe there had been some infidelity in the relationship, perhaps with a neighbour or someone else close by, which would again explain why they were moving. Secret texts and sexy photos stored on a hard drive. The exact same thing had happened to her friend Natalie. *That* had been an ugly divorce.

The house had a basement for storage, which Carrie only showed them after Josh insisted, and then only from the top of the steps. First she'd had to find a set of keys to open the padlocked door.

"Light's broken," Carrie said as the three of them stood in the doorway peering down into the gloom. "Sorry."

"Might convert this into an office," Josh said, and Marion thought she saw Carrie blanch.

"You won't want to spend a lot of time down here," Carrie said. "There's no natural light."

"Maybe not," Josh said, and grinned. "But it'll be the perfect place for hiding the bodies, eh, Marion?"

"Josh!" Marion said, swatting at his arm. "You and your twisted sense of humour."

Carrie showed them a thin, tolerant smile again. "So," she said. "What do you think?"

"I think it's a done deal," said Josh. "Right, Marion?"

Marion turned, and was a little disconcerted to find Wayne and the two children stood close at her back, peering past her into the gloom of the basement.

"Yes, well, we certainly can't argue about the price."

***

Two weeks after they moved in, Josh discovered the hole. He started talking almost immediately about turning the basement into an office. Unnerved at this idea, but not certain why, Marion suggested he convert one of the spare bedrooms.

"You can use the box room. At least, until we need it for, you know…other things."

Marion knew Josh understood *other things* meant babies, but neither of them dared say it out-loud until it became a reality. They had both agreed a family was the next step after buying their own home. Marion was already spending time on-line looking up baby names and window-shopping for cots and cute little clothes, usually when Josh was in the shower.

Josh insisted though he was going to convert the basement. Marion suspected he wanted somewhere all of his own, his shed, his man-place, somewhere she wouldn't go, somewhere he could play computer games which she wouldn't allow him to do anywhere else in the house because the constant noise of gunfire and explosions irritated her. He had started clearing out the junk Carrie and Wayne left behind, when he discovered the hole in the dead centre of the basement floor. It had been covered, he said, by a heavy wardrobe laid out flat on the floor which he'd had to take apart to move. The hole was perfectly cylindrical, and only about a foot in diameter. When Josh pointed a torchlight into it, they saw no bottom.

"Wow!" he said. "I wonder how deep it goes."

He seemed fascinated, but Marion had felt an immediate sense of anger and betrayal. "So that's it then! This is why she didn't want us coming down here at the viewing. I knew there must be something wrong for them to be selling at such a low price. I told you we should've had a full survey done, but oh no - you said we could spend the money fixing anything we found wrong. Well how much is this going to cost us, Josh?"

"Marion," Josh said, looking taken aback by her outburst. "It's just a hole."

***

At work, during what they all called the three o'clock lull when the phones went quiet and her workmate Farrah popped out to buy cakes — most of which she ate herself — Marion liked to check for messages sent to her account on the Soulm8s dating site. She knew she should have closed her account after meeting Josh, but she'd found that when she felt low it gave her a little boost to know men were still interested in her. Farrah was always saying how glamorous she looked, coming into work, it seemed a shame not to get some reward for her efforts. She couldn't remember the last time Josh had paid her a compliment.

There were the usual messages from lonely scaffolders and divorced dads, dull attempts to start conversations. *I like the cinema too*, one man had messaged her. His profile picture had an intense stare. *Maybe we could catch a film together sometime.*

Marion mouthed the word 'No' and continued scrolling through the messages.

Coffee?

Hey, beautiful.

She had no intention of acting on any of the messages. She certainly wouldn't respond to any of them. But she enjoyed reading through them and looking at the men's profiles, imagining what it would be like to go on a date with them. It was addictive, the interest. There was the only word for it. Addictive.

***

On the way home that evening Marion took a diversion through the inner city. Carrie and Wayne — the previous occupants of 28 Arcadia Street — had left in one of the kitchen drawers a scrap of paper with a forwarding address written on it. Marion came across the scrap of paper that morning when she was looking for the spare house keys, and decided she was going to drive by Carrie and Wayne's new place. She didn't plan to call in. No, no. Not yet anyway. All she wanted was a look. Something about the whole situation still didn't add up for her, and she hoped by getting a look at where Carrie and Wayne had moved to all would become clear.

This proved not to be the case.

It wasn't the most desirable part of the city, but Marion imagined the property was cheap. Her car's navigation system, into which she had punched Carrie and Wayne's new postcode, led her to a tower block. It had to be fifteen stories or more. It made sense a flat in this building was all Carrie and Wayne could afford after selling 28 Arcadia Street at such a loss, but why had they done it? What was the urgency? The whole point of buying a home was to get on the property ladder, and the generally accepted idea was you went up the ladder, not down. At least not until you retired and decided to downsize. Otherwise you kept going up.

It was the hole in the basement, Marion was sure of it. That was why they'd moved, and that was why they'd covered it up. The hole had to be affecting the house's foundations or something. It had to be some kind of a hazard. Carrie and Wayne must have discovered it then decided to get the hell out, pass the house on to someone else and let them deal with it. She pictured Carrie, pale and put upon, snapping at her husband to put his phone away. And the children with their waxy expressions and hands they couldn't still. They were an odd family for sure.

***

When she arrived home, she found lights and the TV on in the living room, plus a half-dozen empty beer cans on the coffee table. Her husband was nowhere to be seen. And in the kitchen she saw no attempt had been made to start dinner.

Standing at the foot of the stairs she called, "Josh? You up there?"

No answer.

"Josh? Where are you, honey-bun?"

Nothing.

She sniffed. There was a trace of something pungent, slightly discernible. She knew what it meant.

So Josh was with his deadbeat brother-the marijuana enthusiast. Most likely they had both smoked a couple of joints with those beers, before opening the windows in an attempt to get rid of the smell before she got home. Well, they had failed. There was only one place they could be now. In the basement.

Marion disliked Josh when he was stoned. It made him greedy and selfish. He would get the munchies and eat his way through entire packets of biscuits or anything else sweet he could get his hands on. It was as if he couldn't be satisfied. He'd sit and munch and munch. It was unpleasant to watch. Unattractive.

"Josh, honey?"

She peered into the basement's gloom. With the light entering from the hallway behind her, Marion could make out the two figures sat cross-legged on the floor with their backs to her. Neither turned to acknowledge her. Josh held a torch which he directed into the hole in the floor. Marion moved slowly down the steps.

"Josh?"

Still no change. She saw now she'd been correct. It was Benjamin who squatted next to Josh. He was the only person they knew who wore oversized American ice-hockey shirts. Benny-the-B he liked to call himself, as if he was some kind of gangster, and Marion liked to extend this into Benny-the-Bug. Sometimes she called him The Roach.

She stamped her feet on the concrete floor as she walked towards them, but they continued staring into the hole.

"Josh?" she said, then: "JOSH!"

That did it. Both he and Benjamin jumped and twisted to face her.

"J-Jesus, Marion, what're you trying to do to us? We nearly fell in."

"You wouldn't fit down there, dummy."

"Scared us half to death creeping up."

"I've been calling you for the past ten minutes. What're you doing sitting down here in the dark?"

"I was showing Benny the hole."

Marion tried to avoid looking at the hole, though she found her eyes were drawn to it. The way Josh's torchlight illuminated its smooth interior both intrigued and unnerved her.

"What the hell do you want to show him that for?"

"It's fascinating," Benjamin said. "Take a look."

"Don't be ridiculous. You're both stoned."

"He is," Josh said, pointing at his brother and letting out a childish giggle.

"He is," Benjamin retaliated, also giggling.

Marion shook her head.

"You both are. You should have been getting dinner ready, but instead you're sat down here gazing into this stupid hole. What are you looking for exactly?"

"There's something down there," Benjamin said, though Josh made belated attempts to silence him.

"What? You mean like rats or something?"

"Not rats."

"What then?"

"Something good. We don't know what it is yet. Take the weight off, G. Have a look."

Marion sometimes felt like slapping Benjamin for the silly way he talked.

She began to walk away when Josh took hold of one of her hands, caressing the back of it with his thumb. "Seriously," he said. "It's a good thing. Sit down and have a look. You'll see for yourself."

Huffing, and shaking her head, making a show of her unwillingness but curious nonetheless, Marion sat down on the floor next to Josh. She looked into the hole.

"Well," she said. "There's nothing."

"Wait," Josh said. "Keep watching."

Marion went on staring into the hole. Once, she thought she saw something moving and her heart picked up, but then she realised it was only the torchlight had shifted. Still, it had given her a little thrill. The idea that there *might* be something down there. The possibility of it.

She went on looking. There was nothing there really. She knew there was nothing there. But the more she looked the more she found she couldn't stop. It took some effort for her to drag her eyes away. Reluctantly, she stood.

"Well," she said. "One of us better get dinner on. I suppose I don't need to ask if you're hungry."

***

Josh tossed and turned beside her in bed. She couldn't sleep herself, thinking about the hole and what might be inside it. When Josh got up, she didn't need to ask where he was going.

"One last look," he said. Marion listened to his feet padding down the stairs.

Though she was tempted to get up herself, she realised she had work the next day. It took all her willpower to remain in bed. It was hours before she fell asleep, and Josh still hadn't returned.

A week later, Marion didn't question her husband when he took the mattress off the bed in the spare room and dragged it down into the basement. That same night, she slept there beside him, both of them gazing into the hole by torchlight until they fell asleep. In the morning, waking in the dark basement, Marion would look again. She'd look for as long as she dared, then get ready for work in a rush with no time for a shower or breakfast. A few times she called in sick to work so she could stay with Josh in the basement and stare into the hole. The thing was; she never saw anything. And Josh never saw anything. He kept insisting there was something down there in the hole and if they kept looking, one day they would see it.

***

It was the look on her colleague Farrah's face when Marion arrived for work one morning that finally brought her to her senses. Farrah stared, a cookie raised halfway to her mouth, a look on her face of disgust and disbelief. Marion took herself off to the toilets and in the mirror she looked at herself, really looked at herself, for the first time in weeks. She had lost weight. Her face looked pale and drawn, her skin had a yellowish tint, and there were bags under her eyes. The eyes themselves were glazed and bloodshot. Her hair was greasy and the roots were showing. She'd meant to book an appointment at *Nikki's*, but she hadn't found the time. The worse thing was her clothes. Her blouse looked as if she'd slept in it, had a ketchup stain on the collar, and it didn't match the skirt she wore. The tights were ill-matched as well, and on her feet were the trainers she used to go jogging in. What the hell had she done to herself?

"Something needs to change," she muttered as she went about trying to put things right as best she could. "I'm going to tell Josh. We need to stop. This is…something needs to change."

But she knew she'd never get through to Josh. She pictured him, with his slack, unresponsive face, his eyes trained on the hole in their basement floor. When was the last time they'd made love? When was the last time they'd had dinner together? When was the last time they'd spoken more than two words to each other? All he wanted to do these days was stare into the hole.

There had to be someone else who she could talk to. Someone who could help her. She wracked her brain.

***

When Carrie opened the door, she had the same pale, put-upon look as she had months ago when she showed Marion and Josh around 28 Arcadia Street, but now there was something else in the mix: a look of resignation and defeat.

"Yes?" she said, blinking at Marion, whom she clearly didn't recognise.

"Don't you remember me? My name's Marion Swann. My husband Josh and I bought your house at 28 Arcadia Street." Feeling vengeful, Marion added, "The one with the *hole*."

"Oh," Carrie said. "I wondered how long it'd be until you came knocking."

"You knew about the hole then?" Marion said.

Carrie shrugged. "How could I not?"

"Guess you didn't feel like mentioning it to us."

"Well," Carrie cast her eyes downwards. "I was kind of hoping you wouldn't find it."

"That's why you moved isn't it? That's why you wanted a quick sale."

Carrie looked up again and nodded. "We had to get away. It had them, you see."

"Had them?"

"The girls. And Wayne-it got him too. And I was starting to…we had to get away from it. I wanted us to get our lives back."

"And did you? Did you get your lives back?"

Carrie drew a deep breath. "You'd better come in."

The inside of the flat was cramped and smelled of wet washing. As Carrie led the way along the hall, Marion glanced into the rooms they passed. The living room was small and unoccupied. In the tiny kitchen, crockery was piled up by the sink. The two bedrooms had boxes stacked in them.

"Still not fully unpacked then?"

"Huh? Oh, we've been kind of…uh…busy."

"Don't worry, we haven't fully unpacked either. It takes time. Where's the family? They out?"

Carrie turned and shook her head. "I'll show you," she said.

There was a door at the end of the hall. When Carrie opened the door, Marion's first reaction was one of horror.

She's murdered them, she thought. *She's murdered them and now she'll murder me.*

She had begun to back up, when one of the girls lifted her head and glanced at her. The girl lay on her back on the floor of what appeared to be some kind of storage room. She was almost as long as the room itself, and crammed in beside her were her sister and her father. Neither of the other two acknowledged Marion. They didn't even move. Wayne looked chubbier than he had the first time Marion had seen him, and he had the beginnings of a beard. His attention, and that of the two girls, was held by something directly above them, something on the ceiling of the little room. Though Marion already had an idea of what she'd see, she stepped forward at Carrie's invitation, ducked her head inside the room and looked to see what Wayne and his daughters were staring at.

In the ceiling, a little to the left of the room's single light fitting, there was a wide, circular hole. Marion felt a familiar jitter of excitement when she looked into it and had to wrench her eyes away.

"There's… there's one here too?"

"They're everywhere," Carrie said.

"But what's the fascination? There's nothing there. There's nothing inside."

"There might be."

"There isn't. There—"

"I was about to join them. I don't suppose you want to…?"

Join them? So it had Carrie too now? It *had* her.

Before Marion could respond, Carrie knelt and lay down on the floor of the little room beside her husband. She lay on her back like the others, gazing up into the ceiling hole. Marion had an odd sensation that Carrie had departed. That all that remained of her now was this still and unresponsive shell on the floor.

Appalled, Marion turned to leave. But then she stopped. It couldn't hurt if she had a look could it? Only a few minutes. Where's the harm? Maybe there was something here. Maybe this hole had something inside it. She was tired of sitting in her basement at home, waiting for something. Always looking. Always waiting. And never seeing anything. Perhaps here, in this hole, there would be *something.*

Still unsure, she crouched and squeezed in beside Carrie's two daughters. It felt comforting to lie there with the four of them. She let out her breath.

And together, they looked.

WHO LISTENS TO HUMMINGBIRDS?

By: Sarah M. Lewis

The little girl should have been posing in the bluebonnets, not lying dead in them. A huge black and yellow butterfly, big as a salad plate, lay on her. It didn't fly away. It looked dead too.

It couldn't be her. "Letitia?" EMT Sam Hernandez knelt over the small still form.

"Sam?" He'd come over the instant he heard his fellow EMT Addison calling his name from where she stood on the embankment several feet away looking down at something. She sounded strange.

Only an hour or two ago, that little girl left the hospital happy and alive skipping off with a pretty butterfly fluttering after her. It couldn't be the same butterfly.

Behind him, a twisted SUV wrapped around the guardrail and state troopers blocked off the northbound lanes of I-45 until the coroner got there. Two people dead, on a straight stretch of interstate in the middle of the day.

"How the hell did it happen?"

***

"Do you feel sick, honey?" Sam's fellow EMT Addison asked Letitia while carefully inserting the child's finger into the bio-scanner. They'd arrived to find the little girl conscious but pale, supported by the teacher. Sure enough, the scanner read Leticia as anemic.

They'd already taken several elderly people from assisted living to the hospital that morning because of the anemia. Every spring anemia came north to Texas, along with the hummingbirds and butterflies, hitting kids and old people. You never knew who or when. The experts claimed hotter temperatures were to blame.

Letitia shook her head. "No. Just sleepy."

No surprise. Small traces of something that acted like a narcotic turned up in the blood of those sickened with anemia.

Letitia scratched at her arm.

"What's this?" Sam could clearly see red marks. They looked like insect bites. The bugs were getting immune to the latest oral repellants again.

"I was playing outside and something bit me."

"We'll put something on it." Addison sent a quick message through her intermed link that the oral insect repellant formula needed some bio-chemical updating.

They wheeled Letitia down the hall to the ambulance, passing classroom after classroom of children nodding off at their desks and listless, exhausted teachers trying to concentrate on the lesson.

"Spring fever is really bad this year." The principal apologized. "The kids are fine in the morning, but after recess, it's hard for them to concentrate."

Outside the building, hummingbirds were kicking up a fuss over the flowers and nectar feeders, chasing each other.

"Mine! Mine!" They squeaked angrily when there were plenty of flowers for all of them.

Every now and then Sam caught a word in English or Spanish that made him blush. They were annoying enough without being bilingual. How could Anglos think they were cute?

Talking hummingbirds began appearing in Texas backyards about the time Sam started high school. There were loco stories about how this happened. Everyone had an opinion. Exposure to chemicals causing mutations, secret government experiments gone wrong, Narco Cartels running genetics labs to breed illegal exotic pets, accelerated evolution caused by global warming, you name it.

"I guess the vampires got me."

"Don't believe everything hummingbirds say, sweetie." Sam felt a surge of anger. The damn hummingbirds had started the rumors about vampires. He and Addison had seen plenty of garlic hanging in windows and patients wearing crucifixes, even if they weren't Catholic.

All because that old lady kept posting videos of her talking with the hummers.

"*Hola, Pajaritos y Pajaritas.*" She'd say.

The hummers would swarm about her shrilling, "*Hola. Hola, Senõra.*"

Then she'd posted this video of the tiny nest with two tinier dead baby hummers, brittle like old leaves. The hummers said vampires did it and the video went viral. To top it all off, experts who studied hummingbirds reported finding nests with dead baby hummers.

A hummingbird whirred past them chasing one of those big black and yellow butterflies, the ones with marks like bar codes on the wings. It impaled the butterfly fluttering above the ornamental hedge.

"*Muerte!*" it shrilled.

The little girl looked up as they loaded her into the ambulance. "Why do the hummingbirds fight the butterflies? They've been fighting all morning. Sometimes the hummingbirds poke holes in the butterflies' wings and they die!"

Sam followed the child's gaze and saw hummingbirds darting around the shrubbery chasing the butterflies away from the windows. Dead butterflies carpeted the ground.

As if it heard, a hummingbird came and hovered a couple of feet from Letitia.

"*Mala mariposa!*"

Sam swiped at it. Vicious little pests. "Well, sweetheart, I think they fight over the flowers. They both feed from the flowers."

One of the hummingbirds broke away from the battle and squeaked, "*¡Hombre estupido!*"

***

"*Muerte!*" The hummingbird screamed at Sam.

Sam wished he'd decided to eat lunch inside the hospital cafeteria, but it had been such a nice day, he felt like being outside. He had to keep shooing the butterflies away. For some reason, they kept trying to land on him.

A hummingbird buzzed Sam's head before dive bombing the butterflies scattering them.

"Death!" It screamed.

Sam waved his device at it, splashing his soda on the ground.

His device pinged. He accepted the notice. Letitia, the little girl from that morning had been given an iron infusion. She wanted to say "Bye" to him before leaving with her mother. He wished all his days were like that.

Five minutes later, Letitia came skipping up to Sam clutching a can of soda. What a difference from the pale drooping little girl of a few hours earlier. She still had a slight rash that looked like insect bites. Besides the anemia, Sam kept seeing insect bites on people.

"Thank you, Mister."

"You're welcome, honey."

The mother proceeded to thank Sam and exchange polite small talk.

"Mommy, look a butterfly!" A big black and yellow butterfly hovered in front of Letitia's face to her obvious wonder and delight.

Her mother, who was now looking for something in her purse, didn't give it more than a glance. "It's pretty, Letitia."

"Look, Mommy, it landed on my finger." The child stood there barely breathing as the butterfly perched on her finger fluttering its wings. Sam smiled. The kid must have soft drink on her fingers.

"Finish your drink, we've got to go." Letitia's mother said. The butterfly flew up as her mother took her hand.

"The butterfly isn't finished drinking coke off my finger."

Her mother wasn't going to wait. "Soft drinks are not good for butterflies."

"Mommy, my butterfly is following me!" Letitia looked back. Sam grinned. She wanted that butterfly to come with her and be her butterfly.

"Get in the car, honey, Daddy's waiting."

***

"What are those marks?" Addy asked.

Sam blinked back tears.

On the child's wrist were puncture marks with uncoagulated blood. Then the huge black and yellow striped butterfly opened its wings. It wasn't dead after all. It crawled down the dead child's body, settling itself upon the small wrist. Sam and Addison saw the needle-like tongue extend into one of the puncture marks.

Addison stared. "What is it doing to her?"

"Death! *Muerte! Mala Mariposa.*" Sam remembered what the hummingbirds had shrilled at him. He should have listened.

"That poor kid. She was standing there, so happy when the pretty butterfly perched on her finger. The hummingbirds were right about vampires. I didn't get it! They'd tried to tell us all, but we weren't listening. I am *hombre estupido!* Who pays attention to what hummingbirds say?"

Addison looked at him. "Sam, what are you saying?"

The pieces were all fitting together. "Everybody knows hummingbirds are vicious. I saw the hummingbirds chasing and killing butterflies.

"Remember all those classrooms full of sleeping kids? They were okay until after recess. We saw the butterflies all over the hedges at the school windows. Now Texas is full of kids with anemia. Don't you see? Who would have thought it? Those big butterflies drink blood like mosquitoes. Maybe they need iron. I bet their bite has a narcotic effect."

Addison looked up at him.

"Her mom must have crashed the SUV trying to get that thing off her. Maybe it bit her several times and she lost control. We have to call Homeland Security and Wildlife Management."

"Get away from her!" Addison swatted at the killer butterfly.

It fluttered a short distance away onto the asphalt shoulder where it landed too bloated to fly.

Sam stood over it. "You're not getting away this time."

He lifted his foot and stomped the butterfly into the ground again and again.

GRASSHOPPER

By: Ellen Denton

When I was in my junior year of high school, the factory my father worked at burned to the ground leaving its four hundred employees scrambling to find work. Jobs in a small town are hard to come by, but we all did our part.

I learned from the school guidance counselor that one of the teachers, a Miss Anna Linus, mentioned wanting to find someone to help part time with household chores. She lived with her sister Emily in a large Victorian home inherited from their parents.

I went to Miss Linus' classroom to recommend myself for the job, and assured her, that if hired, I would work diligently at whatever was needed. She was a rosy, rotund woman with an ear to ear smile and laughter in her eyes. She cheerfully hired me on the spot.

I was to work for three hours each day after school, six hours on Saturdays, and was to start the next day.

***

The three story Victorian was on the outskirts of town on two acres of well maintained, landscaped grounds. The house was quite imposing looking from the outside. To the right of it was a neat row of painted sheds, the largest greenhouse I'd ever seen was off to the right, and a fine-looking tack and stable house made from tumbled stone was to the left, now devoid of horses.

If the well-manicured grounds and stately structures hadn't looked as regal as they did, I wouldn't have been so surprised when the front door was opened to my knock by the broomstick-thin, sour-faced sister Emily, and revealed what I can only describe as a vortex of filth and decay within.

On that first day, when I walked into the wide entryway, there were black plastic bags filled with foul-smelling trash piled up against the walls, waiting for monthly transport to the town dump. When I timidly ventured to ask why they didn't place the garbage outdoors in cans, and have the cans emptied weekly by the sanitation department as was the normal custom in town, Emily Linus looked at me with annoyance and pointed out, as though it were obvious, that the big metal trash cans would besmirch the appearance of the grounds.

I was shown into what appeared to be a formal drawing room, that under other circumstance, with its high, ornamental ceilings and breathtaking stained-glass windows, would have been magnificent.

However, the corners of its floors, walls, and ceilings were festooned with cobwebs thick as bird's nests. The threadbare carpet was stained everywhere. A large decorative wood table with a busted leg lay on its side. Stacks of old magazines and newspapers spilled from it onto the floor in a yellowed, haphazard heap (which I later learned had been there like that for the last two years). I could see, peeking out from under a ruffle of floral upholstery at the bottom of a chair, a mousetrap with a dead rat, mostly gristle and bone, in it.

The expressionless Emily Linus gave me a tour through a few other rooms in the house that were on that first floor. Most of the surfaces were coated with inches of accumulated dust, some of it dotted with dead flies.

I had to restrain myself from gagging when I entered the kitchen because of the smell from rotting food left in the stack of unwashed dishes piled up on every counter. Dead cockroaches floated in a cauldron of oily water sitting on the filthy stove. I almost slipped on a chunk of greasy meat on the kitchen floor.

After seeing a few more spaces of similar ilk, I reminded myself how badly my family needed money and how scarce jobs were, forced an eager look onto my face, swallowed hard, and turned to Miss Linus.

"What would you like me to do first?"

I was relieved when she told me to check the flower beds encircling the house for weeds, adding the comment, "You can never put too much time or work into keeping the outward appearance of a home looking lovely." She then explained that her sister, Anna, would be returning late from the school, and she would be the one to assign me further tasks when she arrived.

***

You could have practically gotten down on your hands and knees with a magnifying glass to find any weeds in the beautiful and well-tended beds, which I soon learned Emily saw to personally, along with the lavish plantings in the greenhouse. The rest of the grounds were cared for by a full time gardener.

Anna Linus didn't show up while I was there, but she did on the day after, which was a Saturday.

That's when I got to see the second floor of the house and heard something alive moving around on the third.

***

The second floor was every bit as horrible as the first, and in some cases worse, with one exception.

Emily Linus's bedroom was as fresh, sculptured, and beautiful as the grounds surrounding the house. Not a speck of dust anywhere. The four-poster bed, the slip-covered chairs, and the long, billowing curtains were cheerful looking and spotless. A lovely cherry-wood writing desk sat in one corner and hook rugs brightened the floor. The entire room smelled like springtime, which I soon saw was because of a large vase of lilacs on a bedside table and a bouquet of yellow roses atop a bureau. I was not shown this room by anyone, but took a peek inside when I knew the two sisters were occupied with something downstairs and would not catch me snooping.

I'd been brought to the second floor by Anna, who wanted me to remove all the boxes and trash in the library so she could get at the books. There was a lot to do, and it would take me at least the entire six hours of that first Saturday.

The work was extremely unpleasant because of the rodent droppings and cobwebs. The library smelled so terrible that I began habitually checking my watch to see how much longer I would need to be there before my six hours were up, and was finally relieved when I only had an hour left to go.

I walked down the hallway with one of the remaining boxes to place it in an unused bathtub. I heard a dull thump on the ceiling above me.

I stopped and looked up for a few moments, and heard it again, except this time, it was five thumps in rapid succession. There was an urgency to the sound, like someone pounding on a door who desperately needs to get in or out right away. There was a pause of about thirty seconds, three more slow and deliberate thumps. This was followed by a prolonged wail, muffled by the layers of floor and ceiling above me. This pained sound rose in pitch until it became an unearthly scream, also distant and muffled, but sharp enough to make the hair on my arms stand up.

Sure there was someone alive up there, I raced downstairs to the sisters, who were sitting in the drawing room, and asked them about it.

They both stared at me in silence with identical, emotionless expressions (which is when I realized for the first time that the laughter normally visible in Anna's eyes was actually the gleam of insanity).

It was she who finally spoke. "It's nothing dear, just rats or water in the pipes. This is an old house. Go back to work."

Her usual, merry smile, which had only faltered for a moment, returned to her face, and Emily Linus now looked as stiff as a totem pole.

I did as I was told, but there was something unsettling about what had just occurred. The more I thought about the sounds and the sisters' reactions when they knew I'd heard them, the more I felt there was something wrong going on - more wrong than just two eccentric women living in a filthy, decaying house.

***

I worked Monday through Friday of the following week on both the first and second floors, and never heard those sounds again. I couldn't get them out of my mind though, and never felt convinced by Anna's explanation. There was something too insistent, focused, and human about them.

I decided the next time I was working on the second floor and knew the sisters were busy elsewhere, I would sneak up to the third and look around quickly, just to dispel my concerns.

That day came on Saturday. There was a storage room at one end of the second floor that Anna wanted me to rearrange, which would take me several hours.

After working awhile, I ascertained both sisters were still on the first floor by going downstairs and asking if it was okay to get a drink of water from the kitchen (which I did, from my cupped hands, as I was afraid the smudged, foggy-looking glasses might be diseased). They were both occupied. Emily worked from home as a bookkeeper and was in her office and Anna was in the drawing room polishing her toenails and humming to herself.

When I got back up to the second floor, I made some noise by pushing around boxes in the storage room so that the sisters would assume I had gotten back to work.

I pulled my shoes off and tiptoed back down the hallway to the curving marble stairway leading up to the third floor.

I had, mid-week, casually asked Emily what was up there. She'd told me it was additional bedrooms devoid of any furniture and an office, also now empty, that her late father had used. I remembered that conversation well because of the way she kept staring at me after she answered the question.

I got to the top of the stairs, and in under a minute had checked the doors on the third floor. Unlike the ones in every room below, each door up here was locked.

I was disturbed by this. The situation reminded me of some b-grade horror movie in which a person is being held prisoner in the attic or basement of a house by some crazy person. I kept telling myself there was nothing like that going on here, and I was just letting my imagination run away with me.

Then I would look at some revolting corner of this crypt-like Victorian monstrosity, (which seemed to get darker and dirtier every day), or look at Emily's lined, stark face or Anna's strangely gleaming eyes, and I could again easily believe there was some terrible thing going on up on the third floor. I also, through seeing Anna on almost a daily basis, realized the bright smile she always wore was rigidly fixed onto her face as though glued there. It was even present when I once ventured into a sitting room and found her napping in a chair, her teeth still gleaming brightly from over-stretched lips. If I reported my suspicions, and it turned out it was nothing but rats in an empty room, it would cause needless embarrassment for the sisters and would surely cost me my job.

I needed to find a way to get into the locked upstairs rooms.

***

On Wednesday of the following week, Anna assigned me tasks to do on the second floor and informed me that she had a headache. She would be lying down in her bedroom for awhile, and if I needed something, Emily would be working in her office on the first floor. It was now or never.

Again removing my shoes, I padded up to the third floor and went to the room I thought the sounds came from when I'd first heard them above me the previous week.

I pressed my ear up against the door and knocked gently. No sound came from the room. I decided I was being ridiculous and started to turn away, when I heard a scraping inside, then a feral snarl that crescendoed into the unmistakable scream of a human voice.

I once used my laminated library card to spring the lock on our basement door when I couldn't find the key, and that's what I was going to attempt with this one.

I wedged it into the space by the doorknob and worked it back and forth and up and down, turning the knob this way and that, until I heard a click.

I grabbed the doorknob and then almost jumped two feet into the air when I heard Emily Linus yell "STOP!" from the other end of the hallway.

I turned to see her hurrying toward me with a horrified expression on her face. When she reached the door, she shoved me away so hard that I tripped and fell. She pulled a key ring from her pocket and locked the door with shaking hands.

She looked devastated when she turned to me.

"I'm so sorry. I didn't mean for you to fall, but you have no idea what..."

She turned to look at the door, and then back at me. Her almost impossibly white face was a mask of desperation and anguish.

I'd gotten over my initial shock and stood back up.

"There's someone in there! I know for sure there is now. I heard them. You're keeping someone imprisoned in there!"

"No! I swear to you, it's not what you think. There's nobody in there right now."

"Then why is it locked? Open the door and let me see!"

She looked resigned, and as though every last bit of energy suddenly drained out of her, she bowed her head and slid down to a sitting position against the wall to the side of the door.

"The only thing I'm afraid of is what will happen to you if you go in there. I told you my father had an office up here, but that wasn't true; it was a laboratory and it took up much of this floor. I wasn't lying when I said it's empty. Right now, at this very moment, I swear to you, there is absolutely nothing in there. When there is, you can hear it, just like you did a little while ago.

***

We sat at a table in the breakfast room, which like the rest of the house, was festooned with spider webs, wet wilting boxes of junk, and slime-encrusted pieces of this and that. There were ruffled floral curtains on the window that I could visualize having once been bright and cheerful, but which were now so encrusted with dirt, I had to avert my eyes from them to not feel ill.

Emily Linus poured us both a cup of tea. A few minutes before, I'd watched her use a piece of steel wool to vigorously scrub the insides of the cups, but that still didn't eradicate the black stained-in dirt around the rims. When she placed the tea in front of me on the table, I put my hands around the cup in a show of polite gratefulness, but couldn't bring myself to put my mouth on it.

Emily saw that and smiled sadly.

"Would you believe, just five short years ago, this entire house was as pure and beautiful as the grounds surrounding it?"

"Like your bedroom?" The question slipped out before my mind could get a hold of my tongue.

She looked at me sharply, then nodded with the same forlorn smile. "I guess I do owe you an explanation about…" She looked around and made a sweeping gesture with her arm. "About all of this. I never meant for anyone to come here. Hiring someone was Anna's idea."

She stared down at the table quietly for a while, then with a resigned sigh, looked up at me.

"My father was a scientist and a brilliant man, quite visionary actually. He had some theories though about things considered so farfetched-things like the existence of other dimensions and parallel worlds-he soon became an object of ridicule and scorn in the scientific community.

He became rabidly unrelenting and fanatical in his demands that time and money be invested into researching these areas. He eventually lost his job. Whispers that he was a madman got around, and doors everywhere slammed in his face when applying for further work.

He had a sum of money stashed away and used it to turn most of the third floor into a private lab where he could pursue his research. He became a recluse."

Emily grew silent here, and I saw a true smile flicker across her face for the first time since I'd met her.

"He was an unparalleled genius. During the ensuing years, he created things never before seen in heaven or on Earth.

He came running out of his lab one day holding an object that looked like nothing more than an ordinary fountain pen. He called Anna and me into the parlor to watch as he clicked this pen-like object while aiming it at a vase. The vase elevated three feet into the air. Within a week, he was able to make this table we're sitting at and the four chairs surrounding it rise up to the ceiling and hover there for a full minute, before slowly descending back to the floor.

Another time, he created this little box with wires and lights all over it. The box would make things placed inside disappear. First small, inanimate things like stones or coins. Then living creatures he kept in his lab like mice and frogs.

You see, he truly was quite gifted and brilliant, perhaps more so than anyone else in this world.

He began working on something he said would vindicate him in the scientific community. He never said what it was, but he became obsessed and often would not leave the lab for days, even sleeping there.

One day, there was a sound like the winds of hell, and every window, wall, and floor of the house, and every object contained within, shook so hard, I thought the end of the world was upon us. Things crashed to the floor; even the light bulbs burst in their sockets. This went on for three horrifying minutes. Both Anna and I feared there'd been an explosion in the lab so we ran up and called out to my father. We banged on the door.

There was no response. We were never allowed to enter the lab without his permission, but of course in this case, I pulled out my keys, and fearing the worst, opened the door.

It was a completely empty room.

Every single thing—every object, every counter, stool and tool, every living creature from my father himself to the mice, rats, rabbits, and snakes he kept there for his experiments, every notebook and scrap of paper—it was all gone. Not so much as a curl of dust remained in that room."

Emily now pushed back from the table and stood up. "You don't believe me!"

She was right. I already had my doubts when she started talking about his improbable inventions, but when she told me about the complete vanishment of the lab, I was sure she was making it all up in some desperate effort to keep me from telling anyone about the person imprisoned up there. She read these thoughts on my face.

"I guess I have no choice but to let you see for yourself. We need to hurry before Anna wakes up from her nap."

The last thing I wanted to do was to go up to some makeshift prison with someone I was convinced was completely insane and probably dangerous. I needed to think fast. I looked at her apologetically.

"It's such a fantastic tale. Please continue. I promise to listen with a more open mind."

"You'll listen with an open mind when you see for yourself there is no one in that room."

She took me back up to the third floor, warning me that, no matter what, I must not step one foot into the room.

With one hand, she grabbed my arm with the force of a vice to prevent me from doing just that, while unlocking and opening the door with the other. Standing behind me and grasping me by the shoulders, she positioned me so that I could clearly see the room was completely empty. She quickly closed and locked the door.

"But the sounds I heard—there was a human voice."

Emily Linus looked toward the stairs at the end of the hall and spoke in a whisper. "Things disappear from that room. Sometimes they come back, but not in the same condition in which they left."

What she told me next was so fantastic, that if she hadn't showed me one final thing as proof before I left that day, I would not have believed any of what she said and would have assumed the entire story was only the delusional rantings of a deranged mind.

***

She led me downstairs and out onto the beautiful grounds, and over to the greenhouse. Before she began to speak, she placed her hand against the outside of the glass as though the life and beauty of the flowers and plants within breathed life into her.

"A week after the lab vanished, our pet dog, a regal-looking bloodhound went into the room and he too disappeared without a trace. I kept the door closed after that. A week later, I heard his familiar bark coming from the room.

Overjoyed at his return, I ran up the stairs and threw open the door.

It was him; I knew that unquestionably because he wore the bejeweled collar I'd once gifted him, but he had three heads now, and the arms of a monkey sprouted from his back.

This mutated monstrosity bolted towards me. I slammed the door shut a moment before it leaped out of the room. For the next hour, as I sat outside the door weeping, I could hear all three dog heads howling and whining like a chorus of the damned in hell. When it stopped, I dared to crack the door. The creature was gone.

A month later, our father returned. Anna was closest when we heard his muffled voice coming from behind the locked door. She unlocked and ran into the room before I could stop her. I heard her scream as I reached the door. An insectile, snake-tailed monstrosity, speaking from my father's face and with his voice, writhed on the floor in reptilian slime coiling around Anna's legs. Both of them vanished into thin air.

She returned days later, and through the door, assured me she was okay, and she was, at least on the surface. I cracked the door. I could see her body was not changed in any way. I let her out of the room only to discover that whoever it was that returned was not Anna. A cursed creature, walking death, or demon now crouched in the portly folds of Anna's flesh and proceeded to take over her life. I never opened that door again, no matter what I heard moving or speaking within."

She concluded this bizarre tale by telling me about the house itself.

"Bit by bit, our home turned into what you see today. It began to slowly die, day by day, room by room, becoming filled with the darkness, dirt, and the putridity that had taken over Anna. She would touch something and it would darken or fade. Ever since her return, some force from that room seemed to flow through her hands and press down onto the house.

For some reason though, she had no power or control over the grounds or anything beyond them. Her suffocating influence was confined to the house by whatever forces had her in their grasp. Outside of that, such as at her teaching job, she carried on the charade of being a normal person.

Over time, I came to realize, for reasons I know not, that flowers and plants dulled the fires of her destruction, at least outdoors and within my own room, which is the only place in the house I can counter-balance what she does. I grow them in the greenhouse, to ensure I have flowers to place there year round.

Come with me back to the house. I'm going to pay you for the week you worked. You shouldn't ever come back here; it's not safe."

As we returned to the Victorian, still stately and impressive looking from the outside, I realized the only thing I knew for sure was true because I saw it with my own eyes, was that no one was locked in the room on the third floor. Everything else she told me was too incredible to be believed. I felt sad for this woman, who I now assumed was harmless, but completely insane. Until I remembered one thing she said that nagged at me with a hook of truth.

It was about the inside of the house slowly dying. In the short time I'd worked there, it did appear to get darker and more hideous every time I looked at something newly.

The once cheerful curtains in the breakfast room were filthy the first time I saw them. When I looked at them today while in the room with Emily, I saw they'd become so weighted down with additional dirt and grease in the few short days, that the curtain rod sagged in the middle. Spider webs that festooned the corners of a bedroom on the first floor had, in less than a week, grown and spread by many feet, dangling like sheets of lace from the ceiling. Far faster than any spiders could possibly have spun them.

Once back in the house, Emily started counting out money to give me from a pretty madras purse. She looked pale and sad.

I thought of something to ask that would tell me if there was at least some crumbs of truth to any of her story, or if she truly was, along with the always strangely smiling Anna, insane.

"Miss Linus, why didn't you ever leave this place? Why don't you leave it now?"

She looked at me for a long time, and I could tell she was struggling with something within her own mind, and debating with herself whether or not to tell me something. She looked resolute and turned away. "I can't leave. That's all."

I walked over to her and gently placed a hand on her shoulder. "Tell me."

She turned back to me, starker and sadder than I have ever seen a human being look.

"I told you things disappear from that room, but sometimes come back, just not the way they left. I didn't know that at first. I too once walked into that room.

Some of the things my father kept in the lab before it vanished were tankfulls of bugs that he used for his experiments. He favored grasshoppers. Green grasshoppers."

Emily Linus always wore loose, long-sleeved, high-necked dresses that came down below her knees. She stepped back to put some distance between us, and starting at the neck, began to unbutton the one she was wearing now until the entire front of her body was exposed. As soon as I saw her hinged, green torso and six spindly legs folded tightly across it, I knew every word she told me that day was true.

***

Emily Linus closed the front door behind me. When I left the house for the last time, I knew I would never return. I avoided even passing by it for the remaining four years I lived in town before I married and moved away.

Today, I returned to visit old friends after being gone for almost ten years. The three-story Victorian was gone. I heard it had one day simply collapsed like an imploding star. Rotted timbers and termites were the general consensus in town. No one knew what happened to the two sisters who had lived there. Their bodies were never found in the debris. The two acres of property and the structures that still remained standing fell to a distant cousin.

When I went by there, whatever was left of the fallen house had already been carted away, and there was a "for sale" sign up.

I walked across the grounds, which had been long untended and were now in a state of wild, weedy dilapidation. The greenhouse was still there, and I could see the blackened, wilted remains of the plants and flowers that had once flourished within. There were cracks radiating out across the glass on all sides of it. Outside, on one wall, a scraggly, thorny vine scrambled up to its roof. It bore a single, lovely yellow rose. A grasshopper clung to it as it waved a little in the breeze.

THE CUSTOMER IS ALWAYS RIGHT

By: Sarah Kalin

Prim slung the laptop bag over her shoulder and scooped up her lunch from the backseat. With practiced motions, she locked the car and resettled her badge so the back was showing. It was an old habit to protect herself from passersby, but these days Prim didn't like looking at her smiling face and name. "Prim Rogers" the laminated badge declared; Prim who worked at EduTech Inc, also known as employee 4513.

She had been none of these things at birth. The company was only 3 years old and Prim had started only 8 months before. Even her name was new: 'Rogers' given to her by her husband and 'Prim' given to her by her teenage self when her family had immigrated to America and pronunciation became a problem. She'd picked "Primrose" in her romantic youth and had shortened it to 'Prim' later. Her husband had called her Prima. With this thought, a familiar chasm of pain opened inside her chest. Mostly she tried not to think of her husband.

What am I even doing here? The world was turned completely upside down, her small corner of it was shattered beyond repair, and yet there was still a stream of people lumbering up the concrete steps of the overpass. The cars below were engaged in their usual traffic. Prim watched the glowing brake lights flash in a rolling pattern as she walked over the ten-lane highway. *How can people keep on like everything is normal? Well, I guess I'm doing it, too.* She shook her head, reaching for the lobby doors. *Humans are weird.*

"Well, good morning! Great to see your smiling face again!" A jovial voice called from behind the security desk. Prim nodded to Jacob and carried on to the elevators, too lost in her thoughts to exchange pleasantries today.

"Which floor?" A man in a blue polo shirt, sporting a buzz cut and a fake smile asked.

"Six, please," Prim said. The man pressed the button with gusto and then promptly fell to ignoring her. *Thank God for small favors.* Prim didn't know how she would get through today. Everything felt hard these days. Talking with new people was exhausting, but talking with the ones who knew her was downright painful. She dreaded seeing pity on their faces and the knowledge of what had happened to her. A small part of her wanted to attack and rage at them. It would feel good and so little did these days. *But I know what's coming and they don't. They think they do…but they don't. THEY deserve MY pity.* She thought fiercely. With a visible shake, she straightened up and gripped her bag harder. The door chimed, opened, and she was off through the familiar gray halls once more.

A short woman with curly red hair and tight yet elegant clothing bustled up to Prim as the doors closed behind. "Oh, my word! Aren't you a sight for sore eyes, darlin'!" Her voice came out thick and sweet while her small hands grabbed Prim's own and clutched them against the ample bosom."Cynthia Rose," Prim said, gripping the woman's hands back before letting them fall. "It's good to see you, too."

Cynthia Rose fell into step with Prim, patting her arm solicitously. "Now, I know it's hard after being gone so long. But we're all here for you, girl. If you need any little thing, you just holler." With a quick hug-like squeeze and a sound of sympathy, Cynthia Rose turned and bustled back down the hallway.

Prim nodded to the kindly woman's back in a weak sort of way. *That's the great thing about Mrs. Cynthia Rose Everett - you really don't have to talk.* She was at her cube now. The grey walls were decorated with bright pictures from her nieces and there, next to the laptop dock, was a framed picture of her and her husband on their wedding day. She stared blankly at the happy couple. They were not facing the camera. Their eyes were only for each other on that day and their happiness felt so unreal. At this moment, Prim couldn't reconcile the person in that picture with herself. It felt more likely that the picture had come with the frame. Yes, that was the easiest way to think of it. With a quick motion, she grabbed the frame and shoved it into the top drawer.

Thirty minutes later, as she was still catching up on email, a bald head appeared above her cube wall. "Staff in five. In Vernon," Todd said before lumbering off in the direction of the meeting room. A flash of fondness swept through her, surely the first Todd had ever inspired in her. He at least was unchanged and, while even two weeks ago she would have said that was a bad thing, it was familiar to her. Prim needed that right now. *Why else would I be here if I didn't?* Coming to work certainly felt like an act of insanity when viewed objectively. *Yet here I am.*

In five minutes, she was wedged between Jodi and Patricia in an overcrowded conference room. Jodi chewed gum and tapped her pen on a small notepad as she waited for the meeting to start. She never seemed to write anything down but always carried it with her. Patricia looked worried but she had the kind of face that looked perpetually concerned.

"How are things?" Jodi drawled unconcernedly. Her eyes roamed the room constantly.

"Living the dream," Prim said flatly.

Jodi cackled and Patricia smiled fleetingly.

"Let's get started," Stewart called from the front of the room. *Oh no, it's his presentation shirt!* Stewart always wore the same long-sleeved pink shirt when he wanted to share a formal presentation with the team. Jodi had told her he'd once read an article claiming pink was worn by executives and he had stuck with the ritual ever since. Prim wasn't thinking of his power when she saw it, though. Mostly she was thinking about the grease stains speckled along the bottom of the shirt where his belly rounded the material outward.

"I'd like to start off by welcoming Prim back," he paused to let a chorus of welcomes and smiles fill the room, coming from everyone and no one in particular. "She's been through a lot of changes these past few weeks and she needs our support. So let's all remind her that here at EduTech we are a family, eh?" He finished with a red-cheeked intensity that almost made the last statement a threat. "Prim," he faced her squarely, leaning forward over the table, "if you need anything - I am here for you. We all are."

"Thank you," Prim said. *Dear God, start the meeting already!* She hated feeling everyone's eyes on her. Well, everyone except Jodi whose eyes were busy staring boredly at Stewart. Prim felt another rush of affection. *Everything feels reversed these days. My husband is gone and here I am grateful for the folks that once drove me mad.*

Prim realized she'd tuned out. Stewart had moved on and was gesticulating grandly at a colorful slide on the projector. Stars framed the bold-scrawled words "New Customer Base" and "First to Market" on the screen. " - and the potential gains are tremendous!" He clicked forward to a new slide showing a steadily rising profit line. "If we can be the first in this space we'll be making record-breaking profits!" A helpful dotted red line appeared on the chart labeled 'Record profits' and the profit line plowed right through it.

How can I take this seriously?

" - but we've got an advantage: first-hand knowledge."

It's like everyone here is pretending the world hasn't changed.

"Prim! You're our ace in the hole!"

What?! How did I get into this?

"What can you tell us about the online educational needs of the exciting new body-snatcher customer base?"

Prim's mouth opened and closed several times. Her throat felt dry and swollen and all the words she wanted to say weren't making it past her filter. *Are you insane? No, that sounds a bit judgey. Should I laugh? Nope, everyone sure seems to be taking this seriously. Is slapping him an option?* There was no good direction for this conversation to take. In the space of one sentence Stewart had short-circuited her brain. She sat there gaping at him.

"Don't be shy, Prim! I know it's your first day back, but I really think we can get ahead of this thing while the space is still open," Stewart turned his wide face to her, ostensibly drawn with concern, but also flushed with the fire of his mission.

Jodi clicked her tongue, sighed, and interjected. "Okay, Prim. Start simple. When your husband was 'snatched, what did he most want?"

There it was. The thing Prim didn't think about. In a flash, she remembered that horrible day when James had come home from work, but it hadn't been James. His face was beaded with sweat and he moved differently: more stiffly as if just learning to walk. But the worst part was his eyes. The warm brown eyes that had stared at his bride in the photo; that crinkled around the edges when he saw her each day; that cried with her when their dog, Nixer, had died: those eyes were frozen in an expression of sheer terror. Below them, his jaw hung slack. Prim had thought he'd had a stroke and was reaching for the phone when he lunged for her and —

She yanked herself back to the meeting room. Back to the eager faces in their business casual outfits who wanted more than anything to appeal to the creatures that had murdered her husband. The creatures that were slowly murdering thousands of people and tearing the seams of the human world apart. "What did it want?" She repeated, absently correcting Jodi's pronoun. "Ummmm, mostly to 'snatch my body…" It seemed obvious and maybe it would remind them of the danger they all faced here.

Jodi made another clicking noise as her mouth turned into a leer. "Men-typical," she said, catching the eye of a woman across the room and sharing a snicker.

Prim stared at the small scene, marveling at the blasé attitudes surrounding her. *It's like they're asleep and this is the reality of the dream. They don't think it can touch them - me sure, but not them. I wonder how many people are like that….how many people are walking around this world living their lives but completely asleep?* Prim didn't have to contribute anymore, the brainstorming was in full flow around her.

Patricia hopped up and started writing out ideas on the whiteboard.

A lanky young man raised his hand. "Well, it's like when you move out of your house, right? Like, they need to learn how to cook and stuff. So maybe like a cookbook?"

Great, the intern is in on it, too.

"Great idea, Hank. Building off that, we could do a quick reference for human needs: nutrition, exercise, sleep, etc. These are things we all pick up as we grow but it will be confusing for the newly settled body-snatcher," Stewart chimed in, gesturing for Patricia to write down both ideas. The room was silent for a moment as people thought or tried to look as though they were. "Come on, people, there are no bad ideas in brainstorming!"

That's only your motto because without bad ideas you wouldn't have any!

"Sandra has an idea," Jeff called from the end of the table.

Sandra's hands fluttered up as if they were trying to take flight. "Oh, it's nothing! It's just…well, I've done the online dating thing before, you know?" She flushed and spoke faster. "We could do something to help make matches-humans and body snatchers. Maybe we could make a tool for them to find compatible hosts."

Yeah, and maybe they can do snatcher match-ups bache-lorette-style; the humans can compete and the winner gets 'snatched!

Jodi made a noise of disagreement, her pen poking into her chin. "I don't like that," she began. *Halleluiah, sanity prevails from an unexpected place!* "That's not going to work. We'll have to do *something* about that name. 'Snatcher' and 'Body-snatcher' just don't capture the message we're trying to send. We need something sexier, more modern. What about 'X-packs'? Cause they look like a backpack, sort of, and the 'X' will make it sound futuresque!"

Oh, for fuck's sake!

Stewart's head bobbed exuberantly in agreement. "Yes, yes! You're right. We need to sell not only to our new customers but to the population at large. Jodi, I want you to head this up. Soon everyone is going to want an X-pack…or whatever the final version is. Love the energy, people! Keep those ideas coming!" Jodi settled back into her chair, her pen resting on the blank notepad and her face smug.

The list grew longer. The courses ranged from "Select-ing the Perfect Human Host" to "Cohabitating: The Benefits of Sharing Mind and Body." One man jokingly pitched a "How to Human" course.

Yeah, maybe after it's done, you can all take it. Prim could feel the anger building in her stomach, shooting itchy tendrils down her arms and legs that made her want to run from the room. She clenched down on the rage firmly. All her focus shifted to maintaining a relaxed body posture and keeping her face neutral.

"Oh! It looks like we're losing the room. Great work today, folks! I'll be following up with some of you offline after lunch. Until then!" Stewart closed the meeting and started disentangling his laptop as the crowd milled slowly from the room. Prim sat, letting her coworkers flow around her.

Stewart spotted her as he started toward the door. "Prim, you free after lunch? Say one o'clock? I have some more ideas to run by you." He glanced at the annoyed faces lining the doorway. "We've got to run but I'll see you then!" His pink shirt zipped around the corner.

Prim stood as the next meeting started filing into the room, pointedly ignoring her. She wandered down the hall, past a group of coworkers clustered around Jodi, and into the women's restroom. She closed the stall firmly and latched it. *I just need things to stop for a minute!* Prim closed her eyes and tried to sort through the images in her head. Her husband smiling; his hands gripping her painfully and pulling her toward the door; Jodi's pen; Stewart's grease stains. Her eyes flew open. The stall door was safer to see than what was inside her mind.

Prim focused on her breathing and the beige door, ignoring the sounds of hand-washing outside the stall and idle chatter. *Breathe in.* She pulled the air deep into her chest, expanding her rib cage and stomach. *Hold it.* Prim waited until she could feel her pulse thrumming through her skull and down to her fingertips. *Breathe out.* She pushed from the pit of her stomach upward, squeezing the air out like she was a tube of toothpaste. *And repeat.* Slowly, the world became less overwhelming. She couldn't say how long it had taken. *There. One morning down, the rest of your life to go.* Prim laughed out loud and left the restroom. *However long that life will be…*

When she returned to her desk, she saw that it was 1:25. *Crap! I missed Stewart.* She hurried to his office, an apology on her lips as she walked through the door. The room was strewn with torn papers and the visitor chairs were tipped over. *What happened?!*

"Did you hear about Stewart?" Jodi asked from where she leaned against the doorframe.

Prim turned to her, the small calm she'd obtained fleeing, the chasm opening in her chest again. "Was he - oh god - was he 'snatched?" She dreaded the answer.

Jodi rolled her eyes, "Promoted. Well, 'snatched too, I guess. Lucky bastard. Upper management said something about it showing real initiative and a dedication to understanding the customer journey. Whatever…the important thing is that he left you in charge!" She flashed a wide, false smile at Prim. "Congrats! Now, which do you prefer: 'X-packs' or 'X-tremes'? I can trademark either."

Prim left without a word. She marched past a startled Jodi, an oblivious Todd, and a concerned Cynthia Rose and knew she'd never come back. The emptiness and rage, terrifying memories and present danger - they all seemed the saner choice when compared to the insanity of human ambition.

If they all did get 'snatched…how could you tell the difference? She pondered as she walked back through the overpass and down to her car. Sliding behind the wheel, she glanced up. The clock on the dashboard read 2:10. *One morning and half an afternoon down. The rest of my life to go.* The car rumbled to life beneath her while Prim smiled.

DOME SWEET DOME

By: Turner Campbell

The moment Dan picked Junior out of the pod was the happiest in his life. He was living the dream—a family, a colonial house with the white picket fence, and a geodesic dome covering it all. The face of his son, flesh of his flesh, was lit up by the harsh Martian sunlight that filtered through the window. Marjorie closed the pod and skated on her tracks back over to Dan to admire the baby with him.

"He's beautiful," Dan said, "Can you believe we made this?"

"Yes, dear," Marjorie said, "I will prepare the nutrition solution." She whirred over to the kitchen to make Junior's drink.

Dan was ecstatic. He had been given the whole day off for the birth of his child, his first, and he was ready to make the most of it. He fed him with the bottle and when he was done he picked up his pride and joy and sang and babbled to him about the long full life he would lead, a noble life tilling the Martian soil, with the promise of happiness as pure as Dan felt now.

Within the hour, Junior was crawling from one end of the room to the other, from Dan to Marjorie. Dan picked Junior up under the armpits to stand him up, and he fell back down. It took a few tries, but he was a quick learner.

It seemed that no sooner was he waddling than he was walking and finally running around the room. He had maybe grown twice as big at this point. Another nutrition solution and off to bed. Dan went to sleep feeling like the luckiest man in the world.

***

The next day, Junior was big enough to use the antique mitt and baseball Dan had bought from a collector back on Earth. Before work, they played catch for an hour in their enclosed front yard. Under the safety of their geodesic dome, they ran barefoot through the ten by ten square of astroturf in front of the house. "You've got quite an arm on you, Junior." Dan said, catching the ball and throwing it back, "Just like your old man."

Marjorie came to the window and peered out at them. The grate of her mouth fizzled with static before she let out the stilted morning announcement: "Daily terraforming procedures will begin in… forty-five… minutes."

"Wow. Time flies, doesn't it?" Dan said, "Come give your daddy a hug, Junior. I'll have to be going soon."

His son ran over to his open arms. "I love you, dad," he said.

***

Dan went to his factory in the glacial domes, where he and the other settlers slowly melted the Martian lakes into rivers and streams. He had helped dig out the estuaries that would soon lead towards more congested fields of residential domes to the east. Now they were setting up a filter net that would run across the length of each estuary, ensuring that only thing to pass through would be oxygen bound to two hydrogen molecules.

All day, the guys congratulated him on his new kid. The ones who didn't have a kid patted him on the back and joked that he could say goodbye to a good night's sleep for a while. The ones that had kids gave him a firm handshake and a knowing look.

"They grow up fast don't they?" said one.

"Wait til he starts having kids," said another, "It'll happen sooner than you think."

***

Dan was excited to play more catch with Junior when he got back to the dome, but in the time he was away Junior had become a full-grown adult. Dan had missed it! Puberty, adolescence, and the subsequent solidifying of neural pathways. All precious moments in your kid's life and Dan had blinked and missed it all.

His son sat at the kitchen table, smiling politely, wearing one of Dan's work uniforms, which was a little too tight. "There was nothing else that fit me," he said.

Dan was at a loss. He held up the ball and mitt. "Do you still want to play catch?"

Junior just shook his head. "I don't think that's such a good idea. Look at how big my arms are." He flexed. "I could probably throw it halfway across the world by now!"

"Yeah, probably," Dan said, "What do you want to do instead?"

Junior leaned back in the chair and put his arms behind his head. "I don't know," he said, "I drank my nutrition supplement today, but I still feel hungry. Or maybe thirsty. I don't know. I just want to go out and do something! Can you think of anything?"

"Hmmm. I'm not sure. There's not much to do but work. Maybe I can introduce you to the guys."

Marjorie chirped a short chiptune. "There is someone at the door," she announced.

Dan answered it and found a man in a spacesuit, helmet off, breathing in Dan's private atmosphere. "Oh, hello," the man said, "How are you? I'm looking for Dan Jr, is that you?"

"Close. I'm Dan Sr. Junior, you have a visitor!"

Junior crouched under the doorway to meet them outside. "How's it going?" he said.

"Wow! You certainly are a big one!" the man said as he shook Junior's hand, "Dan Jr., I'm from upper management. We were informed by your Marjorie that you have completed the maturation phase ahead of schedule."

Junior shrugged. "I guess so."

"That's great!" the man said, "We love a go-getter! Now usually there's a waiting list for new adults to receive a personal dome, but considering how efficiently you handled adolescence, we believe it's best to move you to the front of the line!"

"My own place?" Junior said, "That's amazing! When can I move in?"

"Well, the place we have set aside for you is in the southwest quadrant. If we leave in the next hour we can get there by tonight. We set you up in soil nitration. Does that work for you?"

"It sure does!" Junior said.

"Does he really have to leave so soon?" Dan said, "I feel like I just got to start spend time with him."

The man looked at Dan for a minute, then said, "Junior, why don't you go pack your things while I speak with your father?"

"I don't have any things."

"Maybe you should say goodbye to your mother, then. I just want to go over some details with your father."

Junior went back inside, and the two remaining men walked around the small house, shuffling the dust under their feet.

"I would really appreciate just a few more days with him," Dan said.

"Well, every day counts, Dan. Junior is a man now. He has to strike it out on his own. Learn a trade and practice it well. Marry a nice girl that reminds him of his mother." The manager thought for a moment. "Although, maybe he'll choose a Ruth model instead."

"I just… I wish I had more time."

The manager turned to face him. "I'm going to be frank. It seems there's a slight mutation in Junior, Dan. His growth rate is much more accelerated than it should be. It's important that we get him set up as soon as possible, so he can continue our work before he passes."

"Before he… How much longer does he have?"

"According to the data your Marjorie sent, he has another ten days, at most."

"Ten days…" Dan looked out to the distant rusty cliffs, tears already blurring his vision. "That's not enough."

"It's never enough, Dan. Like I said, this isn't normal. But we took a look at your incubator remotely, and our team seems to have fixed the problem. The next few clones will gestate at the normal rate."

"It's just that… he was my first kid, you know?"

"I know Dan," the manager said, putting a hand on his shoulder, "But some things can't be helped. This is the best way for him to live a full and meaningful life. And you'll have other kids! You still have a few good months ahead of you."

Junior came out of the house, empty hands at his sides. "Well, I'm ready."

"Great!" the manager said, "Here, put on this suit."

"I'm going to miss you, son," Dan said as the kid stuffed his legs and arms into the suit's shiny silver sleeves.

"Aw, I'll miss you too, Dad," Junior said, and the two embraced. Dan tried to take in his son's scent, and the feel of his arms around him, like if he breathed deeply enough and held tightly enough he could keep the memory fresh and preserved in the back of his mind.

"Be sure to visit, son."

"I will, Dad."

Junior put on his helmet and left the dome. He and the manager got in the rover and took off, kicking up a stream of dust that dissipated almost instantly. Here one minute, gone the next.

***

Dan sat on the porch and cried. Marjorie came over near him, but her track didn't run all the way to the door. "There, there, dear," she told him from five feet away, "Please enter and inspect the incubator."

Dan got up and followed her to the pod, and peered at the monitor which showed the outline of a burgeoning human, pea-sized and amphibial.

"He will be ready in approximately… five to seven… days."

"I hope so," Dan said, smiling, "I would love for Junior to be able to meet his brother."

ALIEN AVENUE

By: Mickey Kulp

It was another damned holiday, something about the 12,000th anniversary of the Slibs defeating the Parns. The half-grav sidewalk was choked with eight foot tall Slibs and their alien holobanners proclaiming, my smart glasses translated, "Our sponge sacs protrude with glorious pride."

I was stuck on the one-grav sidewalk; the crowd was no thinner. Everyone else had clogged this sidewalk to avoid the damned parade.

I scanned the wide avenue. Two-grav was less crowded, but I'd be a sweaty mess by the time I got to the job interview. And today I needed to look extra sharp. My boss, I called him Dbag, was breaking my back, and I had to get out of there.

Three-grav was out of the question, even though a couple of crossfit lunks were slogging along in their bright red leotards. Four-grav was empty except for a squat Figrene cruising happily on its six elephantine legs.

"Glassy, you gotta get me out of here," I said to my glasses.

"Working on it," Glassy said using a female voice. "The Slibs are eating all the bandwidth." She showed me a few selfies the giants had posted. Their sponge sacs were indeed protruding.

"You are occupying my space, yooman," Glassy said using a generic alien voice, simultaneously highlighting the oncoming man-wasp that was speaking or farting or whatever it did to communicate. I stepped aside and bumped a species with brown fur and tentacles ringed with yellow pigment.

"Greetings, creature. Do you have a moment to discuss our Lord Jesus?" It waved a paper tract that Glassy translated as, "If you were to stop functioning tonight, where would you spend eternity?"

I waved it away and slipped forward, drafting behind a tall, pale humanoid as it moved through the crush of galactic citizens. Then, I caught a whiff of his gamey pungence and dropped back. Couldn't risk getting any of that on me, not today for sure.

"Glassy, how is the time?"

"You have seven minutes left," she said.

"I'm not going to make it." Dbag had just left for lunch and I wanted to finish the interview and get back to the office before him. "Give me a better path."

"Use the magic word," Glassy said.

Shit. "Please."

"In ten yards, go right."

"That takes me in the wrong direction. Are you sure?" I should have loaded that upgrade I promised her, now she's mad at me. Gonna drag me all over the city.

"Are you serious?" Glassy asked. "Of course I'm sure."

"Sorry, I just…"

"You're being a dick," she said. "Turn here."

Glassy highlighted the street sign and added an unnecessary red arrow floating above the sign bearing the words "Turn here, dick."

I stepped off the busy sidewalk and let the descender field lower me to a perpendicular street. I picked the half-grav sidewalk, moving faster but heading away from the job interview. Geez.

A human female was loping in the lower gravity toward me. Glassy projected the personal information that the stranger had chosen to emit: "Name: Mara / Bio Category: Human Female / Home: Mars / Age: 31 / Mating Status: Hetero Unattached (Not Looking) / Hobbies: Redball."

"Hi Robert," she said. Glassy was also emitting my calling card.

"Hi Mara," I said, waving. "Go Mariners!"

She smiled. "They suck again this season. Might have to start rooting for an Earth team."

And that was it. Social interaction concluded. Of course, it was recorded for later review in my ten exabytes of lifetime storage.

"You asked for a five minute warning," Glassy said. The number '5' flashed a couple of times at the edge of my vision.

"Am I going to make it?"

"Maybe," she said.

I loped a little farther, reaching a park, then farmland. Cows and sheep mingled with other exotic food animals that looked like huge armadillos.

"Turn left."

"Here?"

"No, ten miles from here."

Smartass. Glassy highlighted a small shed about twenty yards away. An actual physical sign was planted in the ground beside it. She translated the runny script as, "Timehop for rent. Good prices. Few deaths."

"You must be joking," I said. A '4' flashed at the edge of my vision. Four minutes. "Humans can't timehop."

"Sure you can," Glassy said. "Humans can handle short hops."

"Look, I've seen the videos. Hell, you are the one who found them for me." The last one I saw showed a woman stumble out of the machine with a bloody monkey arm still gripping her hair. She had a huge wet stain on the front of her jeans.

"That was for giggles," Glassy said. Then she took on a sing-song kindergarten teacher tone. "The videos that bubble to the top of the viewlist always have tragedy or hilarity. They are for enter-tain-ment. The ones where the human yawned and walked away don't make the list." She changed back. "Are you new here?"

I thought about it. A '3' flashed at the edge of my vision. Damn. I started toward the shed. Maybe I wouldn't stain my pants.

The alien behind the counter resembled a big-headed ostrich: long neck, pale hide, scruff of feathery, whiskery things all around, mouth in a perpetual frown.

"Howdy, human. How is your digestion today?" The ostrich alien's personal info cloud showed, "Name: (pop)weekneek(pop) / Bio Category: Durgian Not Yet Female." 'She' donned a woven straw sombrero as I leaned on the shed's counter. Probably some marketing app told her that humans liked hats.

I swiped through her catalog, looking for timehops that had been reviewed by actual humans. There was only one. "No problems. A little dizzy afterward. Three stars."

That was the whole review. I checked the reviewer's personal info. It said, "Name: Robert / Bio Category: Human Male / Home: BeggarsCantBeChoosers7 / Age: 34 / Mating Status: Hetero Unattached (Always Looking) / Hobbies: Redball, Time Travel."

I read it again. I'll be... It was from me.

A '2' flashed at the edge of my vision. Two minutes. Now or never. But it would never be never, would it? I looked again, assuming the entry would have vanished if I had bailed. It was still there.

Glassy transferred the necessary personal data and funding info, a princely sum. Yeah, I'd be eating noodles for a month. My travel goal was one hour into the past.

I heard a buzzing sound, and another Durgian strode to the counter. It also wore a sombrero. It's personal info cloud showed, "Name: (pop)weekneek(pop) / Bio Category: Durgian Not Yet Female."

It was the same alien. Or, a future version of the same alien that had gone into the past with me. My brain twisted a little.

"No worries," version two said to version one. "The stir-fry place will have had a special on snail drop soup. It will have been good." I tried to chase down the verb tenses, and my brain twisted some more.

I followed the Durgian (version one) to the back of the shed. She rummaged through a pile of furniture and produced a metal folding chair suitable for a humanoid.

"Sit, please, human." I sat, a nervous queasiness start-ing to churn my innards. She rolled out a mat and settled next to me. "Hold this, please, human." She handed me one end of something like a jump rope. She fiddled with her end, dialing rings back and forth.

"Your heartbeat is approaching exercise maximum," Glassy said.

"No shit." I could still see the part of the sign that said "Few Deaths." I hoped getting out from under Dbag was worth this risk to my delicate skin.

The Durgian spoke into her end of the jump rope. "Scatter path 2389476. Stand clear. Quantum destination check."

Seconds passed. "Clear," came out of her jump rope handle.

"Leaving in three. May Xeron have had mercy on our souls." She pushed a fat red button.

Have you ever bounced your elbow off a door? It felt like that everywhere for just a second. Have you ever stepped off a curb that turned into a 100-foot drop? It was like that too. It was also like a lot of things that had no comparison. I did not enjoy it.

"Congratulations, human. You did not die." The Durgian was rolling up her mat. We were still behind the shed. "Remember that you will have had left us a review."

I released the death grip on my end of the jump rope. "Thanks," I said. I checked my pants. Still dry.

"That was an odd sensation," Glassy said. "Like when your polarity gets turned inside out." But, I was already walking.

Back in town, I made good time. I smoothly avoided the tiny aliens selling aluminum cookies to pay for camp, eventually arriving ten whole minutes early at the Galactic Data Corp headquarters.

I sat in the oxygen-breathers waiting room, feeling confident, and even a little superior. I was quite the daring rogue: zipping around the timescape, overcoming adversity, triumphing against all the obstacles thrown up by a ruthless universe. I was in the middle of entering my timehop review when it all fell apart. Hard.

"What are you doing here, human Robert?" It was my boss.

"What the hell?" I looked up, shocked. What was Dbag doing here? How could I salvage this? What the hell? I was screwed. Quick - lie.

He towered over me, an alien nightmare of a gorilla wearing a crocodile snout and a spiky tail. Glassy highlighted Dbag and stamped, in flashing letters, "Holy shit!" above his hideous face.

"I.. am… here," I said stupidly, my mind racing, discarding excuses that would never work.

"I see. So am I," Dbag said. His breath smelled of raw meat and coffee.

"You… are… here," I said, still trying to formulate an elaborate lie.

"So are you," he said. "Are you intoxicated? Has your mind lost its juices?"

I stopped. My old Scout leader once said, "When in doubt, tell the truth."

"I am here for the job," I said.

"So am I," Dbag said. "Leave now." A clawed finger poked my shoulder.

Glassy removed the highlight over Dbag and stamped "You're fucked." above his hideous face.

I left, mentally kicking myself all the way to my office door. When I tried to get in, the door wouldn't open. Glassy said, "They revoked your credentials."

"Damn."

"They have sent your personal articles to the mailroom for transportation to your apartment."

"Damn." It felt surreal.

"Your final paycheck is already deposited," Glassy said.

That night, I finished my third bottle of mead and stared out the window, hating life and aliens with their protruding sacs and my stupid decisions. My mind rolled back, examining every wrong turn I had ever made since shedding diapers, slathering the pity on thick.

Glassy said, "I just got a message that the Galactic Data Corp job has been filled." I sighed and stared as the rain started. A few minutes later, Glassy said, "I just got a message that Dbag resigned his position."

Well, ain't that just peachy. "Glassy, please set up another job search." It would be tough with the termination on my record. Maybe someone would hire me to sanitize pig pens.

"Alright," she said. "You want to finish that timehop review? The document is still open."

Another regret to pile on with the rest. Epic stupidity. I had essentially paid a lot of good money for a timehop that cost my job and forever tainted my work history.

It was hellishly expensive to live in the city. I'd be out on my arse in a month unless I could land a new job. I wished with all my soul that I had never taken that damned timehop.

Never taken the timehop. Never... Yes!

I re-wrote the review to say, "Hated it. Worst experience of my life. Peed all over myself."

I pressed send.

***

I swiped through her catalog, looking for timehops that had been reviewed by actual humans. There was only one. It was terrible. Screw that.

"No thanks." I waved at the proprietor. The number '2' flashed at the edge of my vision. Two minutes. Not going to happen. Maybe Galactic Data Corp would reschedule me if the job was still open.

I loped back toward town. No hurry. I had plenty of time to get back to the office now.

SECOND SUN

By: Beth Winokur

The fields are in bloom, the sky is cloudless, and Dustin Mulligan is naked next to his wife feeling no closer to her than before they'd made love. The two lay side by side on the disheveled bed; her frigid hand rested on his chest. With closed eyes, he tried to raise gratitude for her, for their marriage. Instead, anger elevated in a series of waves. One surge got the better of him and he shoved her off the bed. She landed on the floor with a thud, followed by cold laughter.

Does she think this is a game? Does she think at all?

"Shut up!" he barked.

Indifference settled on her blank face. It turned his anger into guilt. The air thickened, making it hard to breathe. He left for the kitchen, grabbed a beer out of the fridge and slammed the door. "Damn it." He flicked the beer cap across the room before tilting the bottle to his mouth. The cold bite in the back of this throat offered a release. He swallowed and tried to forget.

This was a bad idea. There's no forgetting. This can never be enough. How can any of this be healing? She's gone. No amount of blue pills, hypnotherapy, or healing dolls can change that.

Five months had passed by with the new Tasha, with *her*. The first two months were great. He was overwhelmed with the program, believed in it - even insisted he needed it. Tasha had wanted this for him. She had wanted him to continue her; begging for reanimation until her last breath. She even asked her father to make sure it was carried out, not because Dustin would be undependable, she explained, but because he would be distraught from the loss.

Dustin wouldn't deny her return. How could any husband tell his wife that he was okay with her death? For two years he sat at her bedside watching her wilt away from cancer, all the while assuring her of a return. He had, after all, made a vow 'through sickness and health,' although lately the part of the vows that echoed through his mind was 'till death do us part.' He shook his head, philosophical debate wouldn't help, not now. Instead, he coached himself with the usual, 'this is a commitment' speech followed by the 'it'll get better' song.

Everything changed when he stopped following the program. At first, he forgot to take the pills, and then he started missing meetings. It didn't seem intentional, but then a week went by, then two, until finally the bottle of pills got tossed into the trash. The revolt led to the return of 'feeling.' He'd become passionate about 'feeling.' He had more love and compassion for her, but it couldn't last. It's impossible to receive love from a program. She could only follow and copy. Deep emotional connection was out of reach for the Mulligans.

Tasha yelled from the other room, "Dustin, you're an asshole, what's your problem?" He looked at the clock. *Hell, a five-minute delay, she's falling apart.* Rummaging through the papers in the junk drawer in search of her manual, he tried to remember the safety phrase.

"Do you hear me? Why are you being such a jerk?" Tasha continued as she stomped into the kitchen.

Dustin turned to his wife. "Twenty worm mud-pies."

She froze in place.

Dustin looked away. He wanted to kick her. He wanted to put her outside and let the trashman haul her away, but knew the consequences.

He found his way back to the bedroom, flopped onto the messy bed and tried to fall asleep. He refused to think about her. Refused to reflect on his behavior. Refused to write about this in his private journal for Dr. Irvin to read next Friday during support group. He was not going to do anything but let sleep come.

***

Dustin slept late into the morning, not waking until his body ached and his mind started to betray him. He could no longer ignore his wife, suspended in the kitchen. Something must be done. Throwing her out was illegal. He shivered when he thought of what his father-in-law would do if he tossed her out. It would be much worse than jail. Everything must remain the same. The red numbers on the alarm clock read 9:28. "Oh Shit." He jumped out of bed and ran to the kitchen.

"Crap!" he shouted. "You were supposed to be at work an hour ago." He glanced at his inanimate naked wife, his eyes hung on her left breast pushed up and in by her arm still raised, pointing accusingly.

He phoned her work.

"Thank you for calling Second Sun Inc...."

He spoke politely and clearly to the receptionist. "Yes, I suspended her last night. She was having glitches, and not responding to mood, or conversation changes."

"Can you bring her down for a diagnosis?"

"Yeah, I'll send her over," he answered feeling like a spineless idiot. He really wanted to tell Second Sun to fuck off, that they're wrong, that all of it is wrong. But it would be wasted, the voice on the other end of the line would never understand. And while the receptionist may be able to respond, it was a response built purely out of programming. As the radicals say, *husks are interactive propaganda.*

Then, like all losers, Dustin remembered the receptionist was also the wife of some poor sap, and he should be nice - even in his thoughts. *It's not her fault life sucks.* Tossing the phone on the counter, he paused to take in his frozen wife. There was something arousing about how angry and yet how vulnerable she looked standing there with her upper lip slightly curled. Something amusing about how he had paused her mid-bitch face. Her furrowed brow, alone, made him smile. She didn't look so perfect like Second Sun insisted she was, not with frizzy hair and smeared makeup; all the ugly of after-sex.

But really, Dustin thought, as he took a second look, she's beautiful. She was always beautiful. She looked better since Second Sun had gotten their hands on her. Her twenty-year-old body returned, much firmer than the one Dustin had grown accustomed to.

He preferred her pre-death body. Familiar; his hands still craved and anticipated it when he reached for her, even now after all this. As though the years of rubbing her, and the countless times they intertwined their bodies, had molded and shaped her custom for them - for him. She was his; she was always his.

This firm thing standing unaware in front of him, was his too. This Tasha was foreign. Months ago, he decided it was wrong to have sex with her. That it somehow betrayed the real Tasha. He would never cheat on his wife, but he was weak; lacking the will and power to resist his urges, especially since this new Tasha was always so willing to oblige. Sex was great after her 'second rising', but it wasn't enough. After a while it became nothing more than a habit.

Standing in the kitchen staring at her, he made a pact with himself; only hand jobs. That's reasonable. After all, it's only right to get something out of this. He deserved some sort of compensation. Plus, she had to account for their sex life to her doctors. He didn't want anyone to get suspicious, because unlike her doctors, Dustin knew why she was having glitches; he had caused them. He switched her pills with aspirin, fed her fake meat, and left her alone for long periods. In short, he had initiated deterioration.

Standing there staring at his naked frozen wife, he thought about what the *living* Tasha would say. Surely, she would have yelled at him for freezing her with that crumpled up eyebrow and giving her premature wrinkles.

A strong desire for a blow job interrupted his thoughts. *Just one more, and only head,* he told himself. *It'll help her forget about being shoved off the bed last night.*

Dustin pulled his boxers off his tall skinny body and walked over to his wife and rubbed her torso and breasts. He reached his hand to her neck where he softly brushed her hair away and whispered, "twenty worm mud pies."

Instantly, she lowered her finger and smiled. Showing no sign of the previous night's anger, she leaned into him.

He gently reached for her and guided her down. She really was having issues. That would help him when they examined her back at the office. His worries abruptly vanished, Dustin stopped thinking about examinations, Second Sun, and his obligation to the real Tasha. Because at that particular moment, the only thing he could focus on was the cool sensation of his dead wife's lips wrapped around his dick.

THE OCTOPUS OF BANGKOK

By: Robert Millet

A knock on the old Victorian door broke the silence that was Saria's day after coming home from school. She quickly forgot her chores and studies as she raced for the door. A quick twist the brass knob on her family's front door, Saria Sinoy opened the door a crack. Just enough for her to peer outside, there on the front stoop sat a wooden box. The wood was old, weathered, and the nail-heads looked like rusty, black spots. The packing straw poked out from between the small gaps in the boards.

Ever since her family relocated from Thailand, her father, who worked in exporting and importing items. He traded goods from all over the world, he would get packages occasionally. This box was different. It had her name scratched into the top of the crate.

Thirteen-year-old Saria glanced outside for a delivery-man or truck but none could be seen. Her brown eyes scanned the streets but no one stood out except for a young man about eighteen years in age. His features stood out for his dark skin, jet black hair and almond shaped eyes along with a fancy top hat. His features stood out among all the other people on the street with their white fair skin. He looked like a younger version of her father. In the blink of an eye, he was gone into the crowd of other finely dressed men with top hats and long coats.

Saria grabbed the old metal handle and drug the box inside, placing it on the dining room table. Deep white scratches left a trail on the polished wooden table top where the box slid across to a stop. She ran into her dad's workshop. She grabbed a heavy, wooden mallet but couldn't find a pry bar. She dashed into the formal dining room and opened the formal dining cabinet. She grabbed a sterling silver butter knife from the dining set. She returned to the crate, she forced the butter knife into one of the box joints. She hammered the knife on the end with the mallet, prying up the nails that held it together.

She repeated the process on the other corners of the box until the nails released the lid. She discarded the knife, which was twisted into a corkscrew shape. She started to quickly rummage through the box pulling out handfuls of straw and tossing it all over the formal dining room. Inside she found a stack of yellowed newspaper clippings written in the Thai language. She would have to ask her father what they said. There was a fancy gold leafed envelope with a red octopus on the cover along with her name on it, a small Saint Gina statue and some Thai trinkets. The last thing was an old tattered cloth. Saria removed the cloth to find a jar filled with a yellow fluid. Contained inside was a severed human hand. It was small and delicate similar to Saria's hand.

"Eww that is disgusting," Saria said, "I wonder what all this stuff is and who would send it to me?" Saria opened the envelope and pulled out a handwritten letter with a small amount of money. She read the letter aloud.

"You have been selected to join an amazing journey around the world. You will experience things you can only imagine." Her mind filled with the images of far off lands.

"Your journey will begin when you arrive at Saint Gina's Harbor. You must bring the hand. This is your invitation." Saria said. Her mouth twisted at the thought of carrying a jar around town that contained a hand but this was a chance to see the world. There was no indication who sent it to her. Her father's voice filtered in from the outside. He exchanged pleasantries with neighbors. Saria scoop up the letter, money, and the floating hand, raced into her bedroom, and stuffed everything under her bed.

Saria barely had time to get back to a standing position when her father burst through her bedroom door.

"When did you get this?" He asked. His voice was loud and forceful his face was a twisted mass of worry and anger. He didn't even take the time to remove his top hat, goggles, or long coat. "Answer me. When did this box arrive?" He asked gripping her tight around the shoulders.

"It…it showed up today shortly after I got home," Saria replied, "I got curious and opened it. I'm sorry Daddy." Her dad pulled her down the hallway passed all the pictures of various Thai gods and goddesses that were to protect the house and family. Saria's heart pounded hard against her small, gold Phra Somdej amulet that hung on a thin gold chain around her neck.

His eye scanned over the items she had pulled out. His eyes grew sad with each item he picked up and every newspaper page that he flipped. "Why?" His voice was soft. His daughter didn't know what to say "Why did you choose my daughter, my only daughter. I prayed to the gods they would protect her. I went to the spirit houses and I prayed!" Her dad screamed. "I stayed until my knees hurt so bad I could barely walk."

"Daddy, what is wrong?" Saria meekly asked. Her father removed his top hat, white cotton gloves, and goggles. He picked up the newspaper clippings. His eyes scanned over the first one and flipped through the others.

"Sit down. Something that I did eleven years ago has come back to exact its revenge upon me."

Saria sat down on one of the formal chairs. The piston legs dipped, adjusted to her weight, and raised her up to the proper table height.

"Many years ago I worked as the supply person for the project Golden Jackal. Bangkok is a major international trading port the government wanted to protect. A group of inventors built several steam powered mechanical elephants to haul troops and supplies. One inventor created a large grand scale mechanical octopus to protect the sea port of Bangkok. It was amazing. Its mechanical arms could crush ships. It could shoot fire from the tips of all eight arms. It could do many amazing things. There was always a human co-pilot in case something went wrong." Her father's face went from bright and cheery to grim and dark.

"One day, there was a giant celebration at its official launch. All the people involved brought their families to see what we had created. Something horrifying happened when they turned the machine on. The octopus went berserk. It wildly flailed its arms crushing people, setting the pier and surrounding buildings on fire. It nearly burned down the whole city. Many died that day including your mother. I'm not sure how you and me survived that day. The lead inventor lost his entire family. He only found the severed hand of his daughter. She was thirteen. The next day he disappeared as well."

Her father paused for a few moments. "The children of people involved with the project started disappearing, it is always the same. This crate shows up and the children are gone. And now it has come for you. It's why we moved almost halfway across the world and why I keep you locked in this house" Her father took the box and all the contents on the table and threw it in the stone fireplace. He ripped the crystal imported oil lamp that hung on the wall off and threw it in as hard as he could. The crystal smashed and set everything in on fire. She watched as her father placed both hands on the mantel to watch everything burn.

Saria sat in silence unsure how to process what her father said and what the note implied. Saria excused herself and went to her room to settle in for the night. She was about to drift off to sleep when a light from under her bed lit up her room. Crawling out of bed she reached under, pulling out the jar with the hand. The yellow liquid glowed, lighting up her entire room. She feared her father would notice the light. There on the palm was written four numbers.

"Ten, zero four, fifty-five." Saria said, "Hmmm those are the numbers of my birthday."

She saw the fingers on the hand wiggle. "But that's not possible, did I just see that? Do it again." She asked the hand but nothing happened. She figured she must be tired and imagining the hand moving but was super excited at the idea that it would move. Saria grabbed a thick blanket and wrapped the jar until no light could be seen. She stuffed it back under her bed. As she climbed back into bed, she saw him. The young man from earlier, standing across the street looking at her window. She ran over and watched as he gave a tip of his top hat. He reached inside his jacket pulled out an envelope like the one Saria had received and tucked it back inside his coat and walked down the street.

The next day Saria did not go to school, teenage curiosity had gotten the better of her. She stuffed her book bag full of clothes, her favorite penny story book, some candy, and the disgusting floating hand. She walked to the center of town, summoned a carriage. She was determined to find out why this box was sent to her. She would go during the day to see if it even appeared which she doubted.

It was probably a trick parents play to get kids to behave, but at the first sign of trouble, she would leave. She would be back before her father returned from work. The steam-powered horse clattered as it came to a stop in front of her. Thick coal smoke poured from the stacks on its back while the gears of hips spun waiting to be engaged. The elderly coachman peered down at her with his soot-covered goggles giving a warm welcoming smile. His yellow tobacco stained teeth nearly matched the black sooth that coated his skin. He pulled a brass lever and the carriage door opened while stairs folded down from the bottom of the carriage.

"Where to young lady?" The coachman asked.

"I want to go to Saint Gina's Port." She said. She took out the money in the envelope and handed it to the coachman.

"This is much more than needed for a round trip young lady." The coachman replied as his old weathered fingers counted the money.

"I know but I like your horse. You can keep it."

"As you wish." He gave a quick tip of his brown derby hat as she boarded the coach. He pulled the brass lever back, closing the carriage door and folding the stairs back into the belly of the coach. Saria sat on the soft goose down seat. She poked her head out the window to look up at the floating balloon above the coach. The balloon kept the carriage off the ground as it traveled since there were no wheels. It was one of the most comfortable ways to travel. It felt like floating down a river instead of being on a road.

She saw him again as the carriage was about to pass the last building in town. The young man stared, watching as she floated past. A slight nod of his head was the only indication he made that he had even seen her. It was then that Saria noticed it. His left hand was missing, could it have been the one in the jar she now carried in her book bag?

Saria sat in silence with the window coverings drawn. Her fingers fidgeting with her jet black hair.

"Okay young lady, you have arrived." She heard the coachman yell. She exited the carriage, walking towards the pier that had the statue of Saint Gina at the end, identical to the one in the box. Her school shoes clacked on the storm weathered boards of the pier. A nervous chill ran down her spine as she neared the statue. It was the middle of the afternoon and there were many people on the pier. Her nerves were getting the better of her with each step.

"I was wondering if you were going to show up, Saria Sinyon." A man's voice said. Saria jumped, startled at hearing her name called. Out from behind the statue stepped the young man. She felt a sudden sense of panic. "But I am glad to see the driver was correct in choosing you to die."

"Die?" She asked.

"Yes, the Boon-Mee comes for you." He grabbed the small watch piece hanging around his neck and clicked the button on top. "We usually like to do this at night but what Boon-Mee wants, she gets." He gestured towards the harbor.

Saria glanced over the wooden railing. At first, she only saw the blue-green ocean water. A large dark mass rose from under the pier. Golden brass accented pieces shined bright in the afternoon sun while the dark red body pierced through the water. Large mechanical tentacles wound their way up. An awful screeching sound could be heard as the tentacles passed over the barnacles that had accumulated on pillars of the pier.

Saria screamed. Her feet were already moving as fast as they would carry her back down the pier away from the creature. People fled as the metal legs flopped up on the pier blocking Saria's path in her effort to escape. She let out another loud scream. There was nothing but silence and the creature was gone. Witnesses would say they saw the octopus swallow the girl and slip back into the ocean.

The local harbor patrol ship gave chase but was quickly outpaced, even the capital airships could not keep track of the creature as it slipped into the darkness of the ocean.

Inside the mechanical octopus, Saria listened to the steady rhythm hums of the engines that powered the creature. She finally opened her eyes. Inside a large metal room streaked with blue-green rust that ran down the sides of the walls.

"Oh good, you're alive," A man's voice said, "I thought I might have killed you since you hadn't moved in a long time."

"Who are you?" Saria asked.

"I am the inventor of this wonderful machine. You may call me the driver." The man was wired into the machine. Brass tubes and wires ran from various parts his body into the wall behind him.

"I...I...I have to ask, did you bring the hand?" he inquired. Sparks shot out from the wall causing him to stutter, his face to twitch uncontrollably. Saria undid her satchel producing the severed hand in the jar. He took it from her.

"Oh, how are you?" He asked tenderly. The fingers wiggled and twitched as he spoke. "I have missed you too my beautiful daughter. It's time to get you back together."

He placed the jar into a compartment next to him. A few loud bangs could be heard then a door next to the man opened. A small automaton walked out. It was completely mechanical except for the human left hand. A tall golden decorative crown on her head, several golden bracelets decorated her arms. She reminded Saria of one of the Thai dancers she had seen in pictures.

"Hello, Saria, I am Boon-Mee. Thank you for returning me to my father."

"Why have you brought me here?" Saria asked.

"Many years ago my father built this machine. It malfunctioned causing many people to lose their lives, I was one of them." She paused for a moment." My father felt so bad he sealed himself inside and became the driver of this machine to control it. He later discovered it requires a human driver or co pilot to operate properly. As retribution, we select one child from people involved in the creation to live here until they are eighteen or they decide they want to leave."

"What happens when I turn eighteen?" Saria asked.

"A new child will be selected and you will leave to live your life. You will be financially set up for life on the one condition that you never return to your hometown. Besides, they would never believe it was really you. They saw you swallowed whole by a giant octopus." Boon-Mee said a slight smile on the little automatons face.

"So, who was the young man I kept seeing around town?"

"He was the last passenger," the automaton replied.

"And what if I hadn't brought the hand with me?"

"You would become fish food." Boon-Mee said, "You would be surprised how many kids didn't return me to my father. A shame they couldn't follow directions."

"Boon-Mee be nice." Her father scolded, "No, if the hand isn't returned, the child is drugged with a serum I created from poisonous fish and seaweed. It makes everything seem like a vivid dream."

"So, will I have to lose my left hand?" Saria asked.

"No," Boon-Mee giggled," He lost his hand in a disagreement with some air pirates in a pub brawl in London. I am sure you won't make the same mistake of trying to cheat some air pirates at dice." Boon-Mee scuttled over to a room. She came back with a fine china tea set on a tray. "I am so happy to have a girl as my companion this time. Would you like some jasmine white tea? It is my favorite. We have much to explore. Where shall we start first?"

GOODNIGHT, PRETTY MOLLY

By: Jill Hand

When you're a robot dinosaur coming off of a twelve-hour shift of patrolling the streets, the last thing you want is to take crap from a parrot, but you put up with it as best you can.

The reason for this is it's just you and the parrot; everyone else is offline. It seems all of planet Earth is offline. It gives you a lonely feeling. That's why you're willing to cut the parrot some slack. It's just the two of you now.

Stev tromped up the cracked and weed-sprouting asphalt of the driveway, his big metal feet going clomp, clomp, clomp. He clomped into the garage, past the ranks of other robot dinosaurs, all of them frozen in attitudes of attack, or consternation, or repose, all of them offline.

The robot dinosaurs' metal bodies were painted a variety of colors, depending on their function. The green brontosauruses were groundskeepers in the public parks. The red ankylosauruses were companions for the elderly and the disabled. Nobody messed with them when they were accompanied by a robot dinosaur guardian with a forest of sharp spikes sticking out of its back.

The yellow pterosaurs kept an eye out for the children, soaring gracefully above them as they played in the playing fields or walked to school. The pterosaurs were equipped with lasers, in case anyone tried to harm any of the children. Kidnappings and violent crimes against the young had declined to the point of near-nonexistence after that innovation.

There were lots of robot dinosaurs in the garage, painted many different colors. Stev was a black tyrannosaurus. He was a public safety officer. Since almost everyone and everything had gone offline there wasn't any crime-fighting for him to do, but he patrolled the streets anyway from 8 a.m. to 8 p.m., his big, taloned metal feet going clomp, clomp, clomp. It was the job he was programmed to do. He had no choice in the matter. He'd keep on doing his job until he went offline, as he surely must someday. He didn't think he could remain activated forever, could he?

Pretzel the African Gray parrot considered Stev from her perch, her head cocked to one side, regarding him with one silvery eye.

"Hello, Dino Cop! Gimme a nut!"

Stev went over to a fifty-pound burlap bag of birdseed and scooped some out. The bag was almost empty.

"No more nuts. We're all out," he told Pretzel, pouring seeds in her dish. "Have some of these."

Pretzel surveyed the seeds unhappily.

"Nut later?" she said hopefully.

"There are no more nuts. Sorry," Stev said.

He went over to the sink and filled Pretzel's water dish. At least the water was still running. That was good.

"Rub my head, you big booger," Pretzel demanded.

Stev reached out a talon and stroked her head. Pretzel's eyes closed blissfully.

"I love you, you big booger," Pretzel told him in her rusty little voice.

"I love you," Stev told her, gently running a talon along the grey feathers on her back. He was careful when he handled her. She was so tiny, compared to his metal bulk.

"Let's go see Molly," Pretzel suggested.

Molly was a technician. She maintained all the robot dinosaurs in the garage, or at least she had until she went offline. That had been… Stev paused to calculate… 728 days, 14 hours and thirty-six minutes ago.

"Molly's sleeping," he told Pretzel.

Pretzel shook herself, the red feather in her tail tapping against her wooden perch.

"I wanna see Molly. Pretty Molly! Where are you, pretty Molly?" she trilled.

Stev sighed. "All right, but just for a minute."

Pretzel hopped onto his shoulder. The robot dinosaurs were much smaller than the real dinosaurs had been. Stev was nine feet tall from his metal feet to the top of his metal head. That was large enough for the purpose of his designer, who, like every other human on Earth, had gone offline.

Stev walked to the back of the garage, his big metal feet clomp, clomp, clomping against the cement floor. It was quiet in the garage. The TV used to be on all the time, giving the news, but it had eventually gone offline too. The last news had been about something called floo. The TV people called it a pandemic.

Floo and pandemic were not words in Stev's data base. He therefore didn't know what they meant, but whatever they meant it made the TV people unhappy. Some of them had cried as they talked about it.

He opened the door to the back room, where Molly lay on a cot. She was on her side, her knees bent, her brown hair fanned out on the pillow under her head. Her eyes were closed. Her skin had changed color in the dry desert air. It had turned leathery and shrunk against the bones that made up her framework. Molly was offline.

"Pretty Molly! Hello, pretty Molly," Pretzel crooned. She hopped down onto the cot and pressed her beak against Molly's cheek. When Molly failed to respond she patted her gently with one grey wing and then fluttered up to Stev's shoulder. She settled herself against him, holding on with her reptilian feet.

"Molly's sleeping," she said.

"That's right. Let's go back in the other room," Stev told her.

"Have a nut?" Pretzel asked hopefully.

"There are no more nuts," he said.

"Hecky darn," she replied.

Turning to the corpse on the cot she said, "Goodnight, pretty Molly."

THE TIME BEFORE DREAMS

By: E.E. King

Once there was a time before dreams. The night was empty. People rested in deep unconsciousness, a preview of oblivion, with no fancies or night terrors to disturb their slumber.

The dreams never left their home, which was and is, in the fog of memory in the valley between reality and imagination.

Here lived all things fantastic, forgotten imaginings and recollections from lives never lived. Souls that might have been, but never were, wander here. Their illusory reminiscences roam the valley like exceptionally unsubstantial ghosts (never tangible at most their solid.)

In this valley dwelled a little girl who made wishes. By this I do not mean she was fanciful, envisioning, or desiring to be a princess or own a pony. But simply that she constructed wishes. She formed them from saliva, fresh basil and salt, mixed under the full moon. They were hardened with twelve drops of hope and shined to a glossy brilliance with fine linen and a thimbleful of trepidation.

She rolled them into translucent bubbles perfect and small as seed pearls. She and the memories played soccer with them, chasing each other full throttle through violet grass, incorporeal lungs expelling wisps of exertion and ghostly laughter. Whispers of their games would float into our world, teasing deep-night slumber to strain senses at this first murmured prelude to dreams.

Sometimes the wishes would go spinning into our world, where they might break beneath your feet when you least expected it, exploding with unconsidered wishes and sometimes even curses.

Many thought the sudden appearance of desire made manifest was caused by ill fate, celestial design, witches masquerading as old women, or even devils.

In truth, they were merely created by the little girl as a diversion.

Every now and then a wild soccer tackle would send a wish whirling into a deep crevice between the worlds, creating a boundary of unwished for desire thick as fog, verdant and fecund as tropical jungle. Inside vast creatures could be heard, though they were rarely visible. Colorful birds and vespertine mammals, wingspans far beyond imagining, sounded like secrets gliding through the twilight. This was an undiscovered country, inhabited by beings not belonging to either land, creatures neither alive nor dead, real nor imagined. No one passed between the worlds. The wishes created an imponderable border and grew crowded with limitless fancies and unconsidered visions.

One dusk, a train appeared, painted with colors so bright you could see them through closed lids, even if all you desired was the dark, even if you were blind. Inside the train, music was playing so sweet, its vibrations echoed in your soul long after the last cord was silent, even if your ears were filled with wax, even if you were deaf. The air was scented with fragrance that remained inside the skin, rising out of pores long after showering, even if you were to drown, its bouquet would rise from the grave like memory and longing. The food from the dining car was served upon delicate china rosebud plates and lingered upon lips and tongue, engulfing your being with hunger and desire long after you were sated. And touch, that most elusive yet tender of the scents, became forever tangible, even in thought.

The train traveled through the undiscovered country past the signpost of oblivion, stopping in a tiny village west of nowhere. Creatures, from all worlds and no world, out of curiosity, or due to overcrowding, began to board the train. Some never left.

No one and nothing saw a driver or crew, but the train's interior was spotless and so sparkling clean, it hurt the eyes of the nocturnal and crepuscular. Inside the train, on white upholstered satin walls, hung dark glasses, to protect the eyes of the unwary and the unprepared.

Inside this train, a cat might turn into a panther, a girl into a temptress, and desire morph into love or versa vice according to the moon and wind. Sometimes a matron would board under a cold night streetlamp and depart to discover herself a lass again, alone in a strange wood. A cat might sniff its way aboard and find itself a panther, depending on the wind, the whispering of ghostly laughter, the breaking of wishes or even how rapidly the night train ran. And run it did. On little cat feet, out of darkness into light and back again. Trailing dreams and sparks that might become glowworms, fireflies and comets, or dragons, chimeras and fire-breathing-Pandas, depending upon which world it was traversing.

Sometimes, someone or something got left at the wrong stop. This is why our world has seahorses, hummingbirds, bats, orchids, butterflies and manatees, creatures too fanciful and strange to have evolved here.

One sleepless night, when dreams glide like the shadows of great seabirds above deep oceans, an old man huddled on the bare landing of a fire escape, beneath an indifferent neon sky. As if in obedience to unseen voices, he slowly unwound his stiff hunched frame and climbed the narrow ladder leading down, down, down, six long stories to the lamp-lit street. He shivered in the lonely, cold dark of the empty city. Buildings towered above him, giant ebony skeletons, with empty eyes and hollow grins.

Suddenly a rush of hot air, like desire, rushed past him and stopped. The night train silently opened its doors and he climbed aboard. It ran into the night faster than time, more incandescent than passion, stopping only once, where a dog snuffled his way into the gleaming dinner. Although his paws were muddy, the prints immediately evaporated into a rainbow mist, dissipating into air.

The train raced through the night, speeding through the vaporous wood between worlds into the land where wishes are made and the memories of the non-existence roam.

It glided to a stop and the once-old man stepped out, now a slight and straight fresh faced boy. At his heels padded a large dog. Their lungs inhaled the fresh air, devoid of buildings, cars and too many lives. They breathed the strange new perfume of that world.

The boy began to race through the violet grass, dog loping at his side. The dog's large paw squashed a seed pearl wish, breaking it into a million bits of rainbow dew. The boy continued his joy filled, lung bursting, run, a silver wolf trotting by his side.

It seemed like many days passed in that land, but time cannot be trusted in any world, not even our own. The boy played with the wolf, feasted upon strange fruits and sucked wishes like gumballs. The wolf disappeared each night and returned at dawn sated. The boy did not know what the wolf ate. He was not sure if he wanted to know.

I say "night" and "dawn, but these are just conventions to make understanding easier, for this was a land of mists and fog. Light was diffused and moist, embracing the skin like remembered caresses of a distant lover.

One dusk, as boy and wolf ran through the fields, they came upon the soccer game. Boy and wolf joined in the fray and soon it was a nightly, or perhaps twi-nightly, occurrence. The girl and boy playing with wishes, memories and the silver wolf.

One night a ball flew wide and far, laughter spurting from every pore, the boy raced after it. The wolf, all wet tongued, panting joy raced with him. And somehow, unseeing they raced into the open, waiting, train. The wish splattered against the white satin interior. Doors closed and the train began its rumble through the night.

The boy wept and banged at the windows and the doors. He flung the fragrant food off of the rosebud plates and smashed the dark glasses hanging from the walls. But they would not break. No matter how the boy raged the train remained spotless, clean, unbroken and unstoppable, racing though the night into the land between the worlds.

The wolf howled, a cry to tear the soul, but even as he wailed forth his anguish to the night, its tremor changed. His howl grew tamer and when the door opened onto the orange neon night out hobbled a bent old man and a sorrowful mongrel. Together they searched for shelter in the cold, iron night. They lived from scraps snatched from trash bins or left at bus stops. But in the night they dreamed. What dreams! They were more solid than life, hotter than fire, longer than love and truer than death.

And so dreams entered our world, showing glimmers of that other land. Making night passage through our souls into this world. And in that other land do dreams and memories and little wishing girls' dream of us? I do not know. But they remember us. Oh, how they remember.

CARRION

By: Simone L W Mounsamy

Hello. Who are you? I don't know you, but you smell like flowers. It's comforting. Have you got a little time to spare? There's something… well, I don't know what it is exactly. Something has been itching on my mind. It's very itchy. I can't figure it out.

Let me introduce myself. I'm Sasha. I am a black and white canine: German Shorthaired Pointer Mix. Most people will say I am a big dog. My girl says I'm the perfect size. I am spayed, which means I will forever stay a puppy at heart, says the boy of my girl. I don't know if that's good or bad, but he gives me a funny feeling when he says it. Like when you finally get into your bed to sleep but it smells moldy. It makes me wonder if I wish I wasn't spayed. Maybe I should become old at heart? I am five, however. My girl made me wear a poky hat with a five on it, she took my picture, and so I am five.

Now you know me. I do wish you would tell me about yourself.

***

I hope you can help me figure out this pickle. Or more like peanut butter sticking in the back corner there.

Where to begin…Before my girl found me I lived in a breathless place. I was young and already taking up too much space. I don't remember much except the way my insides seemed like a twisted-up garden hose. There was a man with a rolled-up newspaper and terrifying, laughing kids. I learned to hide in dusty and forgotten corners under desks and beds. I didn't know what my problem was. My girl tells me they were the problem. She breathes into my heart-tubes and opens it up again. I'll be with her forever.

When my girl found me, she had a different boy. She took me and him running across town. We went in the bright sun among the other people and dogs next to the river under the trees and between the buildings and beside cars. Sometimes we went at night down the sidewalk between the shadows and under the rainbow neon lights. We became a running pack. I could run all day long for days and days, as long as there was food. She made me a muscly dog when I used to be a frail one. We went everywhere. She'd smile and say, "This is training."

Then my girl changed boys. She changed a little too. She even smelled different. Before, she smelled like outside air mixed with sweat. And then she smelled like coconut oil and…eggs? All of a sudden, I had twisted-up garden hose tummy again. But not because of any hitting or poking. This time it was sounds in their voices that touched me. My girl said it was his fear but I know she found some too. This terrified me, which I think made her even more afraid. I could see it in her eyes like broken mirrors. "We do our best," my girl would say.

She's still my angel. She has freckles and round cheeks. Sometimes she stops and remembers us from before, mostly if we're alone. She slips us into our old skins and holds onto me for what might be hours. It warms my tummy with loose breath. I beg her to stay, she doesn't though. I know she can't. But even when she has broken mirror eyes, they are soft. I love her.

We still go running, but not very much. Now she has a baby, and the boy, so we do our best. I do miss long runs though. We really went everywhere. We ran so hard our brains forgot everything. We just let go of everything except brown, crumpled earth that rolled on and on. We flew. And we smelled a million prickly smells that rushed into our noses and our faces. At least we do still go these days. We let go of everything for a little while and fly. I just want more. I think my girl does too. But we do our best.

We left Austin and its urban color to come to a wild, vibrant place. I went in the car with my girl and her boy to a noise and smell charged-up place where they left me in my box with some strangers who moved me into a moving room and I proceeded to spend the rest of my day being moved in my box by strangers and withstanding extreme discomfort. What's more, my girl gave me something to eat that I think made me zone out completely. It felt super freaky. It wore off though and the day finally ended with my girl hugging me and walking me around some unfamiliar earth.

I'm getting to the sticky part I need your help with. I'm giving you a frame of reference first though.

It all started when my new friend showed up. I had some friends before and one best friend, Mila. This new friend dog has been my only real friend in this unfamiliar place. I know my girl loves him too, but she also loves her new baby and her new farm animals. Before there was just me and her boys. Anyway, my new friend showed up at the fence with his little tail wagging and his mouth slobbering. He looks like a hot dog and he is called Vodka.

After I met him I noticed dogs here are different. You see, he's free! That letting go and flying we do when we run? That's what he does all the time and all by himself. And he is not homeless! He has an owner, and he finds holes in their fence or goes out when they open it and they don't mind! He runs and explores the neighborhood all day long. He goes where he wants, he smells who he wants, he even rolls in mud or other hot, wet, musty things if he wants. He is in top shape even if he looks like a fat hot dog. He goes home for food and water I guess. And there are plenty other dogs like him too.

He came to my fence and smelled my nose. His tail said he wanted to play. I wanted to play. Soon he found a hole in my fence and he came inside. We finally got to play. He is short and I am big but he doesn't mind. We had some fun rolling in the wet grass and making noise and running circles around the yard bumping sides. He even let me pin him down and didn't get mad.

He came over all the time to play before but soon I found out he loves my girl back. He wants more love from my girl than he's allowed. She's already given him water, food and affection. He wants to be her dog and he's not allowed. He didn't tell me but I figured it out when he stopped wanting to play and just began following her.

Anyway, one day he came over and he showed me the way to get out of my fence. I followed him. My girl, her baby and her boy weren't home. I felt a little burst of lightning. This day, I followed my hot dog friend out and I was free too! We roamed. We ran a lot. We trotted. We walked. We met whichever dogs we wanted, some free, some behind fences, some chained. Some chained behind fences. They all smelled so interesting. But some of them said the strangest things.

"We out here Sunny."

"Go on and bring me some."

"He he he, think about it then."

"Those shockers, shockers, shockers!"

It creeped me out but my friend just smiled at them, then at me. We ate salty rib bones. We got thirsty and found a ditch humid and alive like a forest in the rain. We drank the tops of muddy water and swam. We dodged cars. We ran some more. The hot dog dog and I really became best friends that day. Vodka. I had a LOT of fun. I love my girl and I didn't think much of it that day. Afterwards, I wondered if I didn't love being free more than I love her. There's just something about it. I felt completely myself.

Something about my hot dog friend though. A car will come by and he runs right out in front of it for no reason at all! I wait for an explanation but he never even gives a sign except a smile. The cars swerve and sometimes honk. I think they are going to hit him every time he does it. I don't know why he does it. But somehow, he lives. It's part of who he is. It's very annoying. What can you do? Every now and then he asks, "How is the girl?" I don't answer and hope he will stop asking.

We met the hot dog dog's other free friends along the way. A white, slender wolf-looking dog came along for a while. We spent all day outside before my girl found me. She seemed afraid. I don't like her like that, all sharp and high pitched.

"Dammit Sasha!" She's better when she's not afraid. Now I know clearly I cannot be free and keep my girl too. I could not live like my hot dog friend. She would not like me to find holes in the fence and sneak out.

Times passed. My hot dog friend came over less and less. I noticed more and more dogs free. Dogs in front of their houses have no leash and come out barking when my girl and me go running by. Dogs at night roam through the streets together in a group. They come up to the fence sometimes to smell me and I can't help myself. I bark and squeal feeling crazed.

"Take me with you!" I plead. They trot away. I long for the feeling again. No leash, no human, no connection to the human's choices and feelings. Forgetting everything, letting go. Flying through fresh air. The social life. The adventure. The exciting unknown.

One night I saw the dog group passing by. My hot dog friend ran among them! He came to the fence and smelled me. He smelled like black, rich dirt. He whined a little bit with me and whipped his tail back and forth. He reminded me where the hole in my fence is that we escaped from together.

"Come on!" He called from the other side while smiling all over. We knelt down touching noses through the hole in the fence. I couldn't help myself. In no time, I found myself darting out.

We caught up with the dog pack. I counted five other dogs!

"Eh," one called back to me. I smelled their butts quickly as I ran from one to the other. Most of them turned back to react or smell me too but none of us broke stride. We ran by the orange light of the street lamps and by the glowing full moon. The streets were almost empty. We trotted down the sidewalks. We smelled the million clashing smells of the trash cans. We peed on stuff to mark the way, to add to the dog pee smell pile, or just because it was so fun! I stayed next to my hot dog friend. The darkness thrilled me like the shadowy sidewalks while running with my girl.

With the pack, nothing seemed frightening. I felt like I had friends. Weird dogs but still friends. Stronger together. Dogs are much less complicated than humans. Maybe even less complicated than my girl. When I'm out with the dog pack we are together yet separate. Unbound but in good company. That night I decided I would go out again with my hot dog friend and the dog pack when they passed by. I would be back before my girl woke up. She would never know and never be afraid. And I would be able to have both my girl and that weightless freedom.

I lie awake waiting in my dog box on the patio almost every night. I listen for dogs swishing through tall grass and trotting by the fence. Most nights I fall asleep waiting. When I hear them, I jump up and run to the hole in the fence behind the banana trees. I sometimes find my hot dog friend's big nose. We stay out with the pack until the moon moves all the way across the dark blue sky. My hot dog friend and I trot back home and say good night. I sleep most of the next day after these nights.

Last week I went out with them. The moon was a skinny sliver of silver sardines. I don't know what day of the week it was but people were out driving. You know, I am one of the first to become distracted by a cat, a squirrel, or a rat. I can't handle myself. They are so fast and smell so specific. I'm fast too though and I want to see who's faster. A red cat hid in the trees and tall grass on the side of the road. It jumped out and sprinted across the street. I took one step running in its direction but the brown boxer dog took ten. The cat crossed the street and the boxer was almost there when BAM. I jumped back on the curb. All of the dogs in the pack stopped. The black truck continued in the opposite direction. No brakes at all.

The boxer laid mangled in a growing pool of red near the far curb. The cat sat on the other side of the street and we six stood on this side. We watched the boxer. The cat flicked its tail and pranced away. The boxer dog was no longer himself, he was a carcass. The dogs slowly turned from the bloody torn-up lump of flesh and fur. One by one they trotted away. Carried on. My hot dog friend and I were the last to go. He waited for me. When the road emptied I slowly walked out to smell the boxer's rusty iron stomach. Finally, my hot dog friend left too.

That was almost me. The boxer dog never got used to cats, like me. I never lived with cats, never got used to them. They trigger a reaction, an animal reflex. I can't stop myself either. Or with squirrels, or rats. I react too, lunge and charge. Was it just bad luck? There are so many cars on this road though, and they go fast. And there are so many small animals that drive dogs mad. Eventually I walked home alone. I slipped through the hole in the fence and into the banana trees. I padded up the stairs to the patio and my box. The iron blood smell turned rancid and stuck to my nose all night. I couldn't sleep. My mind's eye was haunted. Not by the blood and guts but the cat jumping up onto the curb. The truck with its bright lights devouring the boxer dog in slow motion. The free dog was in fact trapped. The stolen boxer dog lying motionless and breathless in the middle of the road.

Since then, I'm also breathless and in a state of shock. When I hear the dogs my heart beats shallow and quick. I have the urge to run to the hole, dart through, and run out after them but my itchy mind stops me and I can't move. This is what has been bothering me. What do you suggest? And what if my hot dog friend is next? He makes bad choices with cars and for nothing at all, not even a cat. What if I saw him get smashed right before my eyes? Or what if it's me? Still, my whole self, every nerve inside me, pulses forward when I see them. I've missed the pack. I feel the energy frenzying all the way into my toes. Some instinct triggers when I hear the swishing grass and the trotting feet past my fence.

BIRDS OF A FEATHER

By: Liz Schriftsteller

<u>Last Tuesday Afternoon</u>

The penguin was not welcome in Mrs. McConnell's flat, let alone sitting on the couch as if it were waiting to be served afternoon tea. It looked up at her expectantly while she sipped from her cup. She glared back over the top of her rimless glasses.

"Gregory!" she called to her son. "I thought we had discussed this unseemly habit of bringing stray animals into my home!"

"We had, mother!" he called back. "You said it was lovely and I should do so more often!"

Mrs. McConnell pursed her lips and shook a bony finger in the direction of the kitchen. "I said nothing of the sort!" The penguin leaned over to examine her cup, which she guarded close to her chest.

The penguin was only the most recent in a long line of exotic houseguests her son had seen fit to bring home, and no amount of, "Not in this household, Gregory!" had ever stopped him in his twenty-seven years. In fact, the matter had been escalating ever since he majored in wildlife conservation studies at the university.

This, however, was a bit extreme, even for him.

"Now, now, mother," Gregory said, joining them in the sitting room. "Don't be rude. Here, have a biscuit." He offered her a ginger snap but before she could take it, the penguin darted forward and snatched it from Gregory's hand.

Mrs. McConnell yelped and scooted farther down the sofa. "Gregory Malcolm Frederick McConnell!" she chastised. "You march out of here right this instant and take that flightless waterfowl with you!"

Gregory Malcolm Frederick McConnell did not march. He elected to set himself down on the couch between his mother and the aforementioned waterfowl. He tossed the bird another ginger snap, which it plucked from the air and swallowed down.

"That's just the thing, mother, I'm afraid he'll be staying with you for a few days until we can get the sanctuary up and running."

Mrs. McConnell raised an eyebrow and set her teacup carefully down on the side table, all while never breaking eye contact. It was a look that suggested the penguin was most certainly not staying with her and if she had to say it out loud, then her son would not be staying with her either; not now, not ever again.

"I hardly think that Mr. Volpi will—"

"I've already contacted the building manager," interrupted Gregory. "It will only be for a week at most and he says he's fine with it."

"*He* says *he's* fine with it?" Mrs. McConnell repeated, her face growing red. "That's all well and good but he isn't the one who will be sharing his living space with it now, is he?"

"Now, mother—"

"Don't you 'Now, mother' me, young man!" she continued, raising her voice. "Don't you think this is something you should have at least mentioned to me before clearing it with my landlord?"

Gregory sighed. He whistled to the penguin, who hopped off the sofa and followed him into the water closet. "Now wait here, Reggie," he instructed the penguin and shut the door behind it. His mother stood between the hallway and the sitting room with her arms crossed.

"Reggie?"

"Yes. Short for Reginald. And as you can see, he does have a fair amount of training."

"I don't care if he's so well trained that he can open his own cans of sardines," she sniffed. "He's not staying here."

"It's just for a few days. I'll be back next week to—"

"You'll be *back*?" she repeated, her eyes wide. "You don't mean to say you're leaving that thing with me?"

"Well, unless you intend to have it as a permanent resident, I'll be needing to oversee the habitat construction," he snipped.

"I don't intend to have it at all!"

Gregory took his mother's hands in his, a look in his eyes harkened back to his boyhood days when he pleaded to take in his first injured squirrel. Mrs. McConnell hated that look.

"Just give him a couple days, mother, at least until the sanctuary is ready. That's all I'm asking."

Mrs. McConnell pressed her index fingers to her temples and rolled them around as she tried to find her boundary lines.

"Three days, Gregory," she said at last.

"But—"

"*Three.*"

"Starting tomorrow?" he asked hopefully.

"Starting now." She pointed to the grandfather clock in the hallway. "If you aren't back here by tea time on Friday afternoon to collect that—thing—" She gestured pointedly to her washroom door. "Then you can find yourself another penguin. Or another mother," she added. "I don't much care which."

"Oh, thank you, mother!" Gregory kissed her on the cheek. "You won't regret this!"

The look on her face however, confirmed she already had.

***

<u>Tuesday Evening</u>

Mrs. McConnell had considered leaving The Penguin (she refused to refer to it as "Reginald," even in her own mind) in the water closet for the entirety of his stay. However, her flat only had one toilet and she would be damned if she would be put out of her own washroom.

She stood in the hallway in her dressing gown and fluffy slippers, doorknob to the washroom in one hand and brandishing an open can of sardines in the other. Before opening the door it occurred to her that this was a penguin, not a tiger, and perhaps she was being a bit jumpier than was absolutely necessary. Still, it never hurt to be prepared.

She threw open the door and cringed, waiting to be trampled. When nothing happened, she cautiously blinked her eyes open. There, on the other side of the door was Reginald, standing perfectly still and looking between her and the open can of fish.

"Ahem. If you wouldn't mind," she said, gesturing toward the hallway.

Reginald continued to stare at her without moving, save for his occasional glance toward the fish with an expectant look in his eye.

"Get. Out." She pointed toward the hall.

Reginald did not move.

"You!" She pointed at the bird. "Get—"

Before she could finish, Reginald snapped at her finger. She stumbled backwards, nearly tripping on the threshold.

"Oh!" she shrieked. "You wretched thing!" She hurled the can of sardines at him. He scuttled out of the way, knocking over the metal trash bin in the process. She slammed the door behind him, muffling the sound of the bin clattering to the ground.

Mrs. McConnell decided it was in her best interest to use the public washrooms at her local health spa and gymnasium instead.

***

<u>Wednesday Morning</u>

Mrs. McConnell had not gone in her washroom since the sardine incident the night before. If anyone asked her why she was frequenting their showers so often, she decided she would tell them the pipes in her building were under construction. She thought this was a terribly good story and was a little put out no one had bothered to ask.

Even so, she did open the washroom door just wide enough to toss in a few open cans of sardines lest the evil thing starve to death. The only thing worse than a live penguin in one's apartment was a dead one.

185

The next morning, Ms. McConnel decided to make kippers for breakfast.

The smell of the sizzling fish permeated her small flat and crept under the doorjamb into the water closet, from which came an insistent tapping. Mrs. McConnell elected to ignore it. The tapping grew louder causing her to worry he would scratch the finish.

She left the skillet unattended and walked across the apartment. "I suppose you're hungry," she said through the closed door.

Tap, tap.

"Are you going to behave yourself?"

Tap, tap, tap.

"Well, then. You may join me if you wish, but if you act like a wild beast I shall send you right back to the water closet, are we clear?"

Tap.

"Very well." She opened the door and Reginald waddled out into the hallway, tipping his beak toward her. Mrs. McConnell had to admit he did look very regal indeed, with his little tuxedo. She gestured to the kitchen. "Go on, then. Take a seat."

He followed her through the apartment and stood by the kitchen table. She returned to her kippers and gave them a turn with the skillet. He nudged the wooden chair with his beak. It was too tall for him to sit on. Mrs. McConnell glanced over to him. "I suppose the step stool will have to do."

Reginald waddled over to the refrigerator and pulled the little stool away from the wall toward the table. With a quick hop, he jumped atop it and stood patiently by the table as Mrs. McConnell seasoned the fish.

"Here you are," she said as she set a platter down in front of him.

The penguin lunged for the fish but Mrs. McConnell swatted his beak with a dishrag.

"Manners!" she scolded. "In this household we say grace."

The penguin bowed his head as she spoke.

"Thank you, Lord, for this food and this... company... to share it with, such as it is. Thank you for my son, and the patience not to wallop him every time he comes 'round, even though he rightly deserves it. In your name, we pray, Amen."

Mrs. McConnell picked up her fork and gestured for him to continue. Reginald darted forward and sucked the fish down his gullet in one quick bite.

Mrs. McConnell frowned. "Chew your food, please. I will not break bread with a glutton."

Reginald blinked at her but said nothing.

"Now," she said. "I shall have to attend the fishmongers tomorrow. I had not budgeted for an extra mouth to feed." She frowned, thinking of her son's imposition.

Reggie squawked in response.

"Well, I suppose you could come with. You did behave quite well this morning. All things considered."

She cleared the table while Reggie waddled off into the living room. "Normally I would insist you clear your own plate but I'm not quite prepared to have you smashing my fine china," she called after him.

He hopped onto the couch and switched on the telly to the Miss Marple Mystery show.

Mrs. McConnell smiled and put the kettle on. "Well," she conceded. "At least you have good taste in programmes."

***

Wednesday Afternoon

Mrs. McConnell had fallen asleep in front of the television when a knock came from her front door. The sound from the set was so loud that she couldn't rightly hear it at all. Reginald, however, did.

He waddled over toward the front door and with his beak nudged the chain bolt out of its cradle.

Reginald squawked.

The door opened, with Mr. Volpi standing on the other side. He looked down at the penguin and grinned.

"Hullo, Missus M! Thought I'd pop over to see how you've been holding up what with your houseguest this week."

Reginald squawked.

"Ah yes, I supposed that might be the case. One day down, though, eh?"

The sound of chatter within her apartment roused Mrs. McConnell from sleep. "Oh?" she said. "What's that?" She pulled herself from the sofa and saw her landlord at the door, speaking comfortably with Reginald.

"Oh, hello!" She waved and started toward the door with a stiff, shuffling gait.

Mr. Volpi looked startled, his gaze shifting from the bird to the woman, and back to the bird again.

"I hadn't heard you knock, I'm afraid. Luckily it seems Reggie here has figured out the locking mechanism."

"Oh my," he laughed. "Forgive me, Missus, I thought you was the bird!"

Mrs. McConnell took a step back. "I beg your pardon?"

"Ah, but I beg yours!" Mr. Volpi gestured to the penguin, who had Mrs. McConnell's red reading glasses perched over the top of his beak. "It's just that he was wearing the glasses, and he *is* a bit taller than I expected and uh…"

"Yes. I see." Mrs. McConnell sniffed, self-consciously noticing her own long, hooked nose in the hallway mirror as if for the first time. "How very droll."

Mr. Volpi grinned. "Maybe next time, keep him from getting at your specs, eh?"

Mrs. McConnell's eyebrows scrunched together. "But then how would he watch the telly? He's terribly nearsighted."

Mr. Volpi's mouth opened and closed a few times before he found his voice. "I—oh. I hadn't thought of that."

"No, I suppose you hadn't, dear. At any rate, thank you for stopping by." She swung the door shut, his muffled protests drowned out by her curt, "Good day."

***

Thursday Morning

A similar incident happened the following morning, only this time it was at the fishmongers. They had traveled down to the docks early that morning to get the best pick of the daily catch, and the attendant kept directing his questions to Reginald, rather than Mrs. McConnell. She had found it cute at first, not realizing he had honestly mistaken one old bird for another.

It was less funny when he handed Reggie the change, and the penguin had nearly nibbled down a five-pound note. She admonished his incompetence, and more than a few unkind words were exchanged between both parties, some which do not bear repeating.

"Well," she said to Reginald. "The nerve of some people."

The penguin cocked his head to one side as she appraised him. She remembered hearing once that people often take after their pets and vice versa. She doubted he was having such an effect on her after no more than thirty-six hours, and yet, there was something about his manner that did echo her own, ever so slightly.

In the end, she shrugged it off. There were worse animals to be mistaken for, and after all, her black and white dress did look rather slimming.

***

Friday Afternoon

Friday afternoon found them sitting on the couch watching Miss Marple mystery reruns on the BBC. Mrs. McConnell was dressed in black and white again, her favorite since she began taking fashion advice from Reginald. She hunched on the sofa, alternatively feeding biscuits to herself and the penguin, depending on which of them leaned forward when she plucked one off the tea tray.

"You know, Reggie, I'm so glad you suggested the sushi for lunch. It was not something I had ever deemed to try before, but it was actually quite pleasant."

Reggie turned to her and blinked.

"Yes, you're quite right. They can never replace hot kippers and tea of course. But it is nice to break from one's routine on occasion." She excused herself to the loo when the next advert came on the telly, and completely missed the grandfather clock chiming four o'clock in the other room.

A shuffling sound came from the front door as Gregory let himself into his mother's flat.

"Hullo!" he called over to the sofa. "I'm here, as promised."

Reginald made a noise as Gregory headed toward the washroom.

"Oh no, I'm afraid I can't stay for tea, mother. I really must get Reginald acclimated to his new habitat." Gregory opened the door to see his mother hunched over the washroom sink, rinsing her hands.

"Gregory! You really must learn to knock!"

He glanced back toward the sofa and laughed. "Now, mother, I know you're keen on manners, but I doubt Reggie will mind." Gregory wrapped his arm around his mother and pulled her out into the hallway.

"Let me go!" she squawked.

Gregory patted her head. "My, Reggie, you don't usually put up this much of a fuss!"

"I am NOT Reggie!"

Gregory ignored her, choosing instead to direct his comments to the sofa, where Reginald sat munching on biscuits. "I do hope it wasn't too much of an imposition," Gregory said as he ushered his mother out the door. "I know, I haven't the right, but I do appreciate it."

Reggie blinked at him from atop the sofa. There was one last cry of protest from Mrs. McConnell, which was muffled by the abrupt sound of the door closing behind them.

***

<u>Friday Evening</u>

Mrs. McConnell sat in the penguin enclosure amongst a dozen other birds of various shapes and sizes. No one had heard her protests, or if they did, no one had cared. In the end, her hoarse cries blended in with the penguins until at last they all settled down and made peace with their new surroundings.

"I'm sure I don't know quite how this happened." Most of the penguins took no notice of her, except for one about her size and shape, who nodded its head sympathetically. "One minute you're in your flat watching telly, the next…" she gestured broadly to the enclosure.

The penguin beside her squawked.

"Yes, I suppose you're right. It isn't quite the same as being uprooted from the Antarctic."

Mrs. McConnell looked around at her new home.

"It's not so bad, really," she conceded. "At least we've got plenty of kippers."

THE PRISONER

By: Valerie Manwill

The cell was bigger than his last, but nonetheless equally horrible. A low hanging metal ceiling matched a cold, hard floor sprinkled with wooden debris. It was a dirty and desolate place with bars that showcased further prison beyond them. There were no windows, only one dim artificial light that hung outside the cell.

An overpowering smell choked Finn as soon as he entered. Salty sweat mixed with stale urine and feces. The stench was overwhelming.

Finn was young and passionate and not ready to throw away his best years looking out at the world from thin slats. He wouldn't stay here. Not this time. This time he would escape, no matter what it took. Finn pushed on the cell door with all his force. The metal bars under his hands hardly gave way.

He hoisted himself on the door to examine the lock on the top. It seemed to be a latch of some kind. He stuck his arm through the bars to reach it. His fingertips grazed the smooth underbelly.

"It's no use," a scratchy voice called to him from the corner of the cell. "There is no way out."

Finn jumped down to see a cellmate. An old huddled figure, with one milky-blind eye and a strip of white in his long black hair.

"Have you used a piece of wood or something to try and reach it?" Finn threw a darting gaze at the rubble between his feet.

"There's no use." The mysterious figure responded with a toneless voice.

"Have you tested for weaknesses?" he asked, running around and shaking random bars for any loose ones.

"There are no weaknesses. There is no escape," he said as he lumbered his way over to Finn, his hip popping out of place with every other step he took.

"Well, c'mon old man! Think! We could wait until they open the door and push our way through. We have to fight!"

"I promise you, there is no escaping." He lifted his head, his nose wrinkled and twitching. "Name's Graft."

"Finn."

Graft let out an acknowledging grunt. "Well. Make yourself comfortable. I prefer this corner myself." He laboriously hobbled to his corner and cleared a spot in the trash.

Finn watched him incredulously. "You're not going to do anything?"

"There's nothing to be done," he said as if it were a solid matter of fact. "Just be glad they've favored you. You're alive."

"I don't want to just be alive. I want to be free! I want to go home!" Finn protested, kicking at the door. Maybe Graft was okay with spending the rest of his life in a small putrid little room, but Finn was young and had so much left to give and do. If he stayed here, it would be as good as death.

"There is no home." Graft's voice suddenly became loud and stern. "They're stronger than us. They're smarter than us and they're better equipped. If you stay they'll give you food and water and if you leave, they'll hunt you down."

Finn slowly sank on his haunches against the wall. In a way, he knew Graft was right. If he made it out of the cell, he would still need to navigate a prison building that he had no knowledge of. His chances were slim, but at least it would be a chance.

"This is your home now," Graft slumped down into the filth and curled away from Finn. "You can have any of the other three corners but this one's mine."

Finn bit the inside of his cheek. "So that's it? Just because they're stronger than us, that's cause to give up trying?"

He shrugged. "You're just a kid. Tell me honestly, do you even know what home is? Or have you been in prisons all your life?"

Finn shifted uncomfortably. "I'm old enough to know there is a home."

"Was a home," Graft corrected him. "They've taken it all now."

An eerie silence fell across the cell until the wheezy snores from Graft eventually filled the space. Why was this old man so demanding that he stayed? Loneliness? Defeat? He couldn't comprehend Graft's complacency, but figured it had to do with the fact that he was physically incapable of such an attempt. He would be on his own for the great escape. And he would have to do it quickly without anyone trying to put a stop to it.

Finn searched for something he could use to reach the latch. That was his best shot. He shuffled through the wooden bits on the floor of the cell. Each piece was soft and bent easily as if left there to taunt his idea of escape.

Eventually, he had sifted through the trash in each area beside Graft's corner. The snore had gone from a wheezing whistle to a full-on roar. Flint tiptoed over to him, careful not to step too harshly on any debris. Something snapped under his foot. He froze. Graft didn't even stir, giving Finn the confidence to advance faster.

Behind the curled sleeping body in the corner a dark crescent moon shape came into view. As Finn grew nearer, it became clear what it was. It was the curvature of a small tunnel. Filled almost to the brim with debris and trash, but a tunnel nonetheless.

The sight took his breath away. This wasn't just any find. This was a way out. This was his chance at life.

But what did this mean? Surely, the old man had known of this opening. Was he planning to abandon Finn and use it himself? Or was his spirit so broken that he had given up on even the easiest of escape methods? Finn was right about Graft. He was trying to keep him there. He was trying to kill him slowly.

Graft's snorted and half opened his one good eye. He twisted toward Finn in confusion.

"Why didn't you tell me about the tunnel?" Finn went into interrogation mode.

He gave him the blankest of stares. "I told you, there's no escape."

Finn flew into a rage and began clearing the rotting debris with his bare hands. Graft got to his feet. "It doesn't lead anywhere. It only goes to more prison cell. It's not a way out."

"Why should I trust anything you say?" Finn yelled over his shoulder. "You hid this from me. You insulted me. You tried to convince me that this place was my home. You're probably working for them."

Graft didn't respond. His front teeth cracked as he ground them back and forth.

The last removed piece made a hollow clank as it fell. The hole was big enough to squeeze through. Finn's eyes narrowed and tensed at Graft. "Fine. You want to sit in here until you die, be my guest. But not me. I'm going to do something about my situation. I'm getting out of here." And with that, he dove head first into the tunnel.

The walls were rough but easy to grab a hold of as he pushed himself along. Eventually, the tunnel curved upwards. He wiped his face with his hand. *Upwards?* Where was this tunnel taking him? For a brief and chilling moment, he realized that Graft might be right. He didn't know where he was going, only that he was leaving his cell. Maybe this was all a trap. Maybe he was climbing right into his own death.

Finn squinted trying to see the other end. Smaller debris shook loose and fell into his mouth, filling it with the unpleasant dryness of sawdust. A faint light shone from the top. He took a deep breath and hoisted himself up. Even if he died, it was worth it to try. He would have to be smart. Get there as carefully and quietly as possible and have a look around before his enemies ambushed him.

The higher he got, the narrower the tunnel became. The hard, ridged wall soon constricted around his body like a boa constrictor and, for a moment, he feared he wouldn't make it. Finn grunted as he pushed through the narrow section. His breaths were becoming quicker now, his chest was tight. What if he never made it out? What if he had willingly crawled into a trap.

He panted to keep the air from leaving his body. The tunnel started to curve backward. He painfully twisted his waist to face the other side and continued pushing himself along.

The light was stronger now. He was close. He crouched low and crawled as quietly as he could, making his way to the end. He peeked around the opening.

"No," he whispered to himself. He stepped onto the debris and into a second but smaller cell, almost identical to the one he had come from. He dropped to his knees. Tears welled in his eyes. Graft had been right. The tunnel led nowhere. Only more prison. There was no out. No life. No freedom. It had all been a cruel mockery. He would get old and depressed and fade away in this cell. He laid amongst the bits of wood, defeated and tired from his ascent.

Something caught his eye. The glimmer he had seen shining from inside the tunnel. There was a large vertical crack in the ceiling, wide enough to let in light. He immediately stood to investigate. The ceiling was much lower than the cell below and he could reach this one easily. He stuck his fingers into the crack and gave it a hard push with his knuckles. A sharp snap echoed through the room as the roof lifted.

This was it. The chance that was worth all the risk in the world. He could smell freedom, taste the outside world, feel his life at his fingertips. It had to be now. Before Graft woke up and stopped him. Before the captors patrolled the area. He couldn't wait for a proper plan. He couldn't mull it over. It was now or never, and he had to take that chance.

Finn stood on the balls of his feet. He stuck his forehead on the crack and pushed with the back of his shoulder. The crack widened. He pushed again. Harder. The crack grew wide enough to get his head through. Jagged edges of the decrepit roof caught and pulled his hair. His arm followed, grasping the smooth side for any kind of hold. He had gotten both shoulders out, the widest part of him. Using all his upper body strength he pulled himself through the opening, scraping and bruising his back as he went.

He was out. Truly out. He stood on the roof of the prison trying to plot his next move. He could either attempt to climb down or jump. If he jumped, he might break a leg and that would make an escape impossible. He would have to find a way to start climbing and jump if he had to.

Suddenly, heavy footsteps approached. Finn scrambled for a way to get off the roof. It was too late. His captor appeared. A huge, bald giant, larger than a hundred Finns. A human. He spotted Finn right away.

"Mary." The human called out. "One of your damn hamsters got out again."

"Oh, yeah, they always get out of that second level in the cage," A young woman's voice replied from afar. "Put a textbook on top when you get him back in."

Finn's mind flew into a haze. He had to get away. He couldn't go back to prison. He couldn't let his life slip away forever. Finn desperately zig-zagged, not knowing which way to bolt. His captor wrapped his hand around his furry little body. Finn tried to wriggle from his grasp, but he was too strong. He scratched at the giant thumb around his waist.

The captor shoved Finn into the cage. Graft startled and huddled against the corner. Finn ran around in circles and kicked up the sawdust bedding on the floor of the cage. He squealed at the man, who waggled his finger in response.

"Aw." The captor smiled. "You're welcome, buddy."

The human closed the latch and sat a thick heavy book on top of the only means of escape.

A STEAK AND A STORY

By: Frank Kozusko

"Old Sarge" was my first story as a summer intern at the San Diego Star. I had completed my junior year, majoring in journalism at the University of Bismarck and was happy to have a job at a newspaper in a big city. I was assigned to John Graves, City Editor, to write human interest stories. I didn't have a desk, only a little countertop attached to the wall. It was as far away from the boss's office as you could get and still be in the City Room. On my first official day of work, I had just set down my Starbucks' and opened my laptop when I heard my name being bellowed by Mr. Graves.

"Miller! Where's Miller?" I scrambled into his office with my iPad ready to take notes on whatever he said.

"Miller, I want you to do a story on this old Marine that hangs out for dinner at Jack's Texas Roadhouse in Old Town San Diego. He says he fought at Iwo Jima and was on the hill when they raised the flag. He'll tell his story if someone buys him dinner. Since this is your first assignment, you can take your time. Let's see, today is Wednesday, I can't expect you to get a story ready for this Sunday's edition. So give me six to eight graphs and some photos on Monday. We'll try for next Sunday. Any questions?"

"No Sir," I replied. Though I had many questions, I would try to get the answers myself.

"Alright, then get outta here and get to work," said Graves as he ushered me out of his office by pushing on the nape of my neck."

"Iwo Jima, the flag, the hill? It took several attempts spelling Iwo Jima before I was able to land on the right page of Wikipedia. Battle of Iwo Jima, WWII, February/March 1945, flag raised on Mount Suribachi, famous photo that raised American spirits. I found in Wikipedia Clint Eastwood had made two highly regarded movies about the battle of Iwo Jima: Flags of Our Fathers, depicting the American side, and Letters from Iwo Jima which showed the Japanese side. I was able to get those two movies to watch as current background and as entertainment.

I had spent my first two days researching for the story. Now it was time to meet my subject. It was 2015, seventy years since the battle. I thought anyone who fought in that battle must be at least ninety years old. I had never known anyone that old. I was excited to talk with someone who had been in combat.

I got to Jack's Roadhouse at 4:00 PM, just in time for the Early Bird Specials and asked to speak to the manager. I introduced myself, my purpose and asked about the old veteran who told his story.

"Oh, yes," said Gary Jones, Assistant Manager (his name and title announced by a name tag pinned above his left breast pocket. "He's been here every evening since we opened three years ago. At first, he would try to sit at the same table, but it wasn't always available. After a while we just marked his table RESERVED. He usually arrives at about five. He puts out his sign that says 'Ask me about Iwo Jima' and waits for someone to ask. He tells them he'll trade his story for a steak dinner. He usually gets a taker. If not, he'll just sit there with his coffee until 7:30 then leave."

"What's his name?"

"Behind his back, we call him 'Old Sarge.' If you ask him his name, he'll answer, 'Just call me Sarge.'"

I asked to get a table where I might observe 'Old Sarge' before attempting to interview him. He arrived on time, ordered a cup of coffee. On his table, he placed a five by eight card that was folded to make his sign. He wore a red baseball cap that featured the Marine Corps symbol bearing 'Eagle, Globe and Anchor' and the lettering WWII and Iwo Jima in bright yellow. He had on a red vest, with numerous military patches, and a denim shirt that matched his slacks. His face was craggy with numerous brown age spots. His right hand seemed to shake a little but he steadied it by using both hands to cradle his coffee cup that rested on the table.

Jack's Roadhouse is a tourist place. The manager had told me Old Sarge usually got a free meal. Tonight, however, he wasn't making it. By 6:45, I was afraid he would strike out for the evening so I decided to go myself. I wouldn't identify myself as a reporter but impersonate an out-of-towner.

"Sir," I said as I approached him. "I know a little about Iwo Jima, but it would be interesting to hear about it from a veteran. Were you in that battle?"

Old Sarge continued gripping his coffee cup, which I suspected was empty by this time, as he looked up at me from his booth. "Well of course I was, why would anyone listen to me talk about Iwo Jima if I wasn't there?" he said with a hint of irritation in his voice.

When I asked if I could join him, he replied staring at me and through me, saying, "We fought those Japs for five weeks. They didn't care if they died. They just wanted to take as many of us with them as possible. I'm probably one of the few left that survived the battle. If you want to hear my story, you will have to buy me a steak dinner."

I smiled a little, feigning surprise, and nodded my head "Yes," as I took a seat across from him in his booth. I was taken aback a little with him referring to the Japanese as Japs, but I realized he had carried that term with him all these seventy years.

"Hey, Jenny give this young fellow a menu. You know what I want."

After I ordered, he began. "Well, everyone knows about the flag-raising on that stinking island. You do know about it, don't you?" I assured him I was familiar with the photo and the monument in Arlington but withheld how I came to this knowledge.

"Thousands of us landed on the beach after the Navy had spent days pounding it with their guns. The Japs hid in the caves but came out at night to fight. It wasn't until the fifth day we took the peak, Mount Suribachi they called it. They raised that big flag. It could be seen all over the island. The landing and support ships off the beach blew their whistles. It made everyone feel good. I was on the hill resting when they raised the flag. I stood and saluted. I did feel good for a while. I know that in a few days that photo hit the states and everyone was inspired. But they all thought the flag meant the battle was over.

"It wasn't!" said Old Sarge, banging his fist on the table. "Thousands of our guys died in the next weeks, 6,800 in all. I lost my best friend from boot camp."

Old Sarge turned away from me as if to regain his composure. He explained how he was transferred back to the states after the Japanese surrendered. "It is a good thing we had the bomb. The Japs lost 20,000 defending Iwo Jima. What if we had invaded their mainland?"

I asked him many questions: What was the landing like? What kind of weapons did he have? He didn't hesitate as his answers came between chews on a rare steak. He only looked at me when I asked a question, the rest of the time he concentrated on cutting his steak or peered at the ceiling as if creating in his mind pictures which supplied the answers. When he finished his steak (I had a burger and fries), he advised me for the first time, "Apple pie à la mode comes with the dinner." Without my objection, he hailed Jenny and told her he was ready for dessert.

I tried to get him to tell me about his personal life after the war. Did he have a family? What kind of job did he do? How old was he? He advised me that he only talked about Iwo. I asked him his name. He replied, "Just call me Sarge."

"Can I get a picture, Sarge?"

"No! No pictures."

He finished his dessert and said, "Well that's it for tonight." He got up and left.

I had learned a lot about the Battle of Iwo Jima but not much about Old Sarge. I didn't even get a picture. The next day I reported my experience to Mr. Graves. "That's funny," said Graves. "You would think talking to tourists for years, he would have been asked and allowed his picture many times by now. Did you tell him you were a reporter and you wanted to do a story about him?"

"No, should I have?"

"If he didn't want a tourist to take his picture, he wouldn't want a reporter to take it. You lucked out and did the right thing."

I took a little pride in having done at least one thing correctly even if the boss attributed it to dumb luck. Graves went silent for a while, looking off to the side and rubbing his chin in thought.

"Look, there may be a story here, maybe not. Since you are not getting paid, it doesn't bother me if you try to run down a story that doesn't pan out. You are here to learn. Do you want to give investigative journalism a try?"

"Yes, Sir! That would be great."

"See what you can find out about this guy, Old Sarge, you said? Report to me each morning at 9:45 after my layout meeting. If you are busy on the job, you can call in your report."

Wow, I thought, investigative reporting: Woodward, Bernstein, and now Miller!

The next day I returned to Jack's with the idea I would try to follow Old Sarge when he left. I sat at the bar where I could see him from behind, hoping he wouldn't see and recognize me. After he found a visitor to buy him a steak, I left and sat in my car, positioned where I could see the entrance to the restaurant.

Old Sarge left the roadhouse a bit before seven o'clock, walked a few blocks, waited and caught the Green line bus. I followed for forty minutes to La Mesa where he climbed out of the air-conditioned bus into the August heat of that desert town. Soon doffing his red vest, he slowly walked several blocks before disappearing into an old looking two-story house. The house, with a wraparound porch, looked out of place as it was surrounded by typical single story California ranch houses. A worn mailbox on a post, set at the edge of the road, displayed the name Beldin in faded black letters. I had a name and an address, what else could I learn now?

I went back to my dorm room at Balboa U., which sponsored the visiting journalism internships in San Diego and got on the internet. It is amazing what information can be pulled up on that little screen. La Mesa property records showed 4711 San Lumis Rd was owned by Dan Beldin as far back as 1930. In 1966, James Beldin inherited the property from the estate of Dan Beldin (his father, I guessed). Peoplefinder.com indicated only one James Beldin in La Mesa, age 91 and he was related to a Rosemary Stimson age 49, who also lived in La Mesa.

On a hunch, guessing the house may have been Old Sarge's boyhood home, I decided to check the 1940 US Census Records, which had recently become available online. Sitting at my laptop in 2015, I was eerily reaching back seventy-five years into the handwritten records of some long departed part-time census taker. The recordings were random within a district, not easily searchable. Finally, I found the entry for 4711 San Lumis Rd: Husband, Dan Beldin age 40; Wife, Harriett, age 38; Son, James, age 16; Son, John, age 16. It looked like Old Sarge had a twin.

The next morning, I arrived at the Star at 9:00 AM and spent my time reviewing my notes and preparing for my meeting with Mr. Graves. He finally called me into his office thirty minutes late, though he could see through the glass walls I had been present and waiting the entire time.

"Okay, Miller, what've you got?" When I finished my briefing, his first response was a questioning, "Uhmm?" He stared silently at me with a wrinkled face that I could have interpreted as a scowl or a pensive. "During the war, the paper was always running stories about the local boys who were in the service. Maybe there's a story about Old Sarge or his brother. Check the microfiche archives for the time frame of Iwo Jima, say January to September 1945."

This new assignment gave me a feeling of validation from the old man, and I was relaxed enough that I thought I could have some fun with him. Dredging up from my memories of those same film noir newsmen stories I had watched as a boy, which made me want to be a journalist in the first place, I recalled a catchphrase and replied to Graves' order, 'Right Chief".'"

Graves gave me a little smirk, "Okay, get going."

Microfiche research is slow and boring. For me, it is also a little nauseating looking at those scrolling pages. When I finally found the story I was looking for, it answered several questions but opened a new mystery.

March 25, 1945. Marine Staff Sergeant John Beldin died February 23, 1945, in the battle for Iwo Jima, the day of the famous flag raising on Mount Suribachi. John's twin brother Lieutenant James Beldin is a US Marine aviator deployed in the Pacific.

Graves received this new information with the same questioning as I had. The man calling himself "Old Sarge" had to be James who inherited the house in 1966. Why would he pose as a Marine survivor of Iwo Jima when it was his brother who fought but died on the island? "Go to his house and try to interview him. If he balks, inform him that it is a crime under the Stolen Valor Act to impersonate a decorated veteran," ordered Graves.

I was nervous as I drove back out to La Mesa, choosing and rehearsing questions in my mind. A pleasant looking middle aged woman answered the doorbell. I showed her my press ID and told her I needed to talk with Mr. Beldin about Iwo Jima. When she said he wouldn't want to talk to me, I told her that I knew his story wasn't true and the paper wanted to give him a chance to explain. She hesitated before replying. "He's in the garden. I'm his granddaughter, Rosemary Stimson. I'll go tell him. Please come in and have a seat."

She left and quickly returned. "He's coming; he has to wash up first." She didn't sit down but went to the mantle over the fireplace and picked up two framed pictures to show me. Each picture looked to be a colorized portrait of a young Marine in full dress uniform. "This is my grandfather, and this is his twin brother, Johnny." The portrait of the deceased brother bore a small red and white flag with a gold star. "My great uncle died at Iwo Jima."

"Yes, I know but your grandfather has been…"

Before I could finish my reply, the old man entered and having recognized me, interrupted with a brusque, "So you're a reporter. And you took the time to see if an old man was telling the truth." He lowered himself into a rocking chair and began to rock.

"The paper got interested when we heard there was an Iwo Jima survivor living here. We were looking for a human-interest piece. When you wouldn't tell me anything about yourself after the war, we wanted to find out why. We now know you've been deceiving people with the story you tell. I'm sorry, sir, this may be the article we have to print."

"So you want to know the truth, uh? I'll tell you everything. You can decide what is true."

The old man stopped rocking and commenced his narrative.

"My brother and me went and enlisted in the Marines two days after Pearl Harbor. Did Rosemary show you our pictures?"

I nodded yes, and he continued.

"Of course they had to separate us after boot camp. Johnny became a grunt. I was a grunt for a while but got picked to fly later. We both fought across the Pacific: island hopping, landings on those bloody beaches. But always without a scratch, the two of us until Johnny got killed on Iwo. I named my only son after him, rest his soul; that was Rosemary's father." He nodded at Rosemary. He looked down and started rocking again.

After a long silence, I asked him why he was telling that story at Jack's.

"You know those movies they made about Iwo a few years ago?"

With a questioning upturn, I replied, "Yes, sir."

"Well, it wasn't just those six guys in the photo that made it up the hill. My brother did too. I wanted to tell his story. I knew it had to be a survivor talking to get anyone interested and if someone bought me dinner, then they would stay and listen to the whole damned thing."

"But how do you know so many details?"

"Oh, after the war, I attended some of the Iwo survivor reunions, got to talk to some guys that knew my brother. Got lots of info from them."

"Did you find out how your brother died?"

He didn't reply right away but continued to stare at me, narrowing his eyes.

"When you were snooping on me, did you see that I was shot down the same day Johnny was killed?"

I silently shook my head no, feeling even guiltier about inquisitioning an old man and World War II veteran.

"Yep, well not really shot down, more shot up. I was in the Philippines with MacArthur, flying aerial support for the ground pounders. I took hits in the shoulder and the leg, my plane was full of holes. I was barely able to make it back to my airfield but crash landed. They pulled me out of the burning wreckage. I took some bad burns to my legs. I was unconscious for three days."

I could see tears forming in the old man's eyes, maybe Rosemary saw them too.

"Grandpa are you okay? Do you want to stop now? You don't have to go on if you don't want to."

He waved her off with the back of his left hand saying "I want to finish this."

"When I was unconscious, I found myself standing next to Johnny on the hill as the flag went up. We were both at attention, saluting. A moment later, a Jap, who had crawled out of his hole, shot Johnny in the back. In my rage, I pulled my service revolver and emptied it into the SOB. When I got back to Johnny, he was barely conscious. As I bent over him, he said. 'I'm not going to make it Jimmy, you have to live. Mom can't lose both her twin boys.' He asked me to light a cigarette for him. I never smoked so I had to dig out his cigarettes and lighter from his shirt pocket. He took a couple of drags and shuddered in pain. He did the best he could to look up at me and say,

'Semper Fi, Jimmy' I replied, 'Semper Fi, Johnny.' The next thing I remembered was waking up in the field hospital with recollections of that weird dream. The medics told me I had come close to death and it was just about a miracle I survived. It wasn't until several weeks later, I got the news from home that Johnny had died on the hill the same day I was shot down."

Not knowing how to respond, I said, "Sounds like a really vivid dream." I asked, "Did you ever find out how he really died?"

"It wasn't until 1955, the Iwo marines had their first reunion. I crashed the party and found some guys from Jimmy's unit. Their memories were fuzzy. They did tell me he died on the hill sometime after the flag raising. After another short silence, he pointed a finger at me and asked with a contemptuous tone, "How old are you?"

"I'm twenty-one."

"Same age as Johnny when he got killed. He made the landing, he stood and saluted and then a photographer made six other marines famous. I have to tell Johnny's story because he didn't live to tell it, but I tell it as if he did live."

"But Mr. Beldin, you really don't know how he died. I think you are making up that part, just like you are pretending to be him as if he survived."

"I told you, I was there when he got it, killed the Jap that did it."

"But it was just a dream."

"Was it? Or was it some kind of twin communication. Maybe as I lay dying, my spirit joined Johnny on the hill. He didn't want both of us dead and sent me back?"

"Still a delusion. You weren't really there."

"You don't think so, hmm. See what's behind Jimmy's picture."

Following the old man's directions, I spotted a small shiny metal case engraved *PFC John Beldin USMC* ".

"Pick it up, have a look. That's the Zippo lighter I gave Johnny after we graduated from boot camp. The same lighter I used to light his cigarette when we were both on the hill."

"I don't understand. If it was his, how did you get it?"

"After I recovered from my wounds and got out of the hospital, they gave me what personal effects survived the crash. Johnny's lighter was with my stuff."

While I tried to think of a reply, the old man got emotional. He sobbed and gasped violently as he kept repeating. "I was there. Johnny wanted me to live."

Rosemary rushed to her grandfather to comfort him. "Grandpa, you should get your nap now, before it is time to get the bus to Jack's."

"Mr. Miller, you must leave now. I hope you can respect my grandfather's privacy."

***

All the way back to my dorm room, I was trying to make sense of what I had heard. What was the real story here? What would I tell my boss?

Back at my dorm, I showered to get ready for the evening get-together planned for the interns. Transferring my wallet etc. to my fresh clothes, I discovered I had taken Johnny's cigarette lighter with me. Curiously, I opened it. Some bits of sand fell out, and the slight odor of rotten eggs hit my nose. I knew from my high school chemistry class that "rotten eggs" is the smell of sulfur and I remembered what I learned about Iwo Jima. In Japanese, *Jima* means island, *Iwo* means sulfur.

The next day, I told my boss about my meeting with "Old Sarge", omitting the part about the "vision" and the Zippo.

"So, Miller, what do you think we should do? Should we out the old man?"

I had thought Graves might ask such a question and had been struggling with my emotions to reach a decision. I had spent a lot of time getting this story. It would be a great addition to my resume. Yet, I respected Old Sarge for what he had been through and sympathized with him.

"I think we should let him be. He is harmless and maybe senile. He is a World War II veteran, a hero in his own right if he wants to honor his dead brother this way, why not?"

"I agree," said Graves. "He's not stealing valor, just preserving it."

POKER NIGHT WITH LOUIE DA SQUID

By: Karen Ovér

How do you get into Miskatonic University? Patience, true believer. First, get accepted somewhere that hasn't lost either its reputation or its location. A school in the same region, like Harvard or Yale, Brown or Mount Holyoke, to throw off parental suspicions. Just another precaution any eager seeker of the Necronomicron should take, to keep them blissfully ignorant of the cosmic path you've heedlessly plunged down.

Basic scrying will locate the main gates. Save your best magic for the journey through them. When you find the campus, you'll know you've been accepted. (By the school, anyway. The dean is another matter.) Good luck, true believer. Miskatonic University awaits your arrival.

This was Tully's mission statement, the home page of his website. As a New Student Adviser at Miskatonic, Tully felt it his highest duty to lure new students to advise. Otherwise, the dean preferred to mistake Tully for a janitor. Tully didn't fancy himself stuck with post-ritual mop up duty.

Of course, if a spell *was* successful, Tully doubted there'd be anyone left to mop up. Lately, it was nothing more sinister than rampant dead professors putting the frights to anyone within reach. Other than the occasional smear of ectoplasm, mop up duty meant bodily fluids.

These days, a summoning counted as a success if the newbies puked and pissed themselves. There was always a great deal of retching, but since the location of the cafeteria was variable, so was the barf output.

Sadly, the Old Ones no longer answered, regardless of the elaborate invocations the students created. There hadn't been a genuine plague of nightmares or psychotic breaks in decades. The last time Tully had seen a shoggoth…

Ah, nooooo. Ain't goin' there. Nice deep breaths, find happy place, get a grip.

"At least the true believers still show up," Tully muttered to himself. "More power to 'em." He glanced at his watch, hoped it was the same time outside the campus as in, then put a hand on his doorknob.

"Buck up," he told himself. "There hasn't been a shoggoth infestation in ages. The worst you might see is that student you lost in the library last year."

I hope.

With another deep breath, Tully stepped into the corridor. So far so good. Staying close to the wall, but not too close, he took a long stride over a nasty stain in the floor, then a hop-skip-jump around a series of unfortunate experiments left to fend for themselves. Somewhat winded, he made the dorm entrance.

After a careful recon of the quad, he moved out. It wasn't always safe in the open, no matter how many people were around. Never knew what you might step in, or what might step in *you*. Another glance at his watch made Tully decide it was worth an expedition in search of the elusive cafeteria.

He hoped it was currently in this universe. He hadn't eaten in hours. Or days, perhaps. It was so hard to tell, here. Head down, intent on his destination, he did his best to dodge the other campus dwellers.

Tully wasn't sure which were more dangerous, the graduate skulkers muttering improvised incantations, or the wide-eyed undergrad dreamers who accosted any creature unfortunate enough to make eye contact. Like the one he smacked into as he dodged a creeper that might once have been someone's pet. Or perhaps a bit of the ivy was out for walkies again.

Tully tried another sidestep, but the kid moved right with him.

"So, the library is off limits? How are we supposed to study the Necronomicron? Or study *at all*? How come Administration is locked? I can't find the dean or even the Student Adviser."

Tully rolled his eyes, waiting for the kid to come up for air. "At ease, newby! I'm Tully, the Student Adviser. You're early. I think. Time's a bit squishy, once you get past the main gates. As for study, I hate to burst your bubble. The Necronomicron disappeared ages ago, along with most of the library. You're lucky you actually reached the campus when you stepped through the gates. Sometimes the whole place pops off into the *never-never*, not just bits of it. That's why the library is off limits. Have you eaten? What is your name, by the way?"

"Herman Newby."

"Seriously?"

The kid put his hands on his hips, otherwise, Tully wouldn't have noticed he had…

Curves. And a ferocious scowl.

"Okay, fine! It's Hermione on my birth certificate, but as soon as I get control of my trust fund, it's gonna be Herman. Problem?"

"Absolutely not, Mr. Newby. Trust fund, huh? Then you've not murdered your parents yet?"

Newby grinned. "Why else would anyone seek the Necronomicron? And no, I haven't eaten, but what's that got to do with the library being off limits?"

"Nothing at all, I guess, but the first survival tip here at Miskatonic U is, any chance you have to find the cafeteria really must be taken. Because you can't always find it, even when it seems to be there. So if you do find it, it's best to eat as much as you can, because you never know when you might find it again. Come along, Newby! On to the cafeteria!"

Since another duty as Student Adviser was to keep newbies alive as long as possible, Tully took him in tow with a handful of collar. "Watch where you put your feet. Some of these potholes are interdimensional. No important engagements in the near future, I hope?"

"Well, uh, I just got here. You were next on the list after I found my dorm. Have you got my class schedule?"

"Class schedule?" Tully winked. "Aren't you here to find the Necronomicron?"

"Well, yeah, that's the most important engagement. Will food interfere with that?"

"Depends. We get into the cafeteria, stuff ourselves silly, might be next week before we get out again."

"You sure take your food seriously around here."

Tully swatted away what might have been a pigeon. Or a really big, ancient bumblebee. Self-preservation stepped aside. His dormant enthusiasm for the quest yawned wide, licked its chops, then swallowed him whole. Alarmed, Tully began to lecture himself as much as Newby. "You don't get it, man. This place is off the map. It isn't altogether *here*. Or *there*, either. The only reason the cafeteria isn't off limits is because we have to eat. The library looks like it's there, but most of the time it isn't. We can pry the boards off a window or cut the chains on the door, but we won't find the library in there."

"But Tully! If we cast the right spell…"

"Dude! You think people haven't tried? You can't just transfer in here expecting an audience with the Old Ones your first day. There's old profs been around here for years, camped out in the corridors because they opened a gateway in their offices and barely got out alive. Oh yeah, don't try to take any leftovers from the cafeteria. It draws stuff to you."

"Right," Newby agreed, much too cheery for Tully's taste. "Don't feed the bears. Got it."

Tully sighed, dragging the young man along to the last known location of the cafeteria. This was gonna be a long day, even if they managed the miracle of a more or less normal meal. Tully heard his stomach growl in reaction to a message from his eyes. With a tug on Newby's collar, he changed course.

"Ha! The cafeteria is in phase. That's at least half the battle. Not so fast, there, Newby. We still don't know what dimension might occupy the *inside*. Never assume you know what's on the other side of any door, or around any corner. Never assume *shit*, around here. You might live long enough to graduate."

"I didn't come here to *graduate*," Newby insisted. "I came…"

"To find the Necronomicron," Tully finished in chorus. "First, we eat."

Tully spotted an empty beer can near the cafeteria door. He stomped it flat, just to make sure it wouldn't sprout jaws full of razor teeth ready to munch his fingers to the elbow. Even then he circled it warily before picking it up.

"What's that for?" Newby bubbled. "Is there a campus recycle program?"

"Dude, shut up and pay attention. What did I just tell you?"

"Never assume. Oh, you mean the beer can might not have been a beer can? Wow, really? That. Is. *So*. Cool."

"Yeah, yeah, it's all cool until a shoggoth shreds you into kibble. Get ready to run."

Tully shoved Newby into position behind the cafeteria door before carefully easing it open. The usual cacophony associated with such places spilled out. Even so, Tully tossed the beer can through the door, then slammed it shut. One hundred woodchucks later, he took a peek.

No change.

"C'mon, Newby. Let's eat." With the door open wide, Tully let Newby enter first. Both made straight for the chow line. When they were seated at a relatively secluded table, trays piled high with food, Newby pulled a notebook out of his jacket, the cardboard cover embellished with runes and other magical symbols.

Tully slapped the book out of Newby's hand.

"Put that away, man! This place is unstable enough without you waving a grimoire around! Are you friggin nuts?"

"I'm not gonna read it. I just wanted to show it to you. See, I've researched sources that contained different parts of the Necronomicron…"

"Stop, okay? What do you think everyone else in this place has done? You see that old white-haired guy gibbering in the corner?"

"Yeah. The one in the drool puddle. So?"

"He's an undergrad, just like you. Transferred in from Yale last spring, ready to dive in for a swim with Dagon. He didn't believe me about the Necronomicron, or the library. Sound familiar?"

Newby nodded. "Yes, sir. What happened, sir?"

Tully raised a disbelieving eyebrow but continued anyway. "One night, he got inside. Wasn't seen again for six months. Lenore happened to walk past the place, just before the holiday break. She saw the board over one of the windows blow out. Like a bomb, except there wasn't any noise. Only a thud, from that guy cratering the lawn. Soaked to the skin he was, not to mention half drowned. By the time we laid down enough temporal stabilization spells to get him to a hospital in Arkham, he was catatonic. Hair turned white at some point. What you see there, that is a vast improvement. Imagine the state he'd be in if he'd returned while everyone was on holiday. Now ask me how he got back."

"Okay." Newby was still completely undaunted. "How did he get back?"

"The Old One threw him out, man. Lenore saw the tentacles."

"What about the Necronomicron? He must have seen it, or at least part of it, right?"

"Forget about the damn Necronomicron, Newby. No one has seen it for like a hundred years. All that guy had was a few scraps of paper, stuff he'd copied down from other people's notebooks. Same as that crap you've got there."

Newby, however, gleaned only what he wanted to hear. "So, maybe he's still got them. Maybe we can get hold of them. C'mon, Tully! I know you want this as much as I do. To search out the secrets. To find the Old Ones."

"Ever occur to you the Old Ones don't want to be found?"

Yet even as he said that, Tully could feel the old thrill sweep over him. The call of Cthulhu welcomed him back into its coils. While they ate, giddy with their conquest of the cafeteria, the new cohorts vowed to search the library. Reckless, they scribbled improvised summoning incantations on the napkins.

It was dark when they finally got out. "Best we stick together," Tully told Newby. "You don't know the ropes yet. The *serious* weirdness happens after dark. We'll make a run for the dorm. Hang onto my coat, so we don't get separated."

They dashed across the quad, not stopping until they reached Tully's rooms. Once there, Tully shuffled their scribbles into an incantation he thought might actually work, while Newby gathered candles, matches, and a couple of crowbars.

Out on the quad once more, they sprinted through undulating shadows to the barricaded library. The screams which echoed across the campus were ignored. They had their own hides to worry about, their own spells to cast. If the ordinary monsters were distracted by others, they stood a better chance of success in their own endeavor.

By moonlight only, they pried loose the boards over a small basement window. Quietly as possible, they lowered themselves through the darkness, only to land with a loud splash in a puddle of cold, stagnant water.

"We must be on the right track," Newby whispered, his voice two octaves higher from excitement.

"Slime track is more like it," Tully grumbled. "I should've thought to wear waders. I think there's algae under my feet. Get the candles lit, so we can see. Mind you don't wet the matches."

After a great deal of fumbling, broken matches, and a couple of dropped candles, they raised their feeble lights. The tiny flames reflected back from the water all around. The two could see each other, but very little else.

"Let's try to find a table or something," Newby said, as he took a tentative step deeper into the darkness.

"Be careful," Tully warned. "This floor's damned slippery, and who knows what's under this water? We might step into more than a puddle, dude. Maybe we should start the ritual right here."

"No, no!" Newby warned. "Not so close to the window! The others might hear us! We should find the center of the room!"

"Come on, man, anyone else out there is only interested in their own summoning. Hold the candles while I get these napkins in order."

"You *did* that already, Tully! Come on!" Newby ventured further into the room even as he turned toward Tully. Tully handed Newby his candle, drawn along with the kid.

They'd barely grunted the phrase scribbled on the first napkin when the floor opened up into icy water. The Old One did not come to them.

The Old One came *for* them.

Thick, heavy tentacles snatched their ankles, pulling them down into the depths of the multiverse.

There was an air pocket beneath the floor, or rather, within the dimensional divide. Both dropped their useless candles, the better to hang onto each other.

"Tully," Newby gasped, "is it supposed to be this dark?"

"How the hell should I know? It's never worked for me before! Wait, there's a light. Looks like…"

"Torchlight," Newby decided.

Before the light, there was more water. Tully got hold of a deep breath. Newby, on the other hand, panicked, struggling against the relentless tentacles.

Tully let go of Newby to clamp both hands over his nose and mouth. He wished he had an extra pair for his ears. He'd never heard anyone scream underwater.

He never wanted to hear that again.

Newby ran out of air before he ran out of panic. A stream of bubbles from Newby's mouth was followed by one huge bubble. Tully screwed his eyes tight shut as Newby's body tried to expel the water he'd inhaled.

Tully gave one last, feeble attempt to break free of the tentacles coiled firmly around his legs. If only he could reach the light which glowed red through his tightly closed eyelids.

With a sudden yank, Tully was flung over the lip of a huge old well, into a stone vault lit with bright torches. He rolled over to cough up water, suck in air, his gag reflex in overdrive. A moment later he made a note to self.

Do not binge in the cafeteria before attempting to summon the Old Ones.

When at last he could crawl weakly away from the mess he'd made, Tully lifted his head toward the light. Smooth stone walls lined with torches, arched overhead like an old forgotten subway tunnel, stretched away in front of him. Flopping over on his back, Tully propped himself on his elbows to look back toward the well.

There it was, a flurry of tentacles high above several human-type figures. Cthulhu's minions, no doubt, with poor Newby their prisoner. Tully blinked away tears, creeping backward, away from the awful scene.

A familiar rattle, like a grocery cart, sounded far down the tunnel. A heartbeat later Tully shrieked as a hospital gurney blasted past his splayed knees.

"Clear!" a voice commanded, like Bela Lugosi on steroids. There came the electric *buzz bang* of a defibrillator, then a string of orders delivered in a Slavic language.

Poor xenophobic Lovecraft's worst nightmare, Tully thought, as a corner of his mind sniggered with enlightened glee. *The Old Ones here are served by the barbaric non-Anglo-Saxons Lovecraft so feared.*

Newby's limp body was lifted onto the gurney. Tully screamed again, unprepared as it blurred past, nearly taking off his leg. The other minions now moved toward him, but his attention stayed riveted on the swarm of tentacles above his head.

Darkness descended like a shroud. Or rather, a blanket, Tully realized as he clawed it into his lap.

A blanket with fluffy bunnies and chicks on it. Bunnies and chicks in little blue uniforms stenciled *NYPD*.

With a whimper, Tully threw the smothering plush away from him. What sort of horrible police state universe had he been sucked into? How did he get from the Miskatonic campus in Arkham to some precinct dungeon in Gotham?

Someone leaned over him. Tully got a glimpse of steel blue eyes above bushy whiskers before the man turned to bellow, "Doc! This 'un's still breathin'!"

A fairy tale character wobbled over to peer at Tully through a pair of granny glasses. "Yep, you're right," Doc confirmed. "Mario!"

The blur that was Mario put Tully in a rescue carry. Time twisted into a corkscrew. In the space of a blink, Mario put Tully on a table. When Tully's eyes focused again his fuddled brain told him he was in a hospital trauma room. Looked like it, smelled like it. Sounded like it too, as the Transylvanians fought to resuscitate Newby.

That droning, flat-line beep couldn't be good.

Dammit, Tully raged silently, *not another one! I'm tired of losing my assignments. Why be a student adviser if they don't even last twenty-four hours on campus?*

Technically, he argued with himself, they had not gone off campus. But could Miskatonic even be said to have a campus, anymore?

Yes! Tully defended his school fiercely. *The biggest campus ever, scattered across the multiverse! Can't get that at those stuffed up, ivy-choked hallows, no matter how much loot your old man hoards.*

Doc the Dwarf climbed a step stool to check Tully's vital signs.

"You'll live," he told Tully, "thanks to Louie. Also no thanks to Louie. He really hates it when you wannabe sorcerers interrupt his poker games. Why do you think he tossed your library into the cosmos before he packed off here? You little smartasses think college is all about throwin' a kegger so you can conjure entities best left undisturbed. Ever consider what the Old Ones think of bein' summoned by every drunken halfwit with a notebook full of consonants?"

"The thought has recently occurred," Tully mumbled. "Where the hell am I? Who the hell are you?"

"I'm Doc. You are in the infirmary of the 86th Precinct, Manhattan. Don't look for us in the city directory, because we ain't there. Just like Miskatonic University ain't there. When you summoned an Old One, you got the one came down here followin' that writer fella. Louie thought ol' H.P. was amusing. Till he got here, anyway. Now he thinks underground Manhattan is much more fun. A lot more water, for one, than the old, slow Miskatonic River. In any case, he needed a lair. Somewhere to hide the Necronomicron from you buggers. As it happened, we needed unlimited storage space, protected by someone who can put a tentacle on whatever's required, at a second's notice."

"Wait a minute - the Old One *works* for you?"

"No way!" Doc admonished Tully. "Louie does it for the fun. He probably discovered poker at Miskatonic, but a cop shop is as good as a campus for that. The table stakes are shellfish and stout. We lose to him, regular. In return, he acts as quartermaster. Trusts us with the Necronomicron, too, since we don't use it like a facebook invite."

Chastised, Tully changed the subject. "Is Newby… Jeez, I can't believe that's his real name! Is he really dead?"

Doc sighed. "He, you say? Explains the failed resuscitation. Can't force an unwilling soul back into the wrong package. Gather your wits to follow me, okay? This gets complicated. In the so-called real world, yeah, Newby is dead. But since we're a paranormal unit, his soul's in luck. The precinct chaplain's havin' a chat with him. Layin' out his options. Not your problem anymore, Tully."

"How do you know my name?"

"Kid, seriously? You got snatched by an Old One in the middle of our poker game. Bet your over-privileged ass Louie knows your name. But don't you worry. He'll drop you right back where he found you. As for your friend's corpse, we'll contact his family to make the notification. We have Authority. He'll be just another casualty of the city."

Tully dropped his head into his hands. "You don't understand. He's the second one in a row I've lost in their first semester. Hell, Newby only just arrived! All he could think about was how to find the Necronomicron. Meet an Old One."

Doc patted Tully on the shoulder. "No worries then, kid. He got his wish. Captain O'Brien wants that book, Louie forks it over. On your feet, then. Time for Louie to toss you back."

"I, uh, no disrespect, sir, but I'd rather take the train." Tully turned out his pockets, came up with a box of matches. Soaked. "Or maybe I'll hitchhike."

"Can't let you do that, son," Doc replied gruffly. "But I can give you a bit of something to make the trip back, ah, shall we say, more of a *trip*." Doc winked. "Might also be enough lobster and Guinness left over to bribe Louie to take it easy on you."

"You can bribe Cth…"

"Hush! Don't get him riled again. We call him Louie da Squid because that's what he calls himself when he's here, and he's always here, except when he ain't, but even then he's here. Understand?"

"Um, yeah. The Old Ones are everywhere, all the time. Space and time are just two of the infinite dimensions they travel through."

"Give the lad a prize," a new voice interrupted. Tully looked up into those steel blue eyes again.

"Padraig O'Brien," the man rumbled, as his meaty paw engulfed Tully's hand. "Captain of the 86th Precinct. Yer lucky Louie just won the pot, not that he ever loses. He's in a reasonably good mood. He couldn't do anything about yer pal, but he can toss ye back before anyone notices ye were gone if we go right now. Mario? I think a bit of assistance is still in order."

A man who matched his name, from his Armani suit to his gelled black hair, materialized behind a wheelchair. Tully sat up, eased himself off the exam table, then gave up and let O'Brien help him into the chair. There was a blur, a breeze, then Tully was back beside the well. O'Brien took Tully's hand, pulling him to his feet as the chair went out from under him.

"How does he *do* that?" Tully gasped when his voice caught up with his body.

"Mario? He's a speed elemental. A city sprite. Looks like Louie's ready ta take ye back ta Miskatonic."

Tentacles oozed out of the well. Some of them twitched as if they wanted to strangle Tully. Tully's eyelids drooped as he flirted with surrender. Then he noticed a pair of tentacles off to one side, shuffling a crisp Tally-Ho Circle card deck. Off to the other side, slightly behind Tully, was a bucket of lobsters, along with a case of Guinness. After a deep breath to dredge up all his courage, Tully attempted the most radical invocation of his life.

"I've been known to play a bit of poker. Not very good at it, I'm afraid."

Tully took a step back, then to the side. He snaked a foot behind the bucket to push the lobsters forward.

A gargle down the well resolved itself into words. "Five card stud. Aces wild."

The cards were dealt, but Louie didn't ante up.

Tully looked at his hand, discarded, and took another deep breath. "Two, please."

Louie flicked a tentacle.

Tully studied the new hand, then raised with the case of stout. Louie discarded, took three cards.

"Cards?" the Old One gargled.

Now Tully understood. All in, this was his cue to fold.

Louie never lost. Louie never bet. Louie knew all the cards, all the time. He chose to accept what they brought as his due. What more could Tully offer?

Amusement.

"I know it isn't table stakes," Tully blurted, "but I'll raise you an idea."

The tentacles thrashed. One of them melted into Tully's forehead for a nanosecond eternity. The gargle intensified.

"Proceed. Poker night is every Thursday. Bring fresh fish."

"We don't get lobster in the cafeteria. When we can find the cafeteria. Begging your pardon."

"Noted. Bring fresh fish from the Miskatonic River. Do not go to the library. You will be collected from the river."

"Please don't drown anyone?" Tully squeaked.

"Take precautions against panic."

"Um," Tully gulped, "noted. Yeah. Next Thursday. River. Fish. No panic. Big poker game. Yeah."

Doc appeared, popping an orange pill onto Tully's tongue. "Have a little Sunshine. It'll help."

Tully barely glimpsed an orange smiley face on the pill before the tentacles ensnared him.

Tully landed with a splash in a puddle of cold, stagnant water. Sunlight streamed in from a window just above his head. It took Tully several minutes to realize he was in the basement of the library. He sat, smiley-faced, mesmerized by the dance of dust motes in sunshine while water soaked his clothing.

Right under the window he'd pried the boards from… When? He couldn't remember. Last night? He pulled himself up to peer out the window. The coast was clear, so he scrambled through. His shoes squished water with every step as he dripped across the quad to his rooms. If he couldn't find his waders, he'd have to buy new ones. Fishing tackle as well. First, he needed to know how long till Thursday.

After a shower, a change of wardrobe, and a few nonchalant inquiries, Tully learned *now* was Friday. Plenty of time to gather the true believers. He found a group of new students in front of Administration, milling in confusion.

The door, as usual, was locked. If you couldn't conjure your way in, the dean didn't want to be bothered with you. All the better for Tully.

"Good morning, my newbies!" he enthused, as they gathered near. "I'm Tully, your Student Adviser. I've got bad news, darlings. That pesky, infamous Necronomicron, well, it can no longer be found at Miskatonic U. The Old Ones cannot be summoned. They are no longer amused by our ritual antics. However, there is one place where an Old One might be found. I shall be your field guide on this expedition. How many of you know how to fish?"

A few tentative hands went up. "Excellent!" Tully boomed, arms wide in welcome to his minions. "Who brought their tackle? Anyone? Well then, my darlings, your first assignment into the unknown will be to get from here to the hardware store in Arkham, acquire the necessary accoutrements, and find your way back into the campus. Accomplish that, then, on Thursday night, you will fish with me in the misty mysterious Miskatonic River."

"What if the fish aren't biting, sir?" One of the minions, a girl in braids, ventured boldly.

"The fish will bite, dude," Tully slipped into comradely slang. "On Thursday night, the fish will *for sure* bite. Once we've caught the fish, we shall see what comes from the deeps to catch *us*. You all know how to play poker, of course? Excellent! Off we go!"

"Yeah man!" Tully's minions exclaimed as the rest of the newbies trailed along. "Field trip! Thursday night! We'll summon the Old One from the depths!"

Transfer enrollment at Miskatonic soared. Tully's newbies soon called him "professor." Tully chose not to correct them. He changed his rooms to a suite on the first floor of Administration. It was mostly in the same dimension and could be entered through a large casement window, thwarting the dean's fetish for locked doors. Professor Tully's only course was the weekly field trip. The only way to flunk was to drown. Successful students often took jobs with the 86th Precinct.

Every semester, he greeted a new contingent of eager young magicians.

"Professor Tully? I don't know how to play poker."

"All the better, dude. All the better. Louie da Squid will *love* you. Oh, by the way, how long can you hold your breath?"

HAROLD'S NOT IMAGINARY FRIEND

By: Pepper Hume

"That is too weird, Harold," Barbara said the first time she came home with me. She had been studying all the oddments poked in and around among my books while I mixed up margaritas. It was a hot night. In more ways than one, I hoped. "Why on earth would you have a real human skull in your home? It is real, isn't it?"

"Why on earth not?" I cleverly countered. "I have all kinds of artifacts around here. You've been university faculty nearly as long as I have. I'll bet you've got lots of books, too. And lots of oddments."

She favored me with that adorable psychologist look of hers and waited.

"Or not. Maybe psych faculty don't collect stuff as compulsively as paleos do. We tend to pick up everything, natural born collectors, pack rats," I finished weakly. Better make those margaritas especially potent.

"A human skull is different. It used to be somebody."

Logic. I didn't need logic tonight.

"Here ya go." I handed her one glass and even managed not to spill any. Her eyes widened a bit on her first sip. A good sign. Suavely, I guided her to my nicely vacuumed couch, and joined her there, with one arm ever so nonchalantly across the back behind her.

During her next sip I could tell those pretty eyes of hers were back on the dratted skull. "Where did you get it? Have you been desecrating Indian burial grounds in those digs you go on every summer?"

"Of course not. In twenty-seven years of paleontology, I have never dug up any human remains of any kind! I only dig for dinosaurs, strictly. None of them were ever people. They weren't even mammals. There were hardly any mammals in existence at all in those times, certainly none even remotely resembling people." I took a healthy drink and moved a tiny bit closer. "So, how's your margarita?"

Knowing eyes smirked at me. She also took a long draft, placed her glass on the side table, and settled nicely into the crook of my arm. "Then where did you get that skull?"

"Someplace in Illinois, not far from Terre Haute." I disposed of my own glass in order to bring both hands into play.

"Terre Haute is in Indiana." She fiddled with the top button on my shirt.

How could she be so maddeningly literal at a time like this, so didactic? I guess it comes with being Chair of Psychology. Okay, I can play that game, too.

"True," I said as my finger traced her neckline down from her far shoulder and brushed across the swell of a breast. "But it's very close to Illinois." Barely touching the cute little crease in her middle where they snuggled together, I added, "I was in Illinois, very close to Indiana." She arched. "Near Terre Haute."

***

Three months later and she's staring at the skull again.

"You've never told me what the provenance is on it."

I cuddled my new bride from behind, resting my chin in the nest of light brown curls on the top of her head. "There isn't any. The junk shop owner didn't know a thing about it."

"You actually paid money for it? Why on earth did you buy it?"

"I don't really know. It seemed wrong to leave it moldering away there. It was a pretty dusty, grimy sort of place. Somehow the thing felt comfortable in my hands. I couldn't leave it. Besides, it made a nice souvenir of when I met Marshall."

"Marshall? Oh, your mythical friend, the one who drops in on you from time to time from God knows where without notice, that Marshall?"

"Marshall Paris is not mythical."

"Then why have I never met him?" She turned in my arms, knowing she had me there, and peered over her glasses at me.

"Come on, I've explained already he didn't come to our wedding because I didn't know where to send his invitation. I still don't know where he lives."

"Yeah, I get it. He never writes or calls, just shows up. Sounds pretty mythical to me." End of discussion colored her voice, so I hugged her a good one.

"In a way, I envy Marshall," I told the little curl wrapping the tip of her ear. "He's the only truly free spirit I have ever known. You should have seen how enormously it amused him when I told him so."

"Whatever," Barbara said. "You still have to make room for my books so we can get those boxes out of the hall. Got a class full of eager young minds waiting to be corrupted. I'll be home around six."

It took most of the afternoon to produce almost three empty shelves and two boxes of my own books to take to the office. Although, God knew where I would put them. I suppose I could weed out some journals and papers. Ugh! That didn't bear thinking about. I surveyed my progress with the bookcases. Aha! If I gathered all my artifacts onto the mantle, sort of like a mini museum display, it could clear maybe another couple feet of shelf space. High time to clean up the catchall miscellany on the mantle anyway. Most of it could go on or in Barbara's fancy hall cabinet by the front door. Funny how one project always seem to lead into another. Probably somebody in Barbara's field had done a study on it. Their tolerance of unturned stones is as bad as us paleos.

I regrouped stuff into its assorted new locations, cleaning as I went—Barbara will be so proud—and stepped back to judge the effect. I wasn't sure I liked the skull with the other items on the mantle though. It didn't relate to anything else.

"Hiya, Doc Harold. What's new?"

After jumping back into my skin, I whirled around to find Marshall standing there. Free spirit or no, I do wish he'd knock before walking right in. It was a rare flaw in his manners.

He looked the same as always, shoulder length hair fuzzy as ever, the usual white t-shirt and faded jeans, standing with one hip cocked out in a loosely strung together way tall, skinny guys stand. Also as always.

"Hey, Marshall! It's been ages. Come on in, have a beer." We talked the afternoon away, over two or three beers. I told him all about Barbara. "She will be delighted to finally meet you."

"Oh geez, man, look at the time." he said. "I gotta split."

"Wait a few more minutes. Barbara is due home soon."

He grinned slyly. "Naw, man, I got a lady waitin' for me."

You could hardly argue with that so I saw him to the door and watched 'til he disappeared past the corner house.

"You'll never guess who was here this afternoon," I told Barbara when she got home. "Marshall Paris, a real case of 'speak of the devil.'"

"Harold, did you have an imaginary friend when you were a child?" She peers over her glasses a lot.

I refused to dignify this with an answer, so she turned on her Sigmund Freud look. Then she spotted the empty shelves.

"Ooh, Harold! You are such a good boy. You shall have two desserts tonight!" Marshall was forgotten.

A week or so later, when it was my turn to come home late from corrupting student minds, Barbara announced, "I have finally met your mythical Marshall Paris. I see what you mean about him being a free spirit. He just walked in and said, 'Hello, you must be Mrs. DeForest,' as though we were meeting on the street. He is a nice kid, though. You didn't tell me he was so young. I invited him to stay for dinner, but he had other plans. Rather an odd duck."

She nailed him there. He had always refused to stay overnight or even for a meal, charmingly but firmly.

Marshall made a record number of visits that fall, but I missed him every time. Apparently he really liked Barbara.

As usual, psychologist Barbara saw it differently. She began to question me about him. Things like, why would he never stay long enough to see his old buddy, me? Where else did he go in town? Where did he stay? How did he travel? Why wasn't he in school or at work? And…

"Why is he such a perfect example of a 1960's flower child?"

"A case of arrested development?"

"He wasn't even born in the sixties."

"Maybe he picked it up from his parents. How would I know? You're the psychology professor."

A few weeks later, her speculation took on a darker quality.

"He was here again today," she said before I could get my coat off. "It was less than fifty degrees out. He had no jacket and didn't seem to notice the cold." She held up her hand to stop my response. "There's more. I've noticed he always arrives soon after I dust the living room. More specifically, after I dust your artifact collection. So I set up a test. I touched only one object on the mantle each day.

"For the last three days, I have deliberately touched only the skull right before you were due home and he was here each time within two minutes. He would not even sit down, saying he couldn't stay. So why did he come at all? Why doesn't he come when we're both here?"

The hairs on the back of my neck prickled. I didn't like where this line of reasoning was going. We were both scientists, tenured university professors, for Pete's sake. We deal in realities. I had to rummage around in my mind to find the word.

"Paranormal. Are you suggesting there's something paranormal about Marshall? Come on, honey, he may be a strange kid, but I'm sure there's a perfectly natural explanation."

"Then you won't object to testing my theory. If I'm wrong, okay. If I'm right…" Heavy implications hung in the air. We looked at each other through them.

"How?" I finally managed to get out.

"Get the skull. First, you hold it alone. If nothing happens, we'll both touch it and see what, if anything, occurs."

I didn't want to turn my head to look at the thing, half expecting Marshall to look back at me when I did.

Feeling distinctly ridiculous, I patted the skull and scanned the room. I paid special attention to the doors and peered out the windows. A car went by.

"Hold it in both hands," Barbara instructed.

I did.

"Maybe you need to be alone," she said, stepping into the dining room.

I actually felt a chill. "I hardly think that's necessary."

She paused at the door to give me a stern look that said "don't be a ninny, I shall be right here, this is all in the name of science," and the rest of those things a wife can say to a husband without uttering a word.

One hundred and twenty seconds had crawled around the face of Barbara's prize banjo clock when she opened the door again. Her eyes swept the room and the clock before she looked at me.

I gave her the time-honored 'nothing's happened, I don't know what else to do, I'm just a dumb husband,' shrug.

Barbara set her sights on the skull in my hands and came toward it. She laid her hands on the skull and we stared into each other's eyes, not really daring to look anywhere else.

"You're a smart lady, Mrs. DeForest. Doc Harold would probably never've figured it out. But that's okay, I doubt if I would have either. Hey! Please don't drop it!"

The skull was dancing precariously between our hands, what with both of us shaking in different rhythms. I could not tear my eyes away from Barbara's which never wavered from mine, either. Part of my mind was fascinated by how wide her eyes could open.

"You don't have to keep holding it. I can stay as long as nobody who hasn't touched it comes in. Did that make sense? I think I got it right. I don't know if it's a rule or what. I've just noticed that's how it works. Nobody who hasn't touched it can see or hear me. Got any beer in the house?"

He moved behind Barbara, to where I could see him. "Come on, Doc. You've known me for years. I haven't changed."

I had to force my eyes to look directly at him.

I realized what he said was quite true. In all the years I'd known him, he had not changed, not even his clothes, his hair was always the same length. It was all true. Carefully, I put the skull down on the nearest table.

A beer suddenly sounded absolutely wonderful. I managed to find the refrigerator and three beers therein. When I returned Barbara was sitting on the couch staring at Marshall.

The beers were promptly opened, half emptied in one continuous swig, not tasted, and yet bringing at least two people back to some sense of normalcy.

"Why didn't you ever tell me?" I asked as soon as I could get my voice to work.

"Couldn't figure out how to, not without scaring the bejammers out of you. I mean… 'By the way, Doc Harold, I'm a ghost and that's my head bone you have in your hands.' Well, I couldn't do it. I mean, you're kind of an old guy. What if you had a weak heart? I couldn't take the chance."

"How old are you?" Barbara had now found her voice as well.

"Eighteen."

"What year were you born?"

"1951."

"Oh my God," I said. My knees buckled. I staggered backward. Luckily a chair was close enough to catch me.

"What happened?" Barbara again.

"I have no idea." The boy took another swig of beer. "I was hitching across country, campin' out along the way to save money. I was on my way home from the biggest rock concert you ever saw. Someplace in upstate New York, out in the country. Gee, that was a fantastic experience. There were thousands of people. I met some terrific girls, if ya know what I mean. And the music was outta sight! All the biggies were there. Booze and girls and pot and the music… I must have been high for days.

"One night on the way home, I felt so good and there hadn't been any cars along for a while so I kept walkin' along the highway. I remember tripping in the dark and falling down a ravine or something.

"Next thing I know, it's daylight and there's this guy wiping muck off an old brown skull. He puts it in a burlap bag. We say hi. He keeps poking around in a mess of old trash that's been dumped from the road. Pretty soon he picks up the bag and goes up to the road.

"I look around a while and then decide to catch up with him. We walk along together, jawing about this and that, 'til we come to a roadside junk shop."

"He could see you? And talk with you?" I interrupted.

"Sure. Why not? I didn't know I was dead. I didn't know anything. It was like I'd woke up brand new. No past, no connection, nothin'. Didn't even occur to me to be bothered about it.

"Anyways, I poked around stuff on the porch while my new friend went inside. The junk dealer scrubbed at the skull with something or other. He thought it might be kinda old so he bought it. My friend bought a round of beers. We hung out and jawed with the junk dealer awhile. Pretty soon my friend decided to leave, but I felt like staying. When the dealer shut shop that evening, I hung around outside and slept on the porch.

"Next day I said hello to some lady who came up to the store and she acted like I wasn't there. So did the dealer. It really rattled me good. It took awhile to figure out what was going on."

"But why?" I asked.

"Why what?"

"Haunt your skull. So to speak."

"I dunno."

My hand obligingly poured beer into my mouth while I contemplated the enormity of it all.

"Christian burial," Barbara said. "Nobody ever found his body. Nobody even knew he died. He's never had a Christian burial."

"But wouldn't his family have had some kind of memorial service since he never came home?"

"They probably figured he'd run away and never gave up hope that he'd show up again someday."

"That must be it." I looked at Marshall, who shrugged.

We talked through most of the night until neither Barbara nor I could stay awake. But we had a plan.

The next Saturday Barbara wrapped Marshall's skull in a dish towel and tucked it into her beach bag. With my small shovel in the trunk, we drove to an abandoned cemetery I'd once run across out along a dirt road. We selected a spot close to the surrounding trees.

"Marshall should be able to rest here undisturbed," Barbara said. I set to hacking through the tight turf to peel back almost a square foot of it. She unwrapped his skull enough for both of us to touch it. Marshall stood quietly a few feet away and watched me dig.

"Looks like hard work, Doc. Ya want me to take a spell at it?"

The idea of letting the boy dig his own grave didn't sit right at all, so I shook my head, even though the ground was tough and hard. "Hey, I'm a paleontologist, remember? Digging in old ground that hasn't been disturbed in thousands of years is what I do," I answered and manfully kept at it. Eventually I achieved a round hole over a foot-square and almost half again as deep.

Suddenly, I wondered why killers always dug square-cornered holes for graves in the movies when there was no coffin. You certainly didn't need sharp corners and straight sides to bury a loose body. Or a skull.

I leaned back on my heels and stretched my back. The sun had moved enough that we'd soon lose the shade of the nearby trees. "Why didn't we bring along something to drink? Or even a little farewell picnic lunch?"

"Stop. You're getting macabre!" Barbara kissed the top of the skull before wrapping it up again. She gently settled it into the tiny grave.

We both pushed dirt in snugly around the bundled skull, settled the turf back into place and scattered the leftover dirt. I finally stood, but Barbara couldn't seem to stop fine tuning the job.

"I think we've done enough, honey." I gave her a hand up. She acted as unwilling as I felt to look at Marshall (one last time?) who gave us a solemn thumbs up gesture. "Good work, Doc. One nice rain and no one will ever know."

"I hope this doesn't require an ordained clergyman," I said. "We most sincerely commend the soul of Marshall Paris into the hands of God." I bowed my head to say the Lord's Prayer.

Barbara's and Marshall's voices joined me. After "Amen" I opened my eyes and raised my head. Barbara and I stood alone.

***

For the next several weeks, I couldn't stop worrying about him. Time and again I'd catch myself staring at the mantle where his skull had been. More than once Barbara caught me at it. I caught her checking it, too. She had rearranged my collection so there was no gaping space but we were both still aware of its absence. At odd moments one of us would mention him, like an on-going conversation we could pick up right where we had left off days before. Finally, she said what we both were thinking.

"We need to go back and check."

"Yeah. What if it didn't work? What if by burying the skull we have only managed to trap him in solitude? What if nobody ever found it again? What if it moldered away and left nothing to connect him to anything at all?" The thought that we might have consigned him to endless limbo was unendurable.

As usual, Barbara thought things through further than I did. "We may need to go to Illinois and find the rest of his... remains and bury him all together in one place."

My heart sank.

"Even assuming we can reestablish contact with him, he had no idea where he was, how far he'd gotten off the highway. He doesn't even know which highway it was. It was dark. It was decades ago. There could be a supermarket parking lot built there by now. I'm not even sure I could find the junk shop again. It was years ago I was there. It could be gone by now, too."

"In the morning," she said. "I'll pack a lunch."

Finding the exact spot in the old cemetery took some time. If we had to hunt for the rest of him with so little information... well, I would never complain about the difficulty of searching for dinosaurs again.

The patch of turf I had so laboriously lifted came up easily this time. It had not yet completely rewoven itself. Unfortunately, there had been rain and enough sun since our little interment for the dirt beneath it to settle dry and hard. And of course, I had forgotten to bring the little shovel. Barbara found a flat, rounded stone with a bit of edge that served as an adequate substitute. I worked the dirt loose with it, taking care not to scatter the dirt into the surrounding grass.

I probed for the towel and worked it around to expose the skull. When my fingers touched bone, I stroked it, feeling stupid. I looked around, not wanting to see Marshall.

"Wait a minute," Barbara said, "He can't appear unless I've touched it, too." She knelt beside me and reached into the dirt.

"Whatchoo folks lookin' fer?"

I nearly yanked the skull out of the ground in my fright. An old man in faded work clothes stood not twenty feet away. Barbara clenched her fists against her bosom.

"An earring," she called, as she slyly slipped one off. I hoped the stranger wouldn't notice the nearly hysterical note in her voice. "I dropped an earring."

"Wahl, I'd be proud to hep you look fer it." He came toward us.

She dropped her hand-the one holding the earring-to the ground and proceeded to run it furiously through the grass.

"Oh, look, here it is." She triumphantly exhibited the "lost" earring and made a great show of putting it on. "Thanks so much for your offer."

The man waved cheerfully and strolled off toward the woods.

"I have never felt so foolish in my life," I muttered. "Thank God no one else has seen us. Two tenured university professors of reasonably mature years, on their knees in an abandoned cemetery, with their hands stuck in the dirt."

We waited for the old man to pass out of sight before resuming our absurd quest down the hole. We remained alone in the headstone-dotted field. No one else appeared in the trees or along the road.

***

"Harold, why on earth did you keep this rock from the old cemetery?"

Things don't go to the cleaners in my pockets any more now that Barbara takes care of me. She handed me the little rock shovel, so I dutifully studied it for an answer to her question. The shallow bowl shape, no larger than my hand, had a broken edge on one side.

"Good heavens! Where did you get this?"

"Out of your jacket." She displayed the guilty garment.

"No, I mean at the graveyard. Where did this come from?"

"I don't know, there was a little outcropping, looked like loose shale or something."

"It's a scapular, a shoulder bone, and I'm pretty sure it's human."

"How do, folks," came a new voice from the doorway. There stood the old man from the cemetery. "The name's Josiah."

I AM BRIDGET

By: Mariah Southworth

The party started at six o'clock. By nine o'clock, everyone agreed that it was the best senior party of the year. At ten o'clock, their father came home unexpectedly. By ten-fifteen, the house was deserted; the remaining mess the only evidence there had ever been a party.

The three girls stood in the living room amongst the debris of crushed cans and empty chip bags, staring at their feet. Better their feet then their father, who frowned down at them with his best disappointed Dad frown on his long, thin face. He was *supposed* to have been at the university all night speaking at some seminar. He still wore his work clothes, and the stiff suit made him even more intimidating, thinning auburn hair and crooked glasses aside.

"Morgan," he said, growling the name out. Morgan, the daughter with the shoulder-length blonde hair scraped into pigtails, looked up with dismay. "Monica," he continued. Monica, the sister with the long, blonde braid, looked up warily. Her face was a mirror of Morgan's; same little nose, same heart-shaped face, same arch to her pale eyebrows, same big blue eyes. Even their clothes were the same—short-shorts and low cut tank-tops.

The twins watched their father expectantly. He pointed to the stairs. "Go to your room," he demanded, before turning to the last young woman in the room. The twins shared a look, then turned pitying gazes to their older sister.

"Now," their father snapped. The twins reluctantly departed, and their father was left alone with his remaining daughter.

She was a bit taller than the twins, and her face squarer. She had the same nose, but it was slightly bigger, and her eyes were the same shape, but they were green. Her deep auburn hair fell in a cascade down the back of her cream colored blouse, and she wore a sensible pleated knee skirt with tights. She stood perfectly straight, ankles together, hands clasped, expression blank.

Her father looked at her, his scowl deepening. "Bridget," he said at last. "I am very disappointed in you."

Bridget's expression did not change.

"For God's sake," her father continued. "You are the oldest; you are supposed to be responsible for them."

Bridget blinked. "Father—" she started.

Her father talked right over her. "I *trust* you to keep an eye on them and keep them out of trouble. I am astonished you not only didn't *stop* them, but you actively *encouraged them.* You are supposed to protect them."

"But…" Bridget began.

"As the oldest, you have responsibility that the other two do not!"

"But Father!" Bridget said again, more forcefully than before.

Her father stopped and pursed his lips at her. "What?" he asked.

"I am not the oldest," Bridget said. "Technically…"

Her father waved a hand to cut her off, glancing fearfully at the stairs.

"They are in their room." Bridget told him. "They can't hear us from there."

Her father lowered his hand, his expression reluctant. "Be that as it may," he continued gruffly. "You are my oldest daughter. You are Bridget."

For the first time in the conversation, Bridget's blank expression cracked. She scowled at her father. "I am not," she said softly. He had been doing this more and more often—she understood that he had to in public, but he could at least stop pretending when it was just the two of them.

The color of her father's face deepened. He was getting angry.

Bridget reached up and unlocked the catch behind her ear, swinging her face forward and off of her head. She let it hang from its nearly invisible hinges. "I am not the oldest," she repeated. Her lips, now facing the stairs and not her father, moved a few fractions of a second out of sync with her teeth and jaw. "I am not. Will you please stop saying that I am?"

Her father flinched at the sight of her without her face, but at least the scowl vanished. Bridget hated it when he scowled at her.

"Close your face," he snapped.

Bridget didn't want to listen to him. She was too angry; at least, her version of angry. She couldn't be sure if it was the same as other people's anger.

When she didn't move, her father stepped towards her and took her face gently in his hands. He swung it back into place, and it locked itself down. Bridget moved her jaw, opened and closed her eyes, and wrinkled her nose. Everything was back in place and she looked perfect again.

"Even if you are not the oldest," her father said, "you are still my daughter." He put a hand on her head for a moment, then stepped back, his scowl returning to a lesser degree. "Regardless, the fact that you allowed this party to take place concerns me deeply, Bridget. I *told* you to keep them out of trouble."

"You didn't say that they couldn't have a party," Bridget told him.

"I consider an unsupervised party trouble."

"It wasn't unsupervised. I was here."

"Bridget…" Her father sighed exasperatedly. He removed his glasses and started cleaning them with his handkerchief. "Alright," he sighed again, replacing the glasses. "From now on, no more parties that I did not give prior, specific approval for. Understand?"

Bridget shifted uncomfortably. His frown was no longer the chiding frown of a father, but the puzzled frown of a scientist. "You shouldn't need such precise instructions. Something must have gone wrong." He chewed on his lower lip, then shook his head. "I'll have to take a look at you this weekend."

Bridget's expression didn't change, but inside she felt an electric surge of alarm. She didn't like it when her father 'looked' at her. It made her uncomfortable. "Yes, Father," she said.

Her father pointed to the stairs. "Go up there and tell them that they are grounded for two weeks."

"Yes, Father," Bridget repeated, then turned and walked up the stairs.

She found the twins in their bedroom. Monica sat on top of the desk, and Morgan perched on the top of the bunk bed. "Two *weeks!*" Morgan exclaimed after Bridget delivered their father's message. She jumped down from the upper bed and landed with her knees bent. "That is *so* unfair," she declared as she straightened.

"No," Monica huffed. "What's unfair is that every time we get in trouble, Bridget is the one that gets lectured."

"Oh, yeah," Morgan said, her pigtails swaying as she shook her head. "Jesus, Bridge, why does he *do* that?"

Bridget smiled shyly at them. "Because I'm the oldest," she said, sitting down on the desk chair that Monica had ignored.

"That's bullshit," Monica said, patting her older sister on the shoulder. "Really—massive piles of bullshit."

Morgan giggled, bounced over and threw her arms around Bridget's shoulders. "Yeah," she said. "We're the ones who always have to talk you into it, and you're the one who always gets in trouble."

"I don't mind," Bridget told them.

Monica shook her head. "Well, *we* do." She leaned down and kissed her sister on the forehead. "We'll toe the line, big sis. We don't want you getting in any more trouble because of us."

Morgan nodded vehemently, her pigtails bobbing comically.

Bridget smiled at them. She felt something inside her relax, and she wondered, *is this love? Or is this me imagining that I am feeling love?* Father said that she could only simulate emotions; she couldn't actually experience them. She liked simulating love, though, and she disliked simulating anger. Did that make it real?

She caught sight of a picture on the desk and felt that relaxing warmth dwindle. It was a picture of the twins and their sister. The sister looked like Bridget, because it *was* Bridget; the Bridget from two years ago.

The Bridget who had died.

***

Bridget sat in her advanced math class and doodled pictures in the margins of her notebook, finding drawing more entertaining than listening to the lecture. The notebook was already full of pictures of Morgan and Monica, pictures of the family cat, and anatomical pictures that would probably get her in trouble with the teacher, just because they were more realistic than the other cartoon versions that people scrawled onto the desks.

"Bridget," Mr. Cohen said suddenly. "Perhaps you can tell us the answer?"

Bridget looked up and swept her eyes over the complex equation on the board. "Twenty over twenty-seven," she said.

Mr. Cohen looked startled; not in a way that anyone else would have noticed, but Bridget saw the subtle widening of his eyes. "Yes, good job," he said. "Glad you're paying attention."

Bridget went back to her drawings. Five minutes before the bell rang, she turned to a fresh page in her notebook and began writing down the answers to the problems that they had covered in class. She copied them down in neat, efficient handwriting, even 'showing her work' off to the side. The bell rang, and Bridget got up and handed in the finished assignment with the other students.

It was somewhat risky for her to do; someone might notice and get suspicious. Bridget didn't care. She was tired of caring.

Technically, Bridget should have graduated already, but her "accident" two years before had made it necessary to take a year off. Now she was a senior at Spring Water High, just like her two sisters.

This has been my entire life, she reflected as she traveled along the hallway with the rush of students. *Two years isn't much of a lifetime, but still...* Her next class was biology. She didn't want to go. She had already downloaded everything there was to know about biology, and it was all there inside her head whenever she wanted it. Why bother going to class just to fill a chair?

Bridget slowed down and allowed herself to drop out of the tide of students. Soon she was alone in the hallway. She stood there for a few moments, enjoying the silence, then resumed walking. Today was Friday. Her father said he was going to take her down into the lab tonight, to take a look at her brain.

Bridget didn't want him to, but she didn't have much choice.

Once upon a time, she told herself as she walked through the empty halls, *there was a girl. She was a pretty girl, and smart too. She lived with her father and her two younger sisters. They all loved each other very much. One day, the girl had a fight with her father. The girl took her father's car, and she drove it off of a cliff.*

Bridget stopped outside one of the classrooms and peeked through the window. She found Morgan, sitting at one of the desks, listening to the start of her chemistry lecture. Bridget caught Morgan's eye, and her sister smiled at her.

Bridget moved on. *The father told his remaining daughters that their older sister was in the hospital, but this was not the case. The truth was that the older daughter had died. The grief-stricken father could not bring himself to tell them this. Instead, he made a replacement. She was just like the girl in every way, except that she was made of plastic, silicone and metal. She would never die like the first girl had.*

Bridget meandered through the school, not really paying attention to or caring where she went. *For a while, everyone was happy. But then the new girl began to feel sad, because she was* not *the original, no matter how much she looked like her. She could not* be *the original, but her father wanted her to be. He wanted her to be the original so badly that he sometimes believed his own lie. The new girl was not the original, and she knew it. She became annoyed at her father, and so she… and so she…*

Bridget stopped. She didn't know how the story ended.

"Hey, you!" someone called.

Bridget turned. A hall monitor stood a few yards behind her. He didn't look happy.

Bridget felt nothing.

***

"This really is the last straw, Bridget," her father said in the car on the drive home from the school. Bridget said nothing. It had not been the first time she hadn't gone to class. In fact, it had been so often now that the school had called her father.

258

"Do you have anything to say for yourself?" he asked her.

"No," Bridget answered.

Her father gave her an annoyed glance. "Well, since I'm away from work now, I suppose we can get your check-up over with."

Bridget felt, or thought she felt, something tighten in her chest. "I don't want to," she said.

"You don't want to?" her father repeated. "You don't *want* to? See, that right there; that should tell you that there is something wrong." He shook his head. "You don't *have* wants, Bridget. Especially not wants that are harmful, and not wanting to get your brain looked at is harmful. So we're going to do it, right?"

Bridget said nothing. She turned and looked out the window.

"And while we are on the subject," her father said, reaching into his jacket and taking out a piece of paper. "What is this?"

Bridget glanced at the paper. "My English homework," she said.

Her father shook the page at her. "Your English homework," he parroted. "Your teacher gave it to me when I came in today. It's yours, and yet I see these drawings along the sides. Why, Bridget?"

"I like to draw," Bridget said.

"No, you don't," her father said, lowering the paper. "More importantly, you *can't* draw. Bridget could *never* draw, but your English teacher told me that I should encourage you to go to an art school. She said that she had never seen such talent before; that they almost looked like *pictures.*" He shook his head. "You are lucky that she didn't know you before. No more drawing, understand me?"

Bridget said nothing.

"I said, do you understand me?" he father repeated with more force.

"Yes, Father," she said.

They had reached home. Bridget got out of the car and allowed her father to lead her inside. At the back of the house was a locked door. Her father unlocked it with one of the keys on his heavy key ring and led Bridget down the set of stairs behind it. When they reached the bottom, Bridget's father turned on the lights.

The basement was a large room with a ceiling higher than average, several work tables, and a storage closet. Every available surface held spare parts, computers, or a mix of plans, tools, molds, and diagrams. Half-finished people hung from the ceiling, their torsos open to reveal a jumble of electronics, their limbs raw and un-textured.

Her father continued into the room while Bridget lingered near the front, staring up at the half-formed mannequins hanging from the ceiling. This was where she had been born.

Bridget's father had, once upon a time, been one of the leading engineers at a major robotics company. He had left for a few reasons; he said the company had dismissed and repressed many of his ideas and hadn't given him credit for most of his contributions. The experience had poisoned him against sharing his work with anyone. He had gone on to teach robotics at the local university and continued his own work in secret.

"Come along, Bridget," her father called. He stood by a chair that looked like it belonged in a dentist's office. There was an array of tools on the counter next to him.

Bridget reluctantly walked over and sat down.

"Okay," her father said, leaning the chair back. "Here we go."

"And awake," her father said. Bridget opened her eyes. She didn't remember closing them.

"Get up," her father said. Bridget got up.

"Spin around," he ordered.

Bridget turned in a circle and looked at her father. He was smiling; that was good. Bridget felt a surge of happiness at the sight.

"Jump on one leg," her father told her. Bridget did just that, without even thinking about it. Her father nodded at her, pleased.

"I couldn't find anything out of place," he told her as he began putting his tools away. "So I increased your obedience levels, among other things. I had originally kept them low to aid in the illusion of life, but things weren't working out with the overabundance of free will."

She didn't like it. She knew that she didn't like it; it was everything that she didn't like about her father examining her head. She didn't *like* waking up and finding everything different, but she couldn't seem to *express* that. She could only return her father's smile.

"Now," her father said. "I have work to do. Run upstairs and make dinner."

Bridget bobbed her head. "Yes, Father."

***

For a time, everything was good. Bridget no longer did anything that annoyed her father. She went to school, paid attention in class, did her school work gradually instead of all at once, and no longer doodled her masterpieces in the margins. She came home and spent the evening cleaning the house, cooking, and doting on her father.

Her father quickly came to enjoy his daughter's increased obedience and began asking her to do more and more. She did whatever he wanted without complaint.

Though her father was happy, Bridget could tell that her sisters weren't. "You should get out of the house more," Monica told her one evening.

Bridget looked up from washing the dishes. "I'm too busy," she said.

Monica frowned at her. "Yeah, that's just it. Father has you doing all of these chores. You need time for friends."

Bridget looked back down at her work. "I don't have any friends."

"Well you used to," Monica said exasperatedly. "Whatever happened to Kyle and Heather, or Dominic? I mean, I know they graduated, but still."

Bridget knew vaguely of those people. They were not her friends. She could only shake her head mutely at her sister.

Eventually, Morgan and Monica were no longer grounded, and Bridget saw less of them. One night she caught them sneaking out late. She stood in front of the door to block their path, and when that didn't work she woke up their father.

"Thanks a lot, Bridget," Monica snapped at her as she walked them back upstairs.

"Father knows best," Bridget said.

"Bullshit," Monica said before disappearing into her bedroom.

Morgan lingered by the door, a scowl on her face. "You didn't used to be like this," Morgan told her.

"We were going to toe the line, remember?" Bridget asked.

Morgan shook her head, scowling. "Ever since you crashed you've been little miss goody two shoes. You used to be *fun*. I mean, I'm glad you didn't die, but now you're always on *his* side."

"That's not true," Bridget said, feeling a surge of alarm go through her.

"What*ever*," Morgan said, slamming the bedroom door.

Bridget stared at the closed door. *It's not true,* she thought. *Father made me exactly like the first Bridget. I am a perfect copy. That is the whole point of me—to have a perfect copy.*

The months went by. Her sisters and her father fought.

"You need to listen to me!" her father yelled one night. "I'm your father and you *will* obey me!"

"Like Hell I will!" Morgan shrieked back. "I can *have* a boyfriend, Father! I am *seventeen,* and you aren't the boss of me!"

"You are *my* daughter, and what I say goes."

"I'm not a child anymore!"

Their father tugged at his hair as if he wanted to pull it out. "God, why can't you be more like Bridget? *She* listens to me!"

"Well *excuse* me for not being perfect!" Morgan screamed. "Maybe you should arrange for *me* to almost drown and then the brain damage will be enough for me to obey you too!"

"Go to your room!" Their father yelled, swinging his arm out to point at the stairs.

"Gladly!"

Later, in his laboratory, Bridget's father sat in the reclining dentist chair and complained about his daughters. "No respect," he said, "that's the problem with both of them."

"Yes Father," Bridget said. She was rubbing his feet.

"I mean," her father continued. "Is it so much to ask for a little obedience? I think I deserve at least *that*."

"Yes, Father."

"God, why do children have to grow up?" he asked with a sigh. "This was never a problem when they were little."

"Mmm…" Bridget said, concentrating on what she was doing. She wondered if the original Bridget had rubbed her father's feet. *She must have,* she told herself. *Father wants me to be just like her. He wouldn't have me be anything that she wasn't. That's why I'm not allowed to draw anymore.*

"I mean," her father said, "you don't have a problem listening to me and behaving. Why do they?"

"I am a robot, father," Bridget said.

It had been a long time since she had reminded her father of this, but he *had* asked. Usually, it upset him, but this time he fell into a thoughtful silence.

"Yes," he said eventually. "You are, aren't you?"

The next week, Monica came home with a tattoo of a butterfly on her bicep. Bridget thought it was pretty, their father didn't like it. He told Monica that she had ruined her body, and she responded by telling him to "shove it."

He demanded that she pay to get it removed, but she refused.

It was all very dramatic.

Bridget loved her sisters. At least, she loved them in the only way that she knew how, and it hurt that they seemed to no longer love her. What choice did she have, though? She *had* to agree with their father. She considered asking her father to remove her emotion simulator to spare her the pain of her sisters' scorn, but the idea of him looking at her brain again frightened her. What if he turned off her ability to think for herself entirely? She liked to at least be able to disagree with him, even if it was only in her own mind.

Monica and Morgan were perpetually grounded now. Bridget was under orders to not let them leave the house. One rainy Saturday afternoon, she couldn't find Morgan. She searched all over for her until she finally found her in the attic.

"What are you doing?" Bridget asked as she climbed the stairs into the dusty, over-warm room.

Morgan sat on a crate, reading a book. She looked up at her sister with a frown. "Did you know this was in here?" she asked.

Bridget returned the frown and approached her. "Know what was in here?"

"Your diary," Morgan said, holding the book out.

Bridget blinked. "I don't have a diary."

"Sure you do," Morgan said, waving the little book at her. "Take it."

Bridget took the small book bound in fake green leather with a rose stamped on the cover. She turned it over in her hands, not recognizing it.

"Father must have put it up here while you were in the hospital," Morgan said.

Bridget flipped open the pages. They were handwritten in a sloppier version of her own handwriting. "I suppose," she said dubiously.

Later, in her bedroom, Bridget read the diary cover to cover. When she was finished, she sat back and stared at the ceiling.

She was not Bridget. She had never been Bridget. The Bridget in the diary complained about her father's overbearing personality. The Bridget in the diary snuck out late with friends, and giggled, and had a secret boyfriend that her father didn't know about. She didn't dress sensibly or like school all that much. She didn't always do her chores when she was supposed to.

The Bridget in the diary was nothing like her.

Why did you make me, Father? she asked inside her head. *I thought you wanted me to be Bridget.*

Bridget got up. She made dinner and did the laundry. She greeted her father when he came home and rubbed his shoulders before bed. Afterward, she waited. When the house was silent, she crept back up into the attic. She looked but found no more hints of the Bridget that had been.

But, she thought, *maybe there are some in the laboratory.*

Her father had never told her *not* to go in there by herself, nor had he told her not to take his keys. Maybe she could find out why she was the way she was in one of those shut cabinets, or hidden in a file on his computer.

Bridget hadn't been in the laboratory for weeks. She unlocked the basement door, went downstairs, and turned on the light. She didn't notice the robot at first. It was in the back of the laboratory, laid out on one of the tables. When she did notice it, she walked over, curious. It was more complete than the rejects that hung from the ceiling; more lifelike, like she was.

The mannequin was naked and hairless. Its face hung open, the skull of black wires and shining metal staring up at the ceiling with large, lidless blue eyes. Bridget, curious, took the face in her hand and swung it back over the exposed skull.

One of the twins looked back at her.

***

"You're a good girl, Bridget," her father told her a few days later. "You know that?"

Bridget looked up at him. "Yes, Father," she said.

He smiled at her. She liked it when he smiled. She was programmed to like it. "Really, the best daughter a man could ask for." He brushed her cheek with his hand. "And you are going to be perfect forever. You're not going to grow any older, or hurt yourself, or do anything stupid. Do you like that?"

Bridget nodded.

"So you're happy as you are?" he asked her. "You're happy listening to me?"

"Yes, Father."

"You're happier than you were before the accident?" he pressed her.

Bridget blinked at him. "Father," she said. "I am not Bridget. I am a robot."

Her father frowned and shook his head. "You *are* Bridget," he said, rubbing her cheek again. "You're my little girl, and you always will be."

"Yes, Father."

Spring Break approached, and Monica and Morgan were finally not grounded. Bridget overheard them making plans to go on a road trip with their friends. They had told their father that they were going to the lake, but in reality, they were going on tours for out-of-state colleges. Their father wanted the girls to go to the local university. He didn't want them to leave home. Morgan and Monica had other plans.

Bridget decided not to tell their father.

The first day of Spring Break came, and Morgan and Monica couldn't be found. Bridget thought that they had left for their trip until one of her sisters' friends called the house. He asked Bridget where the twins were, but Bridget could only tell him that she didn't know.

Her father came up from his lab a few minutes after she'd hung up. "If any of Morgan and Monica's friends call," he said. "Tell them that the girls are sick and can't go on the trip."

Bridget blinked at him. "Yes, Father," she said.

Her father nodded and left. Bridget waited until she knew he was in the bathroom, then she went downstairs to the lab.

Morgan and Monica were there. They were lying on two of the work tables, dressed in sensible clothes. They were also together in a corner, still in their pajamas. Bridget knelt by the two in the corner. They were unconscious and probably sedated.

Bridget stood and walked to the table. She checked over the other Morgan and Monica. This Monica didn't have a butterfly tattoo on her arm.

"Bridget?" asked her father's voice. Bridget looked up from the table. He stood at the bottom of the stairs, watching her.

"I am not Bridget," she said. She took the little diary out of her pocket and held it out.

Her father, frowning, walked over to her and took the book. He fanned it open, saw what it was and shut it with a snap. "You *are* Bridget," he insisted. "And don't ever say otherwise."

"But—" Bridget began.

"Again with the buts!" her father exclaimed. He shook his head. "I hope I've fixed whatever went wrong with you in these models." He looked thoughtfully down at his two new daughters. "If it works, I'll do some reprogramming with you."

Bridget was silent for a moment. "You didn't make me like Bridget," she said at last.

Her father looked at her with pride in his eyes. "I made you better."

Bridget looked over her shoulder at her sisters, the ones in the corner. "What are you going to do with them?" she asked.

Her father placed a hand on the new Monica's thigh. "I made *them* better as well," he said. "I'm almost done. I have a new tool I borrowed from the university. It will make it so much easier to get their memories from the bodies; with you, I had to tell you what you needed to know."

"But what are you going to do with them?" Bridget asked, waving to the Morgan and Monica in the corner.

Her father finally looked at his other daughters, his real daughters. "Oh," he said. "They won't need those bodies anymore. I'll get rid of them."

"You told me to protect them," Bridget said. "You told me I was responsible for them."

"Yes, yes," her father said, looking back to the two on the tables. "You won't need to be anymore when I'm done. They will finally listen to me."

Bridget nodded. Then she stepped forward and wrapped her hand around her father's throat.

He tried to say something, but Bridget's other hand shot out and covered his mouth. She couldn't let him tell her not to kill him. She squeezed and saw his eyes widen with panic as he realized what she was doing. The diary hit the floor with a dull thud as he thrashed and pulled at her, but she wasn't made of weak muscle and flesh. Still, he tried to break her. He hit her in the face over and over again. Something cracked and her face swung off of her head.

His flailing weakened. She felt something break under her hand, and blood trickled out from the corner of his mouth. He stopped moving entirely and after a moment a glaze crept over his eyes, like frost on a windowpane.

Bridget stood for what felt like a long time, holding her father's corpse. She might have stayed there indefinitely, until the flesh rotted and fell away, leaving her holding a skeleton, but someone screamed behind her.

The sound stopped whatever computer glitch had kept her standing there. She dropped the body and turned to find Monica and Morgan awake. They stood huddled in the corner, mute with horror after that first scream.

Bridget took a step towards them and they scrambled over each other in their hurry to flee from her. Bridget stopped and watched as they ran up the stairs and out of the basement.

She realized that her face was still off. She looked around the room, spotted a sheet of chrome on one of the tables, and picked it up. She looked into the shining surface, and her skinless face looked back at her with wide, lidless green eyes.

No wonder the twins had fled from her. She had killed their father and she didn't even look human. *I'm supposed to be human,* she thought. *That's what father wanted, but he didn't do it right. What am I if I'm not human?*

"I am Bridget," she said to the reflection. She tried to call herself something else, because she was, after all, not Bridget. "I am Bridget," she repeated.

Her father had told her that she *was* Bridget, had ordered her to never say anything different.

"I am Bridget."

When the police finally arrived, that was where they found her, standing and staring into the mirror, repeating the same line over and over again.

CAT AND MOUSE

By: David Tallerman

"Would you like to come in for coffee?"

Only, she pronounced it as to two distinct syllables, cof-fee, and I'd never heard anyone make two syllables sound so frankly erotic. Every inch of my body and a good portion of my mind was eager to follow her up that short flight of stairs, through the door, and into the dimly lit, rich-scented depths of her apartment.

But the part of my brain that disagreed was doing so violently. Something about this woman, about the evening we'd spent together, just didn't sit right.

The resisting portion of my brain knew this to be true. Yet when I challenged it to give me a specific example, it floundered. The inner turmoil made me want to howl with frustration. I hadn't had a date in almost a year and now here was this undeniably beautiful woman inviting me into her flat, for something I knew without doubt had little to do with caffeinated beverages.

"Kamrita." Probably I was tired. Probably I was freaking out, trying instinctively to sabotage this good thing that had come out of nowhere into my life. I placed a foot on the first step. "I'd like to…"

My attention drifted, from her face to a point beside her head. I'd have sworn I spotted movement there. Yet when I looked, properly looked, I saw shadows receding into a shallow hallway.

More self-sabotage. I knew it, and the knowledge didn't help. I tried to concentrate, and the itch to stare past her shoulder sent tremors down my spine. I took another step, paused to knuckle my eyes.

For the barest instant, I saw clearly: a pattern of blue and almost-black purple, like…

The thought evaporated. Nothing except shadows. But the damage was done. Those last three steps might as well have been the Gulf of Mexico.

"Ah, I'd like to get an early night. I'm up at the crack of dawn tomorrow, I've a meeting, and…"

Her expression started with surprise and ended with what I could only describe as devastation. That threw me more than anything. Surely a woman like Kamrita could have any man she wanted, and a stone thrown randomly in Leicester Square would be bound to hit a better match than me. I comforted myself with that logic: I was doing her a favour. Perhaps she'd had too much to drink. Maybe she'd built our barely natal relationship into something much more than it was. In the morning, she'd wake up grateful to the asshole who'd turned her down, leaving her to find a partner worthy of her charms.

"Bye," I said. When that didn't seem enough I added, "I'll call you."

I didn't want to see if she believed me. I turned away and started walking, trying not to appear as though I was hurrying and yet hurrying nonetheless. Bad enough that I'd hurt her feelings, bad enough I was acting crazy. Letting her see how frantically I wanted to get away seemed a cruelty too far.

A pause. No sound but the tap of my feet on the pavement. Her voice, lilting behind me: "I'll see you soon."

At first I thought she sounded pitiful. Did she really think I meant I'd call her? Then I realised how she'd said it. This wasn't at all the plea of a woman too desperate to admit she'd been jilted. Surely she wasn't going to start turning up unannounced at my office or loitering outside my flat? No, that wasn't it either. What I'd heard in her voice was simply certainty: the tone in which someone might look at a cloudy sky and say, 'It's going to rain.'

Still, I didn't turn back. I didn't respond, not so much as a nod or shake of my head. I pretended I hadn't heard, or as if she hadn't said anything worth hearing, and I felt like an utter shit. But I made it to the corner, and I couldn't deny that my breath came easier as I turned out of her street.

Finally I slowed down. I let the tension soak out of me and wondered what I was going to do next. The evening was mild, the tail end of an Indian summer that had made the real one look pitiful. Though it was almost October and past eleven, I was comfortable in my T-shirt and light jacket, only shivering a little when the night breeze cut around my collar. I wasn't entirely sure where I was—somewhere near Camden as far as I could tell—and I knew I was a long way from home.

That didn't worry me. I wanted to walk around, to clear my head. I had the frustrating sensation of a word caught on the tip of my tongue; except it wasn't a word, it was the whole of the last few hours. It was like trying to remember a dream, too, except that I could recall everything—*almost* everything—with perfect clarity. We'd met for a couple of drinks in a quiet Soho bar and moved on via a short Tube journey to a restaurant Kamrita knew. She'd offered to order for both of us and I'd agreed. I couldn't remember afterwards exactly what she'd told the waiter, but the result was as near to my perfect meal as I could have hoped for.

Dinner left me mellow, contented, and slightly tipsy. I'd suggested I walk Kamrita home. I don't recollect any ulterior motive; I merely wanted to stretch the evening as far as it would go. Yet even then, doubts were nagging. They'd been there ever since we first met.

How *had* we met?

Looking up, I discovered to my surprise that I was somewhere I recognised. I was walking along Prince Albert Road, with stubby blocks of flats sprouting to my left and on my right the wall of foliage marking the uppermost edge of Regent's Park.

A sudden, mad impulse caught me. Before I had time to question it, I'd already given in and was clambering over the gate into the park. The full moon amid a clear sky was nearly as good as daylight, and I reasoned I'd be able to see and outrun any patrolling guards if there were such a thing. I walked until I was free of the trees around the entrance and abandoned the path. A couple of minutes later, it occurred to me to sit down. Squatted upon the damp grass, I could see nothing of London, though I knew it was out there before me. I tried to guess from memory the locations of all the great, familiar landmarks: Big Ben, Canary Wharf, Battersea Power Station, the Gherkin and the Shard. But the only one I could actually see was the inverted crystalline spike of the Hyde Park Spire, and then only its blunted peak.

Still, it was the Spire that my eyes kept drifting back to. Yet nothing about it seemed offensive or out of place, nor even particularly interesting. I stared at its distant grooves and weird prominences, a half-burned candle sculpted in frosted glass, and wondered what it was that commanded my interest.

Once again, the feeling of wrongness started to creep over me: the sensation, which I now couldn't help but associate with Kamrita, that I was blind to some important detail. It also struck me clearly that a part of my mind had brought me to this spot for a reason. Those two revelations unsettled in one fell swoop the calm I'd managed to accumulate, making the park seem suddenly dark and unfriendly. I stood up and started walking again, as fast or faster than when I'd hurried to escape Kamrita's flat.

I'd gotten turned around. It was years since I'd last been in the park, and now it seemed like a desert of inky grass and trees blotted carelessly onto characterless landscape. I began to jog, though my breath was already coming hard.

Abruptly, a low roar rent the air, hung for a moment as a trembling growl and faded. I almost panicked, until I realised it must have come from the zoo, which lay somewhere to my left—a big cat disturbed from its slumber. Then, oddly, I calmed a little. The scene struck me as almost funny: here I was, running around in London as though it were some tropic wilderness. I took a moment to get my bearings and let the stitch in my side ease. I made a point of not looking back towards the Spire.

Once I settled on a direction, the edge of the park came on me quickly. Clambering over another gate brought me out on a road I didn't recognise. I didn't know this side of London well at all and navigating from a half-remembered childhood visit was getting me nowhere. Even if I was still on edge, it was time I started heading home. The alternative might be a night spent curled up in a doorway if I wasn't careful. Glancing at my watch, I saw that it was coming up on midnight. There should still be Tube trains running if I could find a station in time, and there was bound to be one nearby.

Just as I'd settled on my plan, I heard the growing rumble of an engine behind me, too loud for a car. When I turned, I was dazzled for a moment by the headlights and bright internal glow of an approaching bus. It was the first vehicle I'd seen since I entered the park, and it took me by surprise—all the more so when it pulled to a halt against the curb, for there was no shelter, not even a sign.

Nevertheless, it was a gift horse, and I wasn't about to look it in the mouth. Judging by the destination it was displaying, the bus wouldn't exactly pass near my flat, but it would certainly get me closer than I was now: a reasonable walk rather than an all-night trek.

When I walked round, though, I saw that the folding doors were closed. I was wondering if the vehicle was out of service after all when the driver happened to glance down and notice me. He stared with puzzled consideration for a few seconds, almost as if this were his house I was standing outside of instead of a public transport. Then he moved slightly and the doors concertinaed open.

I stepped up cautiously, conscious his gaze had never left me. I told him where I was trying to get to. He gave the information some thought. As I was starting to despair of getting any sense out of him, he said, "Closest stop's a couple of miles off. That any good to you?"

A couple of miles in London might wind up being an hour's fast walk. "I can live with it."

Abruptly, apropos of nothing, the driver said, "You might want to watch those two at the back. They're a little, ah…" The sentence drifted off. He transferred his gaze to the mirror that let him view the inside of his vehicle, his brow crinkling with worry.

I looked where he was looking, to the two men sat together on the rearmost seat. Though the interior was astringently lit, I found it hard to make them out, as if they'd found a shadow that couldn't possibly be there. If I concentrated, I could see enough of them to think that something wasn't exactly right. But concentrating on them was more difficult than it had any reason to be.

"Sorry," said the driver. "Don't know what I was thinking."

I swiped my Oyster card, wondering which was more bizarre, the driver's confusion or the fact that a London bus driver had apologised to me. Not comfortable at the prospect of being near the two men, I opted for the seat closest the front. A sign told me curtly that it was set aside for the elderly and physically impaired, but the bus was empty except for the three of us, and I figured I could move if need be. Then it occurred to me that I wouldn't recognise my unfamiliar stop in the dark. I ducked back to the driver's plastic window and asked if he'd let me know when we got there.

"Sure," he said, "no bother." He actually sounded pleased, as if the task would be a pleasant diversion from whatever thoughts were rotating in his head.

I went back to the seat I'd picked, saw the sign again and wondered why I'd settled on it in the first place.

Something to do with the pair at the back? But they were only conversing in soft whispers and keeping to themselves. As the driver pulled from the curb, I settled for a spot midway down the bus which would give me a better view of the streets we passed through.

At least, that was the plan. I bore with it for a couple of minutes, trying to draw sense from the blur of buildings and figures, smudged by darkness or bleached into meaninglessness by washes of electric light. I still didn't recognise anywhere. The occasional road signs I saw were scuffed by shadows and the speed of our passage, nonsensical as some alien language. London might have been any city on Earth for all I could make sense of it.

I settled into my seat and allowed my mind to wander. I was confident the driver would hold to his promise, and if he didn't, I wasn't sure I cared anymore. The night had grown too unreal. Did I really want to carry that mood home with me? I knew I hadn't properly processed what I was thinking, or rather *not* thinking ... whatever was untangling itself in the base of my mind.

Kamrita. The name sounded Asian, didn't it? Except I wasn't pronouncing it right. There'd been more there when she'd said it, a throaty resonance I'd known I would never perfect. I tried to remember her accent: to dissect some phrase that she'd spoken in my memory, tease from its innards a hint of accent or clue of nationality.

It worked up to a point. I could hear her voice as if she were sat next to me: its soft vowels and clicking consonants, and its peculiar rhythm, which made the words spin and dance like skaters on a frozen lake. But that didn't bring me any closer to understanding. More and more I found myself focusing on the remembered conversations themselves, how much I'd enjoyed them, and her, and us together. In my mind's eye, I replayed her small and earnest compliments, the bright flares of humour, the way she'd made subjects I'd never bothered to consider immediately interesting.

Kamrita … wherever it came from, it was a nice name. And wherever she came from, it was ages since I'd enjoyed time spent with anyone so much, if I ever had. What was I running from? Was my trepidation really worse than the possibility of living the rest of my life without spending more of it with her?

The bus made a sound of complaint, metal grating upon metal, and slowed rapidly before stopping altogether. I heard the grind and whirr of the doors opening, and immediately after, the driver calling, "This is you, mate."

Caught by surprise—wasn't this the first stop we'd made? —I jerked to my feet, gave the driver a nod and mumbled "thank you," and stumbled onto the curb. Almost before my heels struck tarmac, the doors rattled shut, the engine grumbled back into life and the bus dove back into the road. I looked round in alarm, to watch as its lights receded. It reached the corner and vanished from sight.

Turning back, I saw where the driver had left me: at the foot of the short flight of stairs that led to Kamrita's front door.

This time I really did run. Despite my thoughts of only a few moments ago, the clearly impossible, inexplicable return to Kamrita's home had made the very concept of her downright frightening. I fled with no thought of direction, no thought of anything but placing distance between myself and that innocuous green portal. I ran until stinging sweat blurred my vision, until my ankles and knees felt full of hot lead, until my head swam with the battering of my heart.

I ran until I couldn't run anymore. Then I flopped onto a low garden wall and gasped. I'd never imagined I could be so glad of cool night air. I really believed I could feel it, not only in my lungs but in my muscles and veins, as if my body were a machine being lubricated. I knew I should be cold, I knew my clothes were saturated with sweat, but in fact I felt wonderful, scoured and fresh.

My burst of fear—or perhaps more likely the adrenalin that followed—had done more than any of the night's events to clear my head. I could see the pieces now. The Spire. Kamrita. The men on the bus, not hidden precisely but the exact opposite of conspicuous. I was starting to remember details I didn't know I'd forgotten. I was a part of something, something perhaps out of my control and beyond my ability to resist.

Now that the panic had worn off, I questioned once again why I was trying. If I stopped running, I might at least get some answers.

Sitting in sweat-drenched clothes on an autumn night until I came down with pneumonia, on the other hand, would get me nowhere. I hoisted myself to my feet and set out walking again. Both the fear and adrenalin were gone, leaving in their place a weariness like a hundred tiny weights hung about my body. I was monumentally tired of London streets made dreary and repetitious by darkness. I wanted to be home, or failing that, into a late-night cafe or a takeaway, anywhere I could sit and switch off for a while. But there was nothing; only street after street of houses in increasingly nightmarish succession.

The taxi rank seemed like a vision, an oasis in the urban desert. Three vehicles were pulled up on a tarmac forecourt in front of a small office. From one of the cars, a young man in a white kurta and knitted skullcap was leaning from the open window, his elbow propped on the door's frame and a half-smoked cigarette held between two fingers.

As I approached the office, he called, "Where're you after, mate?"

I told him my address.

He stubbed the cigarette against the outside of the door and flicked the remainder towards a drain. "Sure. Hop in."

I did as he said, opting for the front passenger seat. Struck by sudden doubt, I repeated my address and added, "You know where that is?"

"Yeah," he said, unperturbed, "I know it."

I watched him for a while, as he drove with that peculiar mix of intense absorption and apparent heedlessness peculiar to his trade. On an impulse I said, "Mind if I ask you a question?"

He spared me the briefest flicker of a glance. "Sure, mate."

"Do you remember when the Spire came here?"

"The Spire?"

"The thing in Greenwich Park. It was on the news. Do you remember?"

"Oh … yeah. On the news."

"People were scared. The army were out. And then…"

"Sure. Then." We were pulled up at a red light. He looked at me for a moment, the confusion clear in his eyes, perplexity edging into dismay. The light changed and he turned away. "A while ago, though, all that."

I sensed I was on thin ice, that I could lose his fragile concentration at any moment. "But there were … people … weren't there? Who came out of the Spire?"

"Well, yeah. Of course."

"And they stayed. You see them around." I wanted to add—only, you don't *quite* see them. You see them but you don't.

Slowly, cautiously, as though he was determined to get each word precisely right, he said, "They're no bother, though, are they?"

"No," I conceded. "They're no bother."

"I mean…" He considered. "They want to fit in."

"Yeah. I think they do."

I let the conversation tail off, conscious I was making the cabbie uncomfortable without any hope of a revealing answer. I settled into my seat and let my eyes drift shut, giving myself up to the sounds of the car and the fainter background tremors from outside. It was good to be warm and at rest, cocooned from a nighttime world that had seemed inescapable only minutes before. Warmth soaked into my body, the car hummed and trembled around me, and I thought about what the cabbie had said.

I don't think I slept, but I wasn't quite awake either when the cab pulled up and the driver said, "Here you go."

I knew I wasn't home. Perhaps it was some quality in the street lighting or some internal GPS, but I didn't even bother to look.

Seeing this, the cabbie glanced between the street and his sat nav, presumably unable to reconcile the two. "This is the address you gave me, yeah?"

"Hmm? Oh. Yeah. This is it, all right."

He looked relieved. "Don't know what's got into me tonight. That'll be sixteen quid."

I gave him a twenty, told him to keep the change. I felt, somehow, that he'd earned it. He seemed grateful; but I suspected it was less for the money, more the permission to leave—to return to his normal, day-to-day reality.

As I stepped onto the street, I envied him that a little. But only a little.

I'd reached the bottom step when I heard the sound of the door. I looked up to see it half open, and Kamrita stood in the gap. Our eyes met and held, and suddenly language seemed an inadequate medium for anything significant. When I finally managed to produce the words I'd been storing up, they were quick and garbled and nothing like I'd intended. "Why, Kamrita? Why tonight? Why all of this? Why me?"

"We know our partners when we meet them." Her tone was exactly as calm as it had always been. "And we partner for life."

"You're saying you met me and you decided we had to be together?"

Kamrita shrugged. "I knew." She placed a palm flat on her stomach, as if to indicate this was where her impossible certainty had come from.

I thought about arguing, pointing out what an absurd claim this was. Outside of Hallmark cards and Mills and Boon novels, one look could not possibly assess a lifetime of compatibility, especially when ... especially if...

I let the thought peter out. It wasn't what was bothering me, not really. Maybe it should have been, but it wasn't. "Whatever you're doing to me," I said, "I need you to stop it. I'm not coming in for coffee or any damn thing as long as you're messing with my head."

"It isn't so simple." Her response wasn't an apology or an assertion, simply a statement of fact.

"It has to be. I don't much feel like trying to walk home again, but I swear I will if you can't start being straight with me."

"What we do," she said, "we do together. It's our nature to hide in plain sight."

Could she be telling the truth? Was everything that had happened tonight no more deliberate than a chameleon changing shade to match its new background? "Still. You're smart. You must be able to turn it off."

She cocked her head to one side. Then she gave a small and lengthy shudder, as though an electric charge were running not-quite-quickly up from the soles of her feet. The experience looked uncomfortable, if not outright painful.

There was no sense of change. I didn't feel that a veil had lifted; there was no heat haze transformation before my eyes. I was simply, suddenly, seeing what I'd been seeing all along, what I'd known on some level I'd been seeing—and yet had been unable to see.

Kamrita was taller than me by a clear head, and I was nearly six foot. She was wearing a loose robe, something between a toga and a sari, pale yellow-white and patterned with clustered geometric designs, which left her head and arms and the edge of one leg from thigh to ankle exposed. Every inch of exposed skin was covered with fine fur, a rich cerulean blue overlaid with intricate whorls of purple, like fractal tiger stripes. Her features were somewhat human, but her nose was longer, her ears sharp and tufted, like a lynx's except hanging downward, her eyes larger and the pupils minute amid elliptical irises. Finally, my stare settled on the detail that had unsettled me so badly a few hours ago: the tip of her tail flicking lazily at the air behind her left shoulder.

Although I could catalogue and make sense of all of these details apart, to see them together in a living creature standing not three feet from me was strange beyond belief. Strange—but not unpleasant. Not frightening at all.

"Why do you hide? You shouldn't have to."

"It's our nature," she said again.

I knew I'd asked a foolish question, that there was more to it. How much pain and horror had we wreaked upon ourselves over differences of appearance and culture far, far smaller? Still, there was sense there as well. The woman before me should not have to disguise herself. "You're beautiful."

Kamrita smiled, exposing a mouthful of delicately pointed teeth, a tongue thin and pink as a rose petal. "Would you like to come in for coffee?"

"Of course," I said.

WHY THE LOUISIANA SWAMP CAT HE GO TO TEXAS

By: Sarah M. Lewis

"Damn! An honest to God Louisiana Swamp Cat. What are you doing out by I-10?"

Pretty Boy, he look up at the trucker through his glowing green Swamp Cat eyes. Why the man ask him that? He standing on his hind legs out by the side of I-10 with his thumb stuck out. That extra toe he got on his front paws sure good for opening the refrigerator and cabinets. He even got a back pack. What the man think he doing? People sure not too smart sometimes.

He held up a piece of cardboard fastened around his neck with Mardi-Gras beads.

"Texas?" The truck driving man read the sign. "Whoever wrote that sign can't spell. The 'a' is backward and the 's' looks like a 'z'."

Pretty Boy write that sign himself. It ain't easy making marks that say things to people.

"You meeting up with a cousin or…" the trucker giving him a smirk, "is it a lady cat?"

That cat business. Pretty Boy laid his ears back flat. He don't have to go to Texas for that. He don't have no problem meeting lady cats. Problem is he meet a lady cat ready for lovin, but once he finish up, he got to run for his life cause she ready to kill him.

"It's a lady cat isn't it?"

The man don't get it. Pretty Boy, he a smart cat. God tells Pretty Boy "Go to Texas", he go to Texas.

He turn his back on the trucker, pick up his backpack start walking west, where Texas is, away from the rising sun. He hear the cab door swing open behind him.

"Hop in."

***

Ahhh. That feel so good. He got a full tummy and now waves of *The Blue Danube* rolling out of the radio into his ears. Pretty Boy lay across the Mrs. Satterwhite's and twelve year old Paxton's laps on the sofa gettin a good ole pet and purr. Mrs. Satterwhite so soft and cushiony to lay his head on while she scratch his ears and Paxton give his short water proof fur a good rub down. He stretched out his webbed toes and kneaded his claws.

"You've got good taste in music, Cat." Mr. Satterwhite looked up from his book.

The music ended and the radio began talking in the creaky voice of an old woman. Before Pretty Boy live in the people world, he'd have been scared of hearing people's voices and not seeing them. Now he know voices come out of the radio.

"Eighty two years ago, Ms. Bee, she called me to her bedside. She could lay hands on a wound no matter how deep and it stopped bleeding. 'Lucretia,' she told me, 'I'm passing this gift on to you before I leave this world. Don't ever ask for money for using it and make sure you pass it on. If it's not passed on, it will be lost.'

"I'm fixin to turn a hundred and I must pass on the gift. I've offered it to doctors, nurses, and my grandchildren. Nobody wants it."

Pretty Boy's eyes flew open. That lady say there a gift of touching a bleeding wound and it stop bleeding and nobody want the gift? He see a fellow swamp cat bleed to death after being savaged by a coyote. He taste her blood in his mouth cause he and his fellow swamp cats gather round lickin her wound to cleanse it. Her blood spraying him in fast jets, then spurts, ceasing when her sides stopped heaving.

"So now I'm here offering it to whoever comes."

That was Lucretia Dowd of Cold Spring, Texas." The announcer said.

Just cause they have their machines and science medicines and don't need it no more, people going to throw away that kind of a gift forever like they throw out their trash and there good things in the trash. Pretty Boy knew that for sure. He had a whole stash of good things he got out of the trash on garbage day. Nothing he can do about collecting that gift too."

***

"Go to Texas."

"Who said that?" Pretty Boy sat up from where he lay curled up beside Paxton. There's nobody in her room with its shabby furniture, the shelves piled high with books.

His fur begin to stand up and he lash his tail. Something more powerful than the Forever Cat, locked in his box both living and dead depending on what the people see, speaking to him deep down inside his head.

Pretty Boy never heard of God speaking to a cat before.

"Why not speak to a cat?"

The voice within, it feel good and safe. Like long time ago when he drink milk from his Mama. Or maybe it like when he and Paxton snuggle up and he figure out the marks in the book she read from while the music come out of the box. It feel like love.

"Go to Texas and receive the gift."

"I'm a swamp cat. How I goin to get to Texas? Besides I'm a cunjerred cat. Once I was wild and free, now I'm eatin out of a cat food bowl." He remembered swimming or paddling on rafts through creeks and bayous, beneath the trees. Then he'd crossed over into the people world of Baton Rouge. "I ate food Mr. Satterwhite give me. I let him touch me, and then he name me Pretty Boy. Poof, now I belong to them. You give people that power."

Pretty Boy licked the last taste of fried chicken and gravy off his whiskers and muzzle. He thought about sleeping in their beds. He thought about air conditioning. Being cunjerred ain't so bad.

Most of all, Pretty Boy think about Paxton, his favorite people, sleeping sound while God talking to him. Paxton's always looking out for others. There was the time she and he ran off the coyotes and saved a couple of neighborhood house cats. She save that gal Verity from Hoop Snake. He was about to wake up and go prowling around outside to keep Hoop Snake away if God hadn't started talking to him. Who's gonna look out for Paxton?

"Who helped Paxton face Hoop Snake? Who helped her take on coyotes?"

"If I go to Texas, why would the old lady give me the gift?" Pretty Boy asked.

"Choose to go and receive the gift or stay where you are."

***

It was still dark when Pretty Boy slipped out of the little house at the dead end of Goodwood Drive where the creek runs and the woods begins. He opened his mouth tasting the breezes coming from out of the woods. No taste of snake.

Good thing he still got his claws and balls. He went around the house on all fours lifting up his tail and spraying. This should keep Hoop Snake away if he come rolling out of the woods tonight trying to get even with Paxton.

Course, when the sun come up, Mr. Satterwhite would be getting out the hose and cussing. Yeah, cat piss stink all right, but that's what keep the snakes away.

Paxton, she have good sense. She knows Hoop Snake's still out there, watching and waiting. She'll put mothballs out around the house to keep that crafty snake away.

Next Pretty Boy head up Goodwood Boulevard, the easy way, on all fours, and keep going to the rich folks' houses. He go to the big white house where Paxton's friend Verity live. It was all Verity's fault Hoop Snake all riled up. She had to go in to the woods where she didn't belong and Hoop Snake would have got her if not for Paxton. That young one's mama and daddy need to use the whopping paw on her good. But he spray all round Verity's house too. Good thing he drank a lot of water and saved up enough.

Pretty Boy's kitty cat heart go thump, thump, thump by the time he reached I-10. The white ribbon of interstate stretched out before him. This where so many cats, not just swamp cats, dogs, armadillos and even those dirty masked devil raccoons get mashed flat and smeared on the road beneath them rubber tires. If he going to get to Texas, he had to do this. He stood up on his back legs scanning the dark for approaching headlights.

***

"Boy, I'm sure glad its daylight especially when we hit the Atchafalaya. I used to not mind night driving, but now the trees hate us and cause fogs." The trucker's name was Earl and he sure talk a lot over the country music twanging out of the radio speakers. "I've heard of trees dropping their branches on roads at night."

"Earl sure don't know a lot. The trees sleep at night same as people." Pretty Boy sat up right in the passenger seat watching the trees along the road dance, twirling in blurs, then spinning away behind them. He didn't have a quarrel with the trees. He didn't go around bull dozing trees till they declare war. Make the fogs, make the rains, stop soaking up water, so it flood. He grew up under tree leaves' dappled light and shadows, hearing them murmuring in the wind.

"Then there's the things that live in the swamps, the man-eating pitcher plants, giant snakes, and the Stornes. You have to know about the Stornes, don't you?"

Pretty Boy know more about the big birds with teeth than Earl do. They sure don't like Swamp Cats, but their nests good places to sleep or paddle around the bayou in.

He wished Earl played the classical station instead of country. At least the man didn't play the loud boom boom boom which hurt Pretty Boy's ears.

***

"Here kitty, kitty. Pretty Boy. Pretty Boy, where are you?" At first he hear Mr. and Mrs. Satterwhite's voices. He feel the pull of their cunjur on him. Back in Baton Rouge they calling him for breakfast.

Pretty Boy's stomach churn and growl telling him he want his food bowl. He began moaning in the back of his throat.

Earl heard him. "Easy boy! You going to be sick? I'll pull over."

"Pretty Boy. Pretty Boy." Now he hearing Paxton. He wanted Paxton! He could spend the day listening to her play the violin in the garage. Then they could go out rambling together in the creek and the woods close to home. How'd he get himself into this?

"Eat. You'll feel better." First time God talk to Pretty Boy since he make up his mind to get to Texas.

Pretty Boy fumbled with the zipper on the back pack, his extra front toe not as good as a people's thumb, and pulled out a can of cat food. Good thing the Satterwhites bought cans with pop tops.

The scent of tuna filled the truck cab. Clutching a can of tuna in his front paws, Pretty Boy buried his muzzle in the can, began chowing down. Earl cracked a window.

"Uh."

The cat looked up.

"There's a trash can on the floorboard. I keep talking to you like you understand me, but you act like you do."

Pretty Boy dropped the can in the trash. He pulled a baby bottle of water out of the back pack and began drinking through the nipple.

"I thought cats lapped water with their tongues." Earl said.

Pretty Boy looked at Earl. Drink from a water bowl in a truck? It'd spill. Lucky, he find those baby bottles people threw out and put them in his hidey hole of stash along with the back pack.

When he pack for Texas he get the cat food out of the cabinet and he wash the baby bottles out at the kitchen sink cause Mr. Satterwhite always talking about washing cause of germs and fill them with cold water. He show Earl his spare bottles and cans of cat food in his open back pack.

Earl shook his head. "You're serious about getting to Texas."

What God say is right. Pretty Boy, he feel better after eating and drinking. He still felt the pull of the Satterwhite's cunjur on him, but it more a faraway feeling like him remembering when he a kitten in the swamp.

The trees flew by. They crossed the Atchafalaya. Then that bridge that climb straight up then go straight down. Still no sign of Texas. Finally, Pretty Boy see a sign running toward them saying "Welcome to Texas."

"Time for a pit stop." Earl said and pulled the truck over at another sign that met them saying "Rest Stop."

"Pit stop and rest stop the same thing?" Pretty Boy wondered as he jumped down. "This Texas? Don't feel different from Louisiana."

Normally, he like to do his business outside. Mr. Satterwhite not too happy when Pretty Boy use the toilet when it too cold or a hurricane blowing. People led dogs on leashes to a fire hydrant in a sandy area. Pretty Boy was not a dog. He stood up on his hind legs and followed Earl into the men's room.

"Well, fellow, this is Texas. What now?"

Some of the other men looking at Pretty Boy and Earl kind of funny.

Pretty Boy dug another sign out of his pack.

"Cold Spring? I can take you to Houston."

***

"This is Houston." Earl said.

Pretty Boy thought Baton Rouge was big. When they reach Houston, it go on forever and they still not come out the other side. Buildings and buildings and buildings, if tall stretching up up up, if short stretching out and out.

"There's a bus station across the street. You need to be on one of those buses heading up I-45 to Huntsville."

Huntsville? Pretty Boy needed to get to Cold Spring. He show Earl the sign again.

"From Huntsville, you can take 190 East to Cold Spring."

God wasn't telling Pretty Boy any different. He must be supposed to do that. He climb down from the cab with his pack, check the traffic, than dash across the road on all fours.

***

Pretty Boy's back legs ached from stretching up to look over the counter. The lady, she don't act like she understand he need a ticket. The driver, he stop Pretty Boy from boarding the bus with the big glowing sign in front saying "Huntsville". Said Pretty Boy had to have a ticket. Some nice people on the bus speak up and say that only for people. The driver replied. "The cat rides this bus, it buys a ticket."

Pretty Boy snagged the lady's pen.

"Hey!"

Gripping it hard in his paw he make marks. Two other people behind the counter come over to look.

"He's writing. It's a phone number."

"Doesn't look like it to me."

"Yes it is. I've read worse handwriting. That's a Louisiana area code."

"I've got to be crazy doing this." The lady picked up her phone and dialed.

Even several feet away, Pretty Boy's keen ears picked up Mr. Satterwhite's voice.

"Sir, this is a Houston bus terminal and there's a cat here wanting to board a bus to Huntsville."

"Pretty Boy? Is that you?"

"Rrow."

"Cat, what are you doing in Houston? Do you know I've been driving around looking for you? Why do you want to go to Huntsville?"

Why Mr. Satterwhite ask that? He knows Pretty Boy don't talk people.

"You can write, huh? You could have left a note. Might be we could have made it out."

Trying to write the signs hard enough. Could Mr. Satterwhite have made out a cat note saying, "God tol me, go to Texas."?

"Will you pay for a ticket, sir?" The lady asked before saying a number.

Pretty Boy heard Mr. Satterwhite whistle. "That's for an adult. On his hind legs, the cat's no bigger than a child."

"How's he going to behave?"

"Better than either."

The woman made up her mind. "Okay. We'll issue him a child's ticket."

***

"That's my tail." Pretty Boy snatched his tail away from the grasp of the toddler boy who'd climbed into the seat beside him. He raise his paw and stop himself. He figure he better not cuff the boy's ears even with his claws in. Where's the mama? She need to control her young'un. But she too busy with a crying baby on her shoulder.

"*No toques el gato.*" A little girl caught hold of her brother pulling him away.

Pretty Boy didn't understand her people talk, but he understand she say to leave him alone. The baby screamed louder. With a sigh Pretty Boy went over to the mother. He began purring the way Mama Cats, they purr to soothe their kittens. He reach out and he began rubbing the baby's back with his front paw. He keep it up till the screams became hiccups then heavy breathing.

"Acaricies el gato, como así." The girl showed her brother how to pet a cat. Since they couldn't make him their *gato* Pretty Boy allow it even though they been eating suckers. When he got off the bus though, he going to give his fur a good wash with his tongue. More than one wash.

***

"Adios, Señor Gato." Next thing he know, the kids hugging on him. Their mama have a hard time getting them to come with her. Pretty Boy show them his Cold Spring sign. They shake their heads. Pretty Boy wave bye bye to them and their mama pull them away.

Now what? Pretty Boy, he in Huntsville. This place smaller than Baton Rouge with lots of rolling hills and trees he see from the bus window. He see a bunch of men, some of them mean looking, wearing clothes that don't match heading his way. Pretty Boy fluff his fur out and stand tall to make himself bigger.

He see where they coming from, that building over there, the one with barb wire and towers. A place where people put people in cages.

One of the men stopped and squinted his eyes. "Hey, man. Do you see that cat standing on his back legs holding up a sign? Whattcha doin here, Cat?"

Pretty Boy flex his claws and bristle out his tail. "Hissss." He know a cat hater when he see one.

"You lookin for trouble, Cat?"

Pretty Boy trust God. God give him claws and teeth to fight for himself. He shave those ink drawings off the man's face and arms.

A bigger guy stepped in. "Let it go, man. That's a Swamp Cat. An endangered species. Get the Feds involved and you'll be back inside before you ever see your parole officer."

"Feds nothing." Another man chimed in. "You know how many cat lovers are out there? We don't want some security video of you being mean to a kitty cat. It won't be good for the rest of us."

A car passed by from the direction they'd come from and pulled over. A man in a gray uniform leaned out and looked fixedly at the men. They walked past Pretty Boy and boarded the bus.

The man spoke in yet another strange people accent. "You're lucky I just got off shift and saw what was happening. Who are you and what are you doing here?"

Pretty Boy held up his sign.

"The Bible says 'From him who asketh of thee, turn not away.' My name is Akpobame Okafor."

***

The sun sank toward the horizon. Pretty Boy came up the gravel driveway, walking on his hind legs. His pack slung over his shoulder, the fish he stopped to catch at the lake, where he have Akpobame let him off, tucked under his arm. It'd be easier to carry in his mouth, but people, they don't like that.

Akpobame told him before driving off, "I grew up hearing stories about animals in Nigeria. It was my privilege to wander into your story. God Speed."

Pretty Boy think that fish big enough for a good supper for the lady with the gift and for him. She can't take money.

"Fish all right?" He ask God not knowing if God gonna answer.

God said, "I've given out fish myself."

So Pretty Boy bring the fish, still wriggling, so the lady see it fresh caught.

Sure enough, he'd found the way once he'd gotten to Cold Spring. The old lady was sitting on her rocker on the porch. She rose to greet him. "I knew you would come. I knew today I had to pass on the gift before the sun sets. Thank you, Lord. You didn't send a snake."

FINAL REVIEW

By: Dan M. Kalin

The reviewer finished reading the book "Cosmic Rays; Stellar Empire Series, Volume 1" and deactivated his ebook device, pushing the button in an almost angry way.

Turning to his laptop computer, he logged into the service to start writing his review. He found the author to have a juvenile sense of character development, well-seasoned by a lack of both scientific knowledge and the English language. Perhaps the reviewer was old school, but he felt someone writing science fiction should at least have a working understanding of physics. Failing that, a consistent ruleset within the novel itself would have been an improvement.

The brave new world of Indie book publishing had opened the floodgates for every poseur-at-art to see their works in print. The reviewer suspected most of the new breed of authors spent their time work-shopping with other equally skilled authors or engaging in online contests which were thinly-veiled marketing scams by publisher services companies, rather than actually writing. Talk about the tail wagging the dog! These authors enjoyed saying they were authors, more than having something within them which had to be written.

The reviewer used his customized online tools to learn everything possible about the author. *Good, the neck-*

bearded idiot has an author page on social media! he thought to himself, *Makes it much easier. Right click the mouse, save his photo into the Final Review folder. His bio said he lives in Covina, California with his parrot and Maine Coon cat. Nice. He's twenty-nine, lives in Covina; Ah! here he is.* The reviewer copied the address and telephone information onto a text document and saved it as well. He also made a new folder with the author's name and added it to the rest. Photo and text files were moved to the author's folder. *Time for a road trip,* he told himself.

The reviewer mapped his route to Covina and estimated that it would take two days to get there. Two days to conclude his business and two days to return. His bags were already packed, as his decision was made when he read the first chapter of "Cosmic Rays". One bag contained clothing and incidentals; the second bag was a long soft-shell case. He saved the review in draft form as he would need to add more before it was fully complete. Setting his home alarm, the reviewer loaded up the camper van and set out for Covina.

During the drive, he listened to randomized songs from his extensive music collection. His collection was eclectic, with one exception. He had no rap or hip-hop music as he maintained stolidly that it wasn't music. Artists who couldn't play instruments, were unable to sing without an auto-tune, excessively sampled other real musicians or were little better than glorified DJs, did not receive his custom. Those artists all sang alike, used the same approaches, and often were barely discernible from their competition. The reviewer liked artists whose singing or playing would be uniquely recognizable within the first few bars. The reviewer had a standard, and it was all his own.

Upon arrival near Covina, the reviewer paid cash to park his camper van at Arrow Glen Manor RV Park and hooked the van into the electric power and Internet services provided. He unhooked his small Honda Civic from the tow rig and set out to put the author under surveillance.

The reviewer found the location easily and parked along the street several blocks away. Putting on his walking shoes, the reviewer walked the neighborhood where the author lived, hoping for a sighting in the daylight. As he walked, he appeared to be any resident out for a stroll. He made several rounds of the neighborhood and finally approached the small house. Taking a $50 dollar bill out of his wallet, he folded it in half and rang the doorbell.

The door opened a crack and a middle-aged woman asked, "Yes, what can I do for you?"

"Hello, I was just out walking for some exercise and found this sitting in your driveway. I wanted to see if it belonged to you," the reviewer said, holding up the $50.

"No, I didn't have it to drop, I mostly have ATM $20s," she said.

"Is there anyone else living here who might have dropped it? I know it isn't mine, and would hate to keep it without at least trying to find the owner."

"It might be my son, but I can't imagine him having lost $50, since he mostly mooches my $20s. He's at work, but should return around 6 p.m. If you want, I'll leave him a note."

"Thanks, here, you should hold on to the bill. I'll check back tomorrow when I take my exercise if you don't mind. I'm staying with relatives down the street."

"You know, it is pretty rare around here to find some-one so honest. Thank you. If it isn't his, I'll have it for you tomorrow," she said.

The reviewer waved and walked back down the street. Clearly he would have to come back today around 6 p.m. so he could see the author. Getting into the car, he headed back to the RV park for some lunch and a nap. Since he had a few hours prior to meeting up with the author, there was ample time for more research.

Let's see, he said to himself, *poseur authors often spend a fair amount of their time reviewing other authors' work. Maybe he has an account with the online marketplace and reviews books there. Ah yes, there he is! Let's read of few of his reviews, shall we?*

The reviewer read for a while, shaking his head period-ically when reading something particularly trite. He found a review of a fellow science fiction author, who was a nominal competitor. The author criticized his peer for poor character development and lack of scientific knowledge. *Hah, talk about the pot calling the kettle black!* The review noted the peer author's extensive use of haibunish forms, which piqued the reviewer's interest. He downloaded a copy of the book and searched for the referenced section. Reading through it, he laughed. *What a pretentious wanker! Establishing himself as an expert and then miscategorizing the verse form.* The book section was simply free-verse without the trappings of haibun, no matter how much you squinted your eyes. *He must have heard the term in a workshop and applies it to any unusual verse. This just gets better and better.*

Opening his hacking toolkit, he determined the current IP address for the author's home. Running a scan, he could see they owned several smart appliances which were hooked to the Internet. The reviewer found a TV, security system, thermostat, garage door opener, and multiple video cams. *The new Internet of Things is making this almost too easy!* The reviewer compromised the security system, garage door opener and video cams in short order. Running his commands through a proxy server in Ukraine, he set several events to occur around 9:35 p.m.

At 5:45 p.m. the reviewer parked his car on the author's street, positioned so he had good sightlines to the garage and front door. As he waited, he read the book the author had criticized on his ebook device. Contrary to the author's views, the reviewer felt that the character development was fine and that, while the competing author didn't have a scientific background, he was consistent throughout the book. Definitely not bad enough to be a candidate for one of his final reviews.

At 6:10 p.m., the author pulled his car into the empty garage. The reviewer, seeing him in-person for the first time, had to hold back a chuckle. The pudgy author was wearing a 7-11 clerk smock and a fedora. The hat definitely took the curse off the indignity of being a mere store clerk. The garage door closed, and the reviewer switched to internal video to watch the author going about his business. The author read his mother's note, looked at the $50, and put it in his pocket. Going into his room, he fired up the computer and brought up a document which appeared to be Volume 2 of the Stellar Empire Series. The reviewer rolled his eyes and closed things down. There were several restaurants close by and he had little to do until 9:00 p.m.

After a leisurely meal, the reviewer headed back into the neighborhood and parked on a dark portion of the street. Utilizing the compromised internal cameras remotely, he confirmed the author was still at home. The reviewer donned his dull dark coveralls and assembled the black sniper rifle with suppressor. A small hedge made up of poorly kept trees formed a dark corner in one front yard across the street from the target home. The house had dark windows as though no one was home. The reviewer crawled underneath the hedge and placed the rifle on a brace facing the author's closed garage. Using his range finder, he made adjustments to the scope, and settled in to wait.

At 9:35 p.m. several things occurred in quick succession; the reviewer published his review of the author's Volume 1, titled "Final Review" and the author's garage door started cycling open and closed. The author looked up from reading the bad new review and got up angrily to see what was happening in the garage. Nothing the author did seemed to affect the cycling garage door until he finally got onto a ladder and unplugged the unit.

Waiting for his moment, the reviewer fired with a sharp crack, one round into the author's torso, dropping his ample body to the floor. He shot one additional round into the author's unmoving head. His final review was complete.

Staying in place for a few more seconds to make sure the muffled shots were not noticed, the reviewer gathered the two spent shell casings and disassembled his gun before placing the parts into a shopping bag. He walked at a normal speed onto the sidewalk to his car, and drove away.

The next day, the reviewer hooked up the car to the camper van and headed back home a full day early. During the stops along the way, he looked for more candidates deserving of a final review.

After winning the lottery several years earlier, the reviewer had a lot more time to spend on his favorite hobby, reading. Unfortunately, the authors he followed could only write new books so fast, thus he was forced to consider new authors. Being somewhat methodical, he would finish even the badly written books, and was offended the bad authors would waste his, indeed everyone's, time and money. Taking his cue from the fictional serial killer Hannibal Lecter, he had resolved to improve the quality of the Indie publishing space by removing authors who failed to meet his standards. In order to fail, the author had to be markedly lazy, not spending the time or effort to do a workmanlike job, or have nothing whatsoever to say. If they spent more time in workshops than they did actually writing, they would likely qualify, once published.

The reviewer had all the time in the world to be methodical, but it had not escaped his notice killing bad authors one at a time might not be the best approach in terms of efficiency. As he thought through the problem, he asked himself where such authors congregated? Answer; book clubs and workshops. There the authors sat around stroking each other's egos without anyone ever saying, "Your work is crap, you should stick to a plumbing day job!"

The reviewer experienced an epiphany, *What was it that every faux author wanted? Simple, a publishing house to discover them and come calling, even though they would pretend otherwise. So what if he posed as a talent scout and invited himself to their meetings? Genius!*

He sat down immediately and starting working on a hack of the biggest ebook publishing platform's author database, looking for author names, addresses, titles, revenue generated, and reviews. He was briefly amused with the irony he had used the publishing platform's own cloud computing service for very little cost to hack into their databases, through multiple remote proxies. Downloading the data, he parsed it by geographic locations and started identifying clusters of potentially bad authors. Now he had a list which supported working on group removals.

He focused his search on the Kansas City metropolitan area for his first group to investigate. Perusing social media he could look for commonalities and page subscriptions for writing clubs or workshop groups. Slowly, but surely, he compiled a list of candidates. Figuratively holding his nose, he ordered a copy of each candidate's latest book to read, which doubtless sent them into a frenzy when their online account registered the sale in real time.

Over the next two weeks, the reviewer read each of the books, making notes for his reviews. As he finished a book, he would either circle the author's name on his list or cross it off. Few were crossed off but, for those which were, he wrote an online review stating essentially their book was not terrible.

A group of six terrible authors all met regularly at their writing club, Writer's Muse, stood out as the best candidates for a group review. The reviewer identified the organizer of the group, Patty Brauner and found her contact information on the Writer's Muse website. Doing more research, the reviewer found Patty had written three simply dreadful books about her childhood rise from abject poverty, but all with great cover art and misleading back cover marketing text. He doubted there were many repeat sales. He dialed her phone number and waited for the answer.

"Hi Patty, my name is Judge Smith, I work for a division of Bertelsmann and evaluate Indie authors for possible publishing contracts. The reason I'm calling is that I've noticed a cluster of likely authors are affiliated with your Writer's Muse group," the reviewer said.

"Yes, that is the group I founded. What is your interest?" Patty said, clearly holding back her excitement.

"Well, Patty, it seems to me whatever you're doing there is working. There are a number of published authors in the group I would like to speak with, yourself included. Is there any way I can attend a typical meeting to meet everyone and see how things are done?"

"Why, certainly. This is so exciting! We have a meeting coming up in a couple of weeks being held in my home. We generally work for an hour and a half then socialize until it breaks up."

"Patty, one thing I ask of you. It must be confidential why I am coming to the meeting. Let's just say I am another aspiring author hoping to join the group. The reason for secrecy is I want to see how your journey works, undisturbed, before people start acting strangely because I represent a publisher. We can break the news during the social hour if that works. Landing a cohesive working group into contracts is much more interesting to me than simply finding sole artists."

"I know what you mean. Together we are greater than the sum of our parts. I'll keep it confidential until then, Judge. If I may ask, were you named after the actor?" Patty asked.

"I get that question a lot, especially in the United States. No, the answer is much more mundane, I'm afraid. My mother thought I looked far too serious for a newborn baby, thus the name," the reviewer said thinking fast as he changed the subject. "Are you aware of any agent representation issues that I should be concerned with prior to the meeting?"

"No, none of us have used agents up until now. So far we haven't wanted them," Patty divulged.

"No need for it at this point, although I'm sure agents will approach all of you once our interest is made plain."

Patty provided the reviewer with the date, time and location of the meeting, and they concluded the call.

The reviewer ordered a small batch of business cards for Judge Smith and his fictitious division of Bertelsmann to be delivered to a drop box on the way to Kansas City. He also prepared a disguise that incorporated a temporary change of hair color, close-trimmed mustache, beard, accentuated cheekbones, an expensive fedora, and European-cut business attire with patches on the elbows. *Should fit right in*, he thought to himself.

The day before the meeting, the reviewer packed up his camper van and car with everything he might need. Checking through his list, he set out for the Walnut Grove RV Park in Shawnee Kansas with a short stop mid-trip to pick up his business cards. Upon arrival, eight hours later, he disconnected the Honda Civic for ease in transportation.

Hooking into the RV park Internet services, he established the usual secure access to international proxies and started to review what had taken place with Patty during the last 24 hours. Had she been able to keep her mouth shut? Without too much effort, he was able to enter her email server and started reading. Patty didn't do too badly. She reached out to all the authors and urged them to come, without providing any details. *Good girl*, he thought, *you're still a candidate. My God, she subscribes to about fifty daily writing sites. No emails to Bertelsmann checking into my credentials, good. I think we are a go.*

The reviewer pulled out the package of chocolate chip cookie dough he had prepared the night before, his own special recipe. Cutting the dough in half, he made the first few perfect batches of cookies and set them aside to cool. The final half of the dough required special treatment. These cookies were to be larger than the rest and included macadamia nuts, and a variety of chocolate chip types. The reviewer readied a small HAZMAT chamber for the completed cookies. As they came out of the small oven, he carefully dusted each of them with a powder he kept in a small vial inside the chamber. He watched as the powder was fully absorbed and the cookies cooled inside the sealed chamber. Once he was sure none of the powder had escaped, he purged the chamber with nitrogen gas for several minutes and loaded the cookies into two plastic containers which were placed inside the refrigerator. Now he could eat some dinner and relax with a glass of wine.

The next day, he monitored Patty's compromised email account as well as her text messages. So far, she was living up to the compact. There was no unusual traffic amongst the group other than to confirm that they all would be in attendance. As the sun started to go down, the reviewer started the process of becoming Judge. No one at the park noticed his transformation. He drove off for the meeting.

Arriving in Patty's neighborhood he parked down the street, positioned for an easy exit. Gathering the cookies along with a Moleskine notebook he headed for the front door and rang the bell.

Patty opened the door as if she had been watching for him. "Judge? Hello, I'm Patty. Welcome to our group. What do you have there?"

"Hello Patty, it's a pleasure to finally meet you in person. These are some special treats I prepared for the social bit of the evening. It's just a little something I like to do," Judge said as he handed the containers to her. "No nibbles until after!"

"Certainly. I'll put these in the kitchen for now. Come in and meet the members. Group, this is Judge Smith, a prospective new member to Writer's Muse. Sit, Judge, we'll introduce ourselves as we go through the meeting."

Judge smiled and did a small hand wave to the group while sitting down. The meeting kicked off much as Judge had expected. Each person introduced themselves, made various excuses as to why they hadn't written much during the last week, then read several hundred words of what they had written. The group gave constructive feedback. As each person on Judge's list spoke, Judge wrote notes within his book. Judge smiled as he imagined the meeting to be much like that for Alcoholics Anonymous, "*My name is Joe Blow, I'm an author. Last week was very hard for me and I was unable to write because …*" The room would respond with vocal encouragement, as payment for what they would receive when they too rendered their excuses to the group. *Some of the authors had decent skills, like Patty, but nothing interesting to say. Authors who persist even when they have nothing to say are as bad as those without the skills,* Judge thought. *Regardless, cleaning up this nest will be a service to the arts.*

Finally the meeting closed, and Patty opened up the kitchen for refreshments.

"Patty, do you mind, my process is to make the conversational rounds while handing out cookies?" Judge picked up his containers and opened them. "Patty, as hostess and one of the main reasons I'm here tonight, you get the first one of the special cookies I prepared with my own hands."

"Thank you, Judge! I do love chocolate chip cookies," Patty said as she took several bites. "These are so good! What is your secret?"

"Butter, tender loving care, and my secret ingredient."

Patty announced to the group why Judge was actually there, creating a buzz of side conversations. Judge reiterated what he had said earlier to Patty and he looked forward to speaking with all of them. As he passed by each person he offered up cookies depending on whether they were on his list. If they were not, he would pass them a standard chocolate chip cookie, telling them to take more than one if so inclined. If they were on the list, he would pass the special cookies and insist that they take only take one.

"I must confess my feelings will be hurt if these aren't appreciated," Judge said in a self-deprecating way, "Consider these special cookies the same as receiving a rose, in a different kind of contest." The authors laughed appreciatively and tucked into their respective cookies.

One person on his list refused, citing an allergy to macadamia nuts. *There's always one*, Judge thought, *I'll have to deal with him in a more conventional way.* He was one of those complaining of writer's block during the meeting, but now he was itching to get away from the meeting, saying he had an idea he needed to set down before he forgot it. Judge made an appointment to meet with him the next day.

Judge stayed and made conversation with the remaining authors. He assured the persons who didn't get the special cookie they should stick with the group, as it was clear it was headed somewhere good. Finally, Judge thanked his hostess Patty saying he would be in touch within the next few days. Gathering the empty containers together, he made his way to his parked Honda. Driving away, he pulled into the parking lot of a small convenience store and became the reviewer again by eliminating the beard and makeup by using a container of quick wipes. Looking for any security cameras and finding none, he threw his containers, cards and the spent quick wipes into the dumpster next to the building. Running down his operations checklist, he returned to the RV park and took a thorough shower, washing out the temporary hair coloring.

The reviewer logged into the ebook platform site and wrote final reviews for each of the authors who had eaten the special cookies. The poison they had ingested would not kill them for several days, which was more than enough time to finish what business he still had in town. The final author would require a solution utilizing firearms. Given the time constraints, the reviewer was well prepared for such an eventuality. He wrote the author's final review, as well, but did not publish it.

Using his hacking toolkit, he quickly was able to determine the author lived alone and was a bit of a throwback when it came to new technologies. The author's computer, which he was using to write, didn't have a webcam nor did the reviewer see one within the author's home network. It appeared that he was listening to death metal as he wrote. Of course, the home network had been compromised almost immediately due to the author not changing the router's default passwords. He didn't even seem to have an active mobile phone, or at least one on the network. The reviewer went on to social media, and found the author's business page to be mostly dedicated to his novels without much day-to-day activity.

Taking a deep breath, the reviewer decided to go out once more and see if there was an opportunity to close things out tonight. Failing that, he would have to plan something for the next evening. Putting on his dull black jeans and a long-sleeved black turtleneck, he got back into the Toyota for another drive to the author's neighborhood.

This was a much seedier neighborhood than where the Writer's Muse group met, gang graffiti adorned any wall that would stand for it, and there did not appear to be much late hour foot traffic. Cruising slowly by the author's house, he could see a light in what looked to be a bedroom window. The street itself was dark, as it appeared none of the streetlights were operational. A few lights illuminated the homes willing to have paid for them, but there were not many. *Perfect*, he thought, *I guess we can finish here tonight.* The reviewer parked about a half block down the street, opened his laptop and checked the status of the author. *Still listening to death metal and writing.*

The reviewer took his semiautomatic 9mm pistol from its case and screwed a new canister silencer onto the end of the barrel. Everything in his kit was a dull black, the final touch was to place his black balaclava into his front pocket and the pistol into a shopping bag. It wouldn't be needed until he was off the sidewalk and inside the house. The reviewer exited his car and calmly walked half a block to the author's house. Looking around, there was no one out, so the reviewer moved swiftly to the outside wall of the home.

Putting on his balaclava, the reviewer tested the unlit front door, which proved to be locked. The back door was locked as well. The author was sitting in a bedroom on the first floor.

An in-ground basement had a window well, which was perfect to conceal a forced entry. Scoring a circular scratch onto the glass window using a special key with an industrial diamond tip, the reviewer tapped gently inside the circle until it popped into the basement room with a small clatter. Reaching in through the hole, the reviewer unlocked and opened the window. Using a small flashlight, he looked around the room. It was finished but was apparently being used for long-term storage. Gently stepping down, the reviewer entered the house.

He took out his pistol and placed the empty bag folded, onto one of the open boxes.

Holding the flashlight in his mouth, he walked quietly towards the basement stairs. He walked up the steps slowly, hearing each creak of the stairs as loud as thunder. He paused and realized he could no longer hear the author's death music, realized he hadn't heard it at all inside the house. Perhaps the author was wearing earphones? Turning off the flashlight, he slowly opened the door to the basement stairs and entered the dark kitchen.

The only light came from several nightlights in the kitchen and one in the hallway. At the end of the hall, there was light coming through a partially open doorway. Listening carefully, the reviewer could hear tinny death metal music, confirming headphones were being used.

Holding his gun in firing position, the reviewer looked through the open sections of the door. The author was against the far wall, typing and listening to the music. The reviewer slowly opened the door just wide enough to admit him and, walking softly, aimed the pistol at the back of the author's head as he approached. At two feet the reviewer stopped, braced his hands on the gun and squeezed the trigb6tyg5ytnui8..

[Published posthumously from files discovered by the author's estate]

STORY COPYRIGHTS AND AUTHOR INFORMATION

"Serpent, Wolf, and Half-Dead Thing" by Marie Brennan. Copyright © 2018 by Bryn Neuenschwander.

Marie Brennan is a former anthropologist and folklorist who shamelessly pillages her academic fields for material. She is most recently misapplied her professors' hard work to the Hugo Award-nominated Victorian adventure series The Memoirs of Lady Trent; the first book of that series, A Natural History of Dragons, was nominated for a World Fantasy Award and won the Prix Imaginales for Best Translated Novel. She is also the author of the Varekai novellas, the Wilders urban fantasies, the Onyx Court historical fantasy series, and more than fifty short stories. For more information, visit http://www.swantower.com or her Patreon at http://www.patreon.com/swan_tower.

***

"How Music Moves Us" by Veronica Brush. Copyright © 2018 by Veronica Brush.

Veronica Brush is the author of the novellas "First Grave on Mars" and "Second Deception on Mars", a murder mystery series about the first colonizers of the red planet. Her work has been featured in publications including Literary E-

Clectic, Listverse, and the Mad Scientist Journal. She also has an occasional blog, www.ThemelessWriting.com.

***

"Dome Sweet Dome" by Turner Campbell. Copyright © 2018 by Turner Campbell.

Turner Campbell is a Florida native currently living in DC. They graduated from New College of Florida with a degree in Humanities, where they conducted an undergrad thesis on Mark Z. Danielewski's "House of Leaves". They use strands from the past, present and future to weave their stories. "Dome Sweet Dome" is their first published story. They want to thank their parents for always encouraging their writing, and their partners, Raina and Ashley, for their everlasting love and support. https://medium.com/@turnercampbell

***

"Grasshopper" by Ellen Denton. Copyright © 2018 by Ellen Denton.

Ellen is a freelance writer living in the Rocky Mountains with her husband and three demonic cats who wreak havoc and hell (the cats, not the husband). Her writing has been published in over a hundred magazines and anthologies. She as well has had an exciting life working as a rodeo clown, a Navy seal, and an exotic dancer in the crew lounge of the starship Enterprise. She was also the first person to scale Mount Everest to its summit. (Writer's note: The one-hundred-plus publication credits are true, but some or all of the other stuff may be fictional.)

A long time writer in TV, films, graphic novels, comic books, video games, short stories, and novels for the YA market, Buzz Dixon's credits include such animation classics as Thundarr The Barbarian, G.I. Joe, Transformers, Jem, Batman, and Tiny Toons; the films Dark Planet and G.I. Joe: The Movie; creating the Christian manga category with his hit Serenity graphic novel series; work for Disney and Marvel Comics, the Terminator 3 video game among others; and short fiction published in Mike Shayne's Mystery Magazine, National Lampoon, the Pan Book Of Horror Stories, and Analog. His new YA adventure novel, Poor Banished Children Of Eve, will be published shortly. A husband, father, grandfather, and litter box cleaner for a cranky old cat he inherited, Dixon can be found on his blog http://www.BuzzDixon.com, Facebook, Instagram, and Twitter.

***

KG Finfrock is the author of the horror thriller House of Redemption and host of a podcast series Spooky Tales. An avid supporter of other writers, she is the organizer of a local writer's group and has published The Ten-Minute Writing Prompt (Volume 1). She is currently working on a paranormal ghost novel.

Website: https://kgfinfrock.wordpress.com

Twitter: https://twitter.com/Abigail_Fin
Instagram: https://www.instagram.com/kathy_finfrock/

***

"Goodnight, Pretty Molly" by Jill Hand. Copyright © 2018 by Jill Hand.

Jill Hand is a member of the Horror Writers Association. Her work has appeared in dozens of publications and in many anthologies, including Test Patterns, Mrs. Rochester's Attic, Stories From the Near-Future and Postcards From the Void.

***

"Harold's Not Imaginary Friend" by Pepper Hume. Copyright © 2018 by Pepper Hume.

Pepper Hume is an artist who deals in pictures and words, do not trust her with numbers! Being a refugee from the gypsy life of professional theatre design, she tends to think in four dimensions, often in reverse. Add compulsive people-watching and an addiction to reading, and that's why she writes. She is also addicted to the conversational dynamics of classical music and plans to write a story someday that exactly matches the dynamics of Ravel's Concerto for the Left Hand. Nonetheless, the only Pepper Hume on Facebook is a nice little old lady whose cat, a notoriously picky eater, recently gifted her with a headless dead squirrel on her birthday.

***

"The Hole" by Tim Jeffreys. Copyright © 2018 by Tim Jeffreys.

Tim Jeffreys escaped the north of England more than a decade ago, and now lives in the greener surrounds of Bristol. Despite valiant efforts including studying Graphic Arts and Design at University, his original career plans went completely wrong and he ended up working in a tiny office in a Dental Hospital. The screams he sometimes hears from the clinics occasionally make it into the strange stories he writes when no one's looking.

His short fiction has appeared in Weirdbook, Not One of Us, and Nightscript, among various other publications, and his latest collection 'The Real Rachel Winterbourne and other stories' is available now. Follow his progress at www.timjeffreys.blogspot.co.uk.

***

"Budget Demon" by Dan M. Kalin. Copyright © 2018 by Dan M. Kalin.

"Final Review" by Dan M. Kalin. Copyright © 2018 by Dan M. Kalin.

Dan Kalin is a retired management consultant, publisher, and occasional author. He can be contacted through https://dmkalin.arbitor.com/. Dan resides in Melbourne, Florida under the seemingly constant direction of two herding canines, Annie and Stella. His upcoming novels "Martyrs al-Sabra" and "Pandora's Children" will be released in the first quarter of 2019.

***

"The Customer is Always Right" by Sarah Kalin. Copyright © 2018 by Sarah Kalin.

Sarah Kalin lives in Denver, Colorado with a rigorously-guarded, dragon-sized hoard of books. In addition to writing, she operates Dreamlined LLC - an editing business specializing in services for self-publishing authors. (www.dreamlined.com)

***

"The Time Before Dreams" by E.E. King. Copyright © 2018 by E.E. King.

E.E. King is a painter, performer, writer, and biologist - She'll do anything that won't pay the bills, especially if it involves animals.

Ray Bradbury calls her stories "marvelously inventive, wildly funny and deeply thought-provoking. I cannot recommend them highly enough."

Her books include Dirk Quigby's Guide to the Afterlife, Electric Detective, Pandora's Card Game, The Truth of Fiction and Blood Prism.

She's worked with children in Bosnia, crocodiles in Mexico, frogs in Puerto Rico, egrets in Bali, mushrooms in Montana, archaeologists in Spain, butterflies in South Central Los Angeles, lectured on island evolution and marine biology on cruise ships in the South Pacific and the Caribbean, painted murals in Los Angeles and Spain and has been published widely. Check out paintings writing and musings at www.elizabetheveking.com.

***

"A Steak and a Story" by Frank Kozusko. Copyright ©
2018 by Frank Kozusko.

I am a retired US Navy submarine officer and nuclear
engineer. After the Navy, I spent 20 years as a university
math professor. A few years back, I started writing poetry. I
have self-published several collections. In full retirement, I
am exploring all my artistic talents: painting in acrylics,
sculpting and expanding my writing into short stories. So
far I have published in Bewildering Stories, 50 Word
Stories and Ariel Chart.

***

"Alien Avenue" by Mickey Kulp. Copyright © 2018 by
Mickey Kulp.

Mick is a writer, father, and effing bug slayer who is not
allowed to buy his own clothes. His creative nonfiction,
fiction, and poetry have appeared in numerous consumer
magazines, newspapers, literary journals, and three books of
poetry. He is a member of the Gwinnett County Writers
Guild and founding member of the Snellville Writers
Group. In 2018, he created a quarterly reading series to
benefit the local food co-op.

He lives with his wife and a dozen larcenous squirrels in
Atlanta, GA. His next book is coagulating nicely. More at
www.MickeyKulp.com.

***

"Who Listens to Hummingbirds" by Sarah M. Lewis.
Copyright © 2018 by Sarah M. Lewis.

"Why the Louisiana Swamp Cat He Go to Texas" by Sarah M. Lewis. Copyright © 2018 by Sarah M. Lewis.

Sarah Lewis has a BA in Art History and an MA in history from the University of Mississippi. She's employed by the state of Texas and is a member of the Woodlands Writing Guild.

***

"The Prisoner" by Valerie Manwill. Copyright © 2018 by Valerie Manwill.

Valerie Manwill writes YA thrillers, coming of age novels and other quirky stories in between. She was a contributing author for the play Breakfast with Shakespeare, which won the 2014 Best of Utah State award for Playwriting. Valerie also runs a comedic blog in which she exploits some of her most embarrassing moments. Information about her work can be found at http://valmanwill.wordpress.com.

***

"The Octopus of Bangkok" by Robert Millet. Copyright © 2018 by Robert Millet.

Robert Millet is an author and photographer, originally from Southern California. He first fell in love with Steampunk while making Cosplay outfits for his kids. Although he adores Steampunk and all things Victorian era, he also writes Horror and Dystopia. After studying Radio and Television production in university, he switched careers and became a professional chef for thirteen years.

When he isn't writing Robert can be found concocting new recipes, spending time with his family or hanging out at the

328

local comic book store. His other Steampunk work Ormand's Emporium of Oddities is an interesting read.

***

"Poker Night With Louie da Squid" by Karen Ovér. Copyright © 2018 by Karen Ovér.

Karen Ovér is currently living and writing in New York City. Her work has appeared in Collective Fallout, Sweater Weather, and Sci Phi Journal, in the anthologies Fairy Tale Riot and From a Cat's View, and is available at amazon.com and balletsandbogeys.weebly.com/golemwerks

When not in the midst of negotiating with the cat for desk space, she can sometimes be found clinging to a ballet barre, attempting to realign the vertebrae sent in all directions by hours of maniacal word processing.

***

"Birds of a Feather" by Liz Schriftsteller. Copyright © 2018 by Liz Schriftsteller.

Liz Schriftsteller hails from North Carolina but these days 'home' is anywhere the wifi automatically connects. Her published fiction includes works found in Daily Science Fiction, HAVOK magazine, and The Arcanist. When not writing she enjoys going to the theater, binge-reading stacks of comics, and over-analyzing the plot elements of her favorite TV shows. Follow her on twitter @LizSchriftstell or online at lizschriftsteller.wordpress.com.

***

"I am Bridget" by Mariah Southworth. Copyright © 2018 by Mariah Southworth.

Mariah Southworth is a long time horror and science fiction fan from Northern California. When she's not writing or reading, she enjoys long walks in the redwoods and binge-watching cartoons. Her previous short stories have appeared in CuppaTea Publication's Humans Wanted anthology and in Flame Tree Publishing's Supernatural Horror Anthology. It is still up for debate whether or not she actually exists or is in fact a figment of the collective imaginations of her cats.

***

"Cat and Mouse" by David Tallerman. Copyright © 2018 by David Tallerman.

David Tallerman is the author of the recently released crime thriller The Bad Neighbour, ongoing YA fantasy series The Black River Chronicles, the Tales of Easie Damasco trilogy, and the novella Patchwerk. His comics work includes the absurdist steampunk graphic novel Endangered Weapon B: Mechanimal Science, with Bob Molesworth.

David's short fiction has appeared in around eighty markets, including Clarkesworld, Nightmare, Alfred Hitchcock Mystery Magazine, and Beneath Ceaseless Skies. A number of his best dark fantasy and horror stories were gathered together in his debut collection The Sign in the Moonlight and Other Stories. He can be found online at davidtallerman.co.uk.

***

"The Way It Was With Jonah" by Art Weil. Copyright © 2018 by Art Weil.

Art Weil is a retired history teacher whose interests include astronomy, railroad history, and seashells. A frequent contributor to the Hawaiian Shell News, he co-authored The Wentletrap Book, which features a seashell named in his honor. His son is artistic director of Falcon Theater Company, and his daughter is bestselling science fiction author D.W. Vogel. He lives in Cincinnati with his wife, Virginia, and recently celebrated his ninetieth birthday.

***

"Carrion" by Simone LW Mounsamy. Copyright © 2018 by Simone LW Mounsamy.

Simone L W Mounsamy began reading poetry from her journal to her close circle a decade and a half ago. She branched into fiction in Academialand, specifically Austin Community College, where she obtained an Associate's degree in Creative Writing. She holds another Associate's degree in Musical Theatre and a Bachelor's degree in French. She has been off writing in caves on islands in the French Caribbean since then and is now happily peeking her nose out to explore the publishing world. Simone proudly announces this is her debut publication. Her stories and translations are, or will be, forthcoming in many other literary journals.

***

"Second Sun" by Beth Winokur. Copyright © 2018 by Beth Winokur.

Beth Winokur writes short stories, novels, children books and travel articles. She enjoys writing and reading across multiple genres. Published works include; Sunshine in Darkness, and The Willing Stone (Book 1 in the Abby and Sofia Adventure series) and numerous articles. Beth lives in Southern California where rain is magic.

Find Beth online at her website , Twitter @Bethwinokur , or at her Amazon Authors page amazon.com/author/bethwinokur

***

Cover Art by Priscilla Thomas

Priscilla Thomas is an illustrator and graphic designer. Her work has been featured in such periodicals as Times Publishing for feature stories, and Colonial Williamsburg Foundation for illustrations in 'Trend and Tradition' magazine. She maintains a website at www.priscillathomasvisual.com.

www.ingramcontent.com/pod-product-compliance
Lightning Source LLC
Chambersburg PA
CBHW051212190726
48288CB00006B/1933